N. A. Cole grew up in a small college town in Pennsylvania, United States. She is an author of new adult and contemporary romance. Her love of reading and writing stemmed from a very early age, with her dream always being to publish a novel. Spoiler: her books will always contain happy endings. Of course, the road won't always be easy. Aside from reading and writing, N. A. Cole enjoys spending time with her two dogs, binge-watching K-dramas, and crushing on fictional characters.

This is a work of fiction. Names, characters, businesses, places, events, and incidents are either the product of the author's imagination or used in a fictitious manner. Any resemblance to actual persons, living or dead, or actual events is purely coincidental.

CREEK CAMPUS SERIES

Always,
From Then
Until Now

N. A. Cole

CREEK CAMPUS SERIES

Always,
From Then
Until Now

Vanguard Press

VANGUARD PAPERBACK

© Copyright 2023
N. A. Cole

The right of N. A. Cole to be identified as author of
this work has been asserted by them in accordance with the
Copyright, Designs and Patents Act 1988.

All Rights Reserved

No reproduction, copy or transmission of this publication
may be made without written permission.
No paragraph of this publication may be reproduced,
copied or transmitted save with the written permission of the publisher, or
in accordance with the provisions
of the Copyright Act 1956 (as amended).

Any person who commits any unauthorised act in relation to
this publication may be liable to criminal
prosecution and civil claims for damages.

A CIP catalogue record for this title is
available from the British Library.

ISBN 978 1 80016 990 6

Vanguard Press is an imprint of
Pegasus Elliot Mackenzie Publishers Ltd.
www.pegasuspublishers.com

First Published in 2023

Vanguard Press
Sheraton House Castle Park
Cambridge England

Printed & Bound in Great Britain

To my sister, Taylor, for helping me to breathe life into this story. Prim, Myles, and I will be forever grateful.

ACKNOWLEDGEMENTS

Prim and Myles will always have a special place in my heart. Their love is pure and unconditional. They are what started it all for me. A special thanks to my sister, Taylor, who answered my never-ending questions during the writing process. To my beautiful mother, Beth, thank you for teaching me how to read all those years ago. This wouldn't be possible without you. To my readers, thank you for wanting to dive into this story. I hope you enjoy Prim and Myles just as much as I do. I can't wait to give you the next three couples I have planned. And finally, I want to thank everyone at Pegasus Publishing Company for wanting to publish this novel. From editing, to production, to design. And everyone in between. Thank you for taking a chance on me. You have all made this author's dream come true.

Prologue

Prim
Ten Years Ago (Third Grade)

"Shit, shit, shit!" I hear as the boy; Myles runs around the swing set and screams during recess.

"Hey, that's a bad word, you know. I could tell the teacher on you!" I say.

"It's not a bad word! My mom says it all the time," replied Myles.

"Well, my mommy said that it's not a nice word and that we shouldn't use it in public."

"Shit, shit, shit!" Myles screamed as he continued to run around the playground.

Even after only knowing him for half of a school year, I realize that I don't think that I like that boy very much. I know what's right. My mom said so. That is a bad word. I'm going to go tell Mr. Keller.

"Mr. Keller, Myles keeps saying a bad word."

"Where is Myles right now, Prim?" asked Mr. Keller.

"He's over there running around by the swings."

"What is he saying?"

"Umm. He's saying, 'shit, shit, shit.'"

I see that Mr. Keller laughed when I said this. He shook his head and looked back over at me. I'm sure he could see the look of panic on my face.

"I'm sorry, Mr. Keller. I was just trying to tell you what he was saying," I said, a little panicked. I didn't know if I was also going to get in trouble for saying a bad word. But he did ask me what Myles said so I figured that it was okay.

"I know, I know, Prim, don't worry," replied Mr. Keller. "How about we go over and have a chat with him, okay?"

We walk over to where Myles is still running around and saying, "shit, shit, shit."

"Myles, now you know that word isn't one that someone your age should be saying, right?" asked Mr. Keller.

"But I hear my mom say it all the time. Why can she say it and I can't?" asked Myles.

"Well, umm, usually those words are something that only adults say."

"Well, I think that's stupid," replied Myles.

"Hey, that's not nice either. Mr. Keller, he keeps saying not nice words. Are you going to call his parents?"

"Why don't we all go inside and call home to explain the situation?" asked Mr. Keller.

"But Mr. Keller!" pleaded Myles.

"Hey. No one is in trouble. I just want to get this sorted out, so it doesn't keep happening, okay?"

Mr. Keller took me and Myles inside the classroom and sat us down on the chairs beside his desk. I wasn't exactly sure why I also had to come inside, but I wanted to see what happens.

"Now, let's see if anyone is home just so that we can get this all figured out and move on with our days," said Mr. Keller.

Mr. Keller picked up the phone to dial. I heard him say that it was Myles's mom. He explained everything to her and what had happened and then he said that she wanted to talk to Myles.

"Hi, Mom," said Myles as he took the phone from Mr. Keller.

"We'll talk about this after school. You better listen and behave the rest of the day, okay?" said Myles's mom, Mrs. Ariti.

"Yes, Mom," replied Myles as he handed the phone back to Mr. Keller.

After school, I saw Myles walk up to his mom's car. He got into the back seat, and I could see that she started yelling at him when he closed the door. Maybe I shouldn't have said anything to Mr. Keller. As the car drove away, I could see Myles in the back seat wiping away his tears.

The next day before the bell rang, I decided to go up to Myles to tell him that I was sorry. I didn't want him to cry. I never meant for that to happen. Sometimes I'm a little more stubborn than I want to be. My mom says that I need to work on it.

"Hey, Myles," I said as he was hanging up his backpack on the hook.

"Oh. Hi," replied Myles, looking back down at the ground.

"I'm sorry about yesterday. I shouldn't have told the teacher about you. I thought I was doing the right thing. And, umm, I didn't know you would cry."

"I didn't cry!" yelled Myles, looking up at me with red cheeks.

"I saw you in the car," I replied. His ears were now turning bright red.

"Oh, well, I just cried a little bit."

"I don't want you to cry anymore, so I won't tell on you again."

"You promise?" asked Myles.

"Pinky promise," I replied as we both hooked our fingers in the air.

"Do you want to sit with me for lunch today? We could even play a game during recess if you want to?" asked Myles.

"Yeah! I'm having peanut butter and jelly for lunch. What about you?"

"Me too! My dad made it for me this morning," replied Myles.

"Me too! Now we're twins!" I replied, clapping my hands.

We gave each other a high-five and walked to our desks together.

***

Over the next couple of years, we had lunch together every day. We went over to each other's houses for slumber parties, and Myles's parents always had the best snacks. We had other friends, of course, but Myles and I were friends who always stuck together and shared everything with one another. Even when we got into middle school. We were afraid that we weren't going to be put on the same school team, but we were and had most of our classes together. Myles and I both played sports so we always had some kind of practice after school, and then our parents would take us to get ice cream some days.

When we got into high school, Myles shot up, but I pretty much stayed the same height. So, of course, he would tease me about how short I was. But I was faster than him, so I joked right back. I didn't joke too much though. We always took care of each other and that was one of my favorite parts of our friendship. I was on the high school soccer team and Myles was always there for all my home games, cheering me on. And then he would always call me after I got back from our away games to ask me how it went.

During our junior year, Myles started dating a girl from our biology class. We didn't get to spend as much time together during that year because he was with Brynn, but that was okay. He did his thing, and I did mine. We didn't have to be together all the time. I would sometimes hang out with both of them, and they seemed to work really well together. Toward the end of the year, Myles experienced his first relationship crisis.

"Shit, shit, shit!" Myles said as he barged into my bedroom.

I couldn't help but laugh. "Jesus, what happened?"

"Brynn broke up with me," replied Myles.

"What? Why?"

Myles looked nervously around the room. "Umm, she said that I didn't spend enough time with her."

"What do you mean? You both have hung out with each other a lot this year," I replied.

"She said that sometimes when I was with her, it didn't feel like I was actually present with her, like mentally. She told me I would apparently zone out a lot whenever she was talking to me."

"Umm, okay? I'm not really sure what to say to that. Were you paying attention to her when you had conversations?" I asked.

"I thought I was. She didn't think so."

"Well, I'm sorry she broke up with you. I thought you two were doing well."

"Yeah, I thought so too," replied Myles.

The weirdest part of our friendship was during our senior year. I got my very first boyfriend and Myles wasn't his biggest fan.

"Chad? His name is Chad. That is on the list of the top names for fuck-heads and douchebags. You know I'm right," said Myles, pointing a finger at me.

"He's not a douchebag or a fuck-head. You would know that if you ever met him," I replied.

"I don't know if I want to," said Myles.

"And why is that? Afraid he's more handsome than you?"

"Oh, please. No one could compare to this face," Myles said as he raised his eyebrows up and down in a teasing manner and circled his face with his finger.

"Okay, tough guy. But seriously, it would be nice if the two of you met. You're my best friend. I want you to be involved. Please?" I asked.

He sighed and that could only mean one thing. Victory. "Fine. I'm not making any promises about the guy, though."

"I wouldn't expect anything less from you," I said.

They did not, in fact, get along very well. I don't know what it was, but Myles kept interrupting Chad whenever he was talking and saying things to try and one-up him. It was really immature, and I did yell at him multiple times because of it. Let's just say that there weren't any group outings after that meeting.

The middle of our senior year started to roll on and, by the time we knew it, we had to choose which college we were going to. Myles and I didn't really have to worry about that though. We were both going to Silver Creek University in Pennsylvania, only a two-hour drive from home. I got a partial scholarship to play soccer there, and Myles told me he applied there as well because his school counselor told him they have a great psychology program. So, it worked out nicely for both of us. He told me that the two-hour drive was close enough to home that he could go back and forth easily enough if he wanted to.

"You ready to submit these acceptance responses and continue our best friendship?" I asked as Myles came into the room.

Myles just shook his head and laughed.

"Yes, ma'am," replied Myles.

Then I saw him click "accept" on the computer screen. I clicked on mine right after he did.

Myles
Highschool: Freshman Dance

I don't even want to go to this stupid dance. The only reason I'm going is that I was forced into it. By Prim, of course. I don't even have a date. Prim does though. Jasper Nelson. They sit next to each other in algebra, and he slipped her a note in her textbook asking her if she wanted to go to the dance with him. I'm sure there was a better and less cliché way to ask her to the dance but, hey, what do I know?

I had just gotten back from grabbing a drink at the table when I saw Prim standing still in the frame of the doorway. She was looking at something. No, she was looking at *someone*. I glanced over to where she was looking and saw Jasper. He was dancing with another girl. I looked back at Prim, but she wasn't there anymore. I ran over and out the door. I ran through the hallway and stopped when I saw her sitting on the stairs leading to the second floor of the school.

"Prim, what are you doing there?" I asked as she started wiping her face. She was crying.

"I just needed a dancing break," she replied.

"Are you okay?" Normally, I hate when people ask this question to people who are visibly *not* okay, but I really didn't know what else to say in this situation.

"I'm fine," she replied as she wiped away another tear from the corner of her eye.

"It doesn't look like you are. Tell me what happened."

Her face wrinkled up and she started crying again.

"Please tell me what happened so I can help you." I sat down beside her on the stairs and put my arm around her shoulder.

"It's Jasper," she replied.

"What about Jasper?"

"I thought we were going to come to the dance together, just the two of us. We've been getting along so well recently that I thought something was going to come out of it. But I just saw him dancing with another girl. I know it's just dancing, but it still hurt."

"I'm sorry, Prim. I'll sit out here with you if you want me to. Did you want to leave, or do you want to stay? Just tell me what you want and that's what we'll do."

"No, I want to stay. My parents spent too much money on this dress for me to go home early."

"Do you want to sit here a bit longer or do you want to go back inside?"

"I'll go back in. Can you come with me?"

"Of course, I can. Do you want to go dance with me instead?" I didn't mean for this question to sound so weird, but I could feel heat prickle up my neck after I asked it. Prim didn't seem phased. Not surprising though.

"Yeah, let's go," Prim replied as she took my arm and led me back into the gym.

When we walked back in, there was an upbeat song playing so we went out into the middle of the dance floor. Prim started flailing her arms around in the air and I couldn't help but laugh. Tears still stained her cheeks, but she at least looked like she was having fun. A minute later the song ended. I heard a slow ballad come out of the speakers and looked over at Prim.

"Let's dance," she said.

"But it's a slow song. You still want to dance with me?"

She nodded and came over and wrapped her arms around me. "Thank you for being here."

"Anytime," I replied, having a hard time understanding why it was getting so difficult for me to breathe. I looked straight ahead of me and saw Jasper looking at us. I glared right back at him, and he must have gotten the message because he turned and walked away.

I rested my hands in the middle of Prim's back and continued swaying to the music.

"Why is your heart beating so fast?" she asked, looking up at me.

"I think I'm just out of breath from dancing to the last song," I replied, knowing full well that wasn't the reason at all.

***

Myles
Highschool: Graduation Day

I only had two more hours before I needed to be at the stadium for graduation. If I were late, Prim would kill me. I know that for sure. Plus, I didn't want to upset her today. She's so excited to be done with high school. Honestly, I am too but she's like over the moon about it. She deserves it though. She got a soccer scholarship, so she is going to do great. And we're both super pumped that we're going to school together again. Prim is going to her first-choice school, and me? Well, Silver Creek University was actually my second-choice school, but I didn't tell Prim that. My dream has always been to go to Lakewood University for psychology. They have one of the best psychology programs in the country. I may have told Prim that

that was what my school counselor told me about Silver Creek, but she doesn't need to know all the small details.

I was really struggling with that decision. I got full scholarships to both schools, so it was completely my choice. On the last day to submit our acceptance responses, I was on my way to tell Prim that I was going to accept to go to Lakewood. I knew she was going to be upset and hurt that I waited until the last minute to tell her, but maybe she would understand since it was my dream school. When I got to her house, she already had her parents' laptops opened up to the Silver Creek University website.

"You ready to submit these acceptance responses and continue our best friendship?" asked Prim.

I saw how big her smile lit up on her face and I knew the answer to her question. I shook my head and laughed to myself.

"Yes, ma'am." And I clicked "accept" on the Silver Creek University website.

Now, four months later, I am standing in line at Target getting Prim the stupid elephant stuffed animal she wanted as a graduation present. So, even if I were late for graduation, hopefully, giving her this gift would make her less annoyed. As I leave the store, get in my car, and pull out my phone, I, to no surprise, have a text from the one-and-only Prim.

Prim–You better not be late. I just talked to your mom, and she said you weren't home. Where are you?

Me–Just relax. I went to Target quickly. I'll show you what I got before graduation. Meet me outside the gate. I'll text you when I get there.

Prim–Okay. See you there.

An hour and a half later, I was standing outside the stadium gate waiting for Prim. I saw her turning the corner and parking in front of the tennis courts. She got out of her car already in her graduation outfit and jogged over.

"Now, who's the late one?" I asked.

"Shut up, asshole. You got here quicker than I thought you would," Prim replied.

"Always underestimating me, I see."

"Anyway, what did you want to show me?" asked Prim.

I took out the bag from behind my back and handed it over to Prim.

"What's this?" she asked.

"I got you a present," I said.

"Really?" she asked.

"Yep. Open it. Go on."

Prim opened the bag, took out the elephant stuffed animal, and held her hand up to her mouth.

"I can't believe you remembered. I said I wanted this like months ago."

"Yeah, well, I pay attention," I replied.

"I guess you do. You shouldn't let any other girls tell you that you don't pay attention. You clearly do. I don't know what Brynn's problem was," Prim said as she held up the stuffed animal.

"Yeah, well, it was important," I replied. As I said that, I could see that a tear was forming in Prim's right eye.

"Well, thank you. It means a lot," Prim said and then she came over and hugged me.

Peaches. She always smelled like peaches. When the hug went on longer than I expected, I pulled away.

I cleared my throat. "So, are you going to meet Chad somewhere before the ceremony?" I asked.

"Yeah, I told him I would meet him inside the school after I saw you," Prim replied.

"Ahh, you should probably go see him then."

"Yeah. Okay, well, thank you for this gift again. What should I name him?" asked Prim.

"Hmm, how about Mr. Tusky? Short, sweet, and to the point," I replied.

Prim started laughing. "You know, that's perfect. Mr. Tusky, it is then. I'll see you after the ceremony, okay, Myles?"

"Yeah, see you then," I said as I watched her walk away into the school.

***

After everyone had gotten their diplomas, the ceremony ended and all the caps were thrown into the air, I looked around to try and see if I could find Prim to congratulate her again. And, of course, she was so short, it was hard to spot her in the crowd. People were hugging and crying all around me. I looked over to the left by the bleachers and spotted her. But, of course, she wasn't alone. Chad was walking up to her and pulled her in for a hug. They broke apart and then he took her face, tilted her back, and kissed her. Any excitement that was showing on my face was long-gone by now. Nausea crept up. He *kept* kissing her. She looked so happy.

This girl is never going to know that I'm hopelessly and completely in love with her, I thought to myself as I turned around, put my head down, and started walking to my car.

"Goodbye, school. Thanks for nothing," I said as I threw up my middle finger to the building on my right and drove away.

CHAPTER 1

Prim
Present Day - Freshmen Year of College

"Are you sure you packed enough? I think you have an outfit for literally every day. You won't have to wear a single outfit over again," said Myles pointing at my overflowing suitcases. "At least you'll save money on laundry." He winked.

"Shut up. I like to have all my options. You're going to regret not packing enough. Mark my words, friend," I replied.

"Are you nervous?" asked Myles.

"For which part?"

"All of it. Soccer, new school, another life milestone, all of that."

"I am a little nervous, but I'm excited to move on, I guess. It helps that you'll be there with me."

"I wouldn't have it any other way," replied Myles. "So, have you heard from Chad recently?"

Chad. The first guy who has ever broken my heart. The guy that dumped me two weeks after graduation. *"I just want to be able to have fun at college without being tied down to a relationship."* That was the excuse he gave me. We had been dating for almost a year at that point. Did I really expect to be with him forever? No. But I also thought he would have at least put in a little more effort. I mean, we had a lot of fun senior year and I kind of figured it wasn't going to last much past high school anyway. But it still hurt, nonetheless. We both agreed to remain friends and catch up whenever we had a break at the same time. Did I love him? Honestly, I have no idea. I don't even know what love feels like. I liked him a lot, absolutely, and I enjoyed the time we had together. Another thing. I don't think that sex is supposed to be like that. I didn't have an orgasm once with him. It was always over within a minute or two, so it's really hard to know if it was good or not. Well, he seemed to think so. He obviously got off every single time with no great effort. Must be nice. I've never told any of this to Myles because I don't know if it would make him uncomfortable or not. But I do know that, from my research, sex is supposed to be at least a little better than what I had experienced.

"Nope. Haven't heard from him since we broke up in June. I see him sometimes out and about, but I've never talked to him or anything like that," I replied, brought out of my own thoughts.

"Oh, well, that's good then."

"Of course, you would say that. You hated the guy," I said.

"Yeah, because he's a tool. You're too good for him," replied Myles.

"Maybe I should aim for someone who can at least give me a good orgasm once in a while," I joked, looking right at Myles after I said it.

Myles spat out the water that he had been drinking and his cheeks turned bright red. And that was the exact reaction for which I was hoping.

"Uh, what?" he managed to say after having a coughing fit.

"You heard me. I never had an orgasm with Chad."

"Wait. Not once?" he asked.

"Nope, not even once," I replied.

"So, what? He just got his and then was done?"

"I guess. It only lasted like two minutes, so it wasn't really a big deal or anything. Well, okay, I guess it is a little bit of a big deal. It's not like I have anyone else to compare it to, so maybe it's just me."

"I doubt it is you. Did you ever talk to him about it to tell him what you wanted?"

"No. It's okay, though. That's what this little guy is for," I replied as I pulled out my vibrator from my top dresser drawer and held it up to show Myles. The look on his face was priceless and his cheeks turned even more red than before.

"God, Prim. You did not need to tell me about that. This is crossing some kind of friendship boundary line," Myles replied, covering his eyes.

"What boundary? We don't have any," I said.

"Well, I just set one. No sex or vibrator talk with me. Please. I don't want that image in my head."

"Okay, okay, no more sex talk. Promise," I teased. Of course, I didn't mean it. I promptly turned on the vibrator and started to chase him around the room with it on full blast.

"I swear to God, Prim. I'm going to kill you."

We both collapsed on my bed, stomachs aching from laughing so much.

"Or maybe I'll just use it right here and now," I teased again. "I've been pretty lacking in that area recently."

"You better fucking not," replied Myles.

***

"Are you gonna miss me?" I asked Myles.

"Oh, shush, it's only going to be two weeks and then I'll be here too."

Soccer preseason. Two weeks of grueling work on and off the field. But it does mean that we get to be on the Silver Creek University campus two weeks before everyone else moves in, so it'll be nice to have at least a little bit of peace and quiet before the crowds come in. Myles decided to drive me here because both of my parents are away at some kind of medical conference this weekend. They were sad that they couldn't bring me, but we all said our goodbyes this past week. I told Myles I could drive myself, but he insisted. My parents are going to bring my car here when Myles comes to school in two weeks, so I'll have my car and more freedom then.

We grabbed the boxes and suitcases out of Myles's car and then started walking to my dorm building. Out front, there was a huge red and black sign with the words, "Welcome to Silver Creek University! Home of the Wolves."

"You excited to be a wolf?" asked Myles.

"I am as fast as one," I replied, winking at him.

We got up to my dorm room and, when I opened the door, the room was still empty. My roommate isn't here yet. This building and the one next to it housed both the women's and the men's soccer teams. Each building has a couple of floors specifically designated for the teams. Since these are both freshmen dorms, it'll be nice to bond with the other freshmen girls on the team.

"Maybe your roommate won't show up and you'll get the room to yourself," said Myles.

"I highly doubt it. Everyone has until tomorrow to get here so I'm sure she will be here by then."

I walked over to the desk by the window and put my two boxes on top. The best part about coming early is that I get to choose which side of the room I want. I choose the window side. Our window looks right out to the campus quad. Right in the middle of campus. I walked over to the desk on the other side of the room and pick up the note laying there,

"Welcome to the team, Prim, and Remington. Hope you're excited to start practice. See you tomorrow!

—Coach Wimble."

"Oh, my roommate's name is Remington."

"Nice name," replied Myles.

"Look, it has our phone numbers on here. I should send her a text."

"Or you could just wait to see her tomorrow like a normal person?" asked Myles.

"Fuck off. I'm sending her a text," I replied, picking up my phone and opening the messaging app.

Me–Hi Remington! This is Prim O'Brien. Surprise! I'm your roommate. And soccer teammate, of course. I'm already here in the room so I'll see you soon, I guess.

A minute later my phone buzzed on the desk.

Remington–Hey Prim! I'll be there first thing tomorrow morning. Can't wait to meet you!

"Do you want me to walk you down to your car?" I asked as I turned toward Myles.

"Wow. Already kicking me out, huh?"

"No, I didn't mean it like that. I just meant I don't want you to have to drive in the dark the whole time. It's getting late."

"Nah. Two hours will fly by. But, uh, yeah, you can walk me out, if you want."

We walked to his car, and I turned to give him a hug.

"What was that for?" asked Myles, releasing me from the hug.

"A thank you for bringing me. And, also, I can't remember the last time we spent two weeks apart, so I'll miss you, punk," I replied, punching his shoulder.

"Well, I'll only be a phone call away and you'll be busy running and such, so you won't even notice I'm gone."

"Myles, do you think things will change?" I asked.

"What do you mean?"

"Since we're in college now. Do you think things are going to change between us? I mean, we've been in such a comfort zone back at home and in school, but now things are different."

"I think it's going to take a bit to get fully adjusted to being on our own here, but I don't think things are going to change between us, if that's what you mean."

"You're right. Forget I said anything. I think I'm just nervous."

"Don't be nervous. Everything is going to work out."

"Okay. Well, thanks again for bringing me here. I'll see you soon, all right?" I asked.

"Have a good time, Prim. Let me know if you need anything."

"I will. Be careful driving home."

Myles got into his car, I waved and then turned to start walking back toward the dorm.

"Prim!" Myles called as I turned back around. "Did you remember to pack Mr. Tusky?"

"Of course, I did! He's right inside my duffel bag," I replied.

"He'll help if you're lonely."

"I'll pretend he's you and talk his ears off," I said.

"I don't doubt it. 'Bye, Prim."

"'Bye, Myles. I'll see you soon. Love you."

"Love you too," replied Myles.

I waved again as Myles started the car and drove away. I felt a knot in my stomach as I saw his car turn the corner out of sight. See you soon, best friend. Now, off to my home-away-from-home.

CHAPTER 2

Prim

The next morning, I woke up to the sun beaming through the window and a girl with red hair laying on the other bed typing on her phone. She looked over at me as I sat up in bed.

"Oh, great, you're awake!" she said. "I'm Remington. You can call me Rem. Everyone else does."

"Hi, Remington, or Rem. Sorry, I probably look like a mess," I replied.

"Oh, girl, you're fine. I didn't want to wake you, so I was just hanging out until you woke up. Mind if I turn some music on?" asked Rem.

"No, go ahead. Do you need help unpacking or anything?" I asked her.

"No, I'm okay. Thanks though. So, tell me all about you. Obviously, your name is Prim. What's your major?"

"I'm doing a double-major. Education and English. I can't decide yet if I want to do elementary or secondary education, but it's always nice to have that English major just in case I teach middle or high school."

"Oh, well, that sounds fun! My mom is a secretary at an elementary school down the street from here, so she tells me all kinds of stories about the kids. I'm studying to be an accountant. Runs in my family apparently. My dad, uncle, and brother are all accountants," replied Remington.

"Well, I will definitely be calling you when I need my taxes done."

"Free of charge! Well, maybe some booze wouldn't hurt as payment," laughed Remington.

We both laughed as I got out of bed and put on my robe.

"You sure you don't want any help?" I asked her.

"No, it's okay. I have a whole system," she replied.

"I completely understand that. I have some cereal and milk in the fridge if you want some breakfast?" I asked.

"Oh, I would love that, thanks. What time do we have to be down on the field for practice?"

"Oh, shit, that's right. Let me look quickly," I replied.

I walked to my desk and grabbed the stack of papers that Coach Wimble sent us over the summer.

"We have to be at the field by twelve-thirty p.m."

"That's perfect. We'll have time to get to know each other a little more before we must head out," she replied.

"Sure! What else would you like to know?" I asked.

"Hmm, well, for starters. Who's that handsome guy in the picture beside your bed? Sorry if I'm being nosy. It's just all part of my personality," laughed Remington.

I start laughing. "Oh, no, I don't mind. I want to get to know everyone too. And that," I say pointing to the picture, "is Myles. We've been best friends since third grade."

"Just friends?" replied Remington.

"Yes, absolutely. We get mistaken for a couple a lot, so you aren't the first. We're just close, that's all."

I saw Remington raise her eyebrows at me. Since almost everyone Myles and I have run into has given us this same look, I just start laughing.

"What? I swear, there's nothing going on between us. If something were supposed to happen, it would have already happened by now," I replied.

"Not necessarily," she said.

"Well, not for us. Anyway, what about you? Are you seeing anyone?" I asked her.

I could see that Rem's face changed a bit at that question. Should I not have asked? Please don't be awkward already. I just met this girl.

"I was dating someone from high school, but we decided to go our own ways for now. He plays soccer too and our schools are far apart so we wouldn't be able to see or talk to each other a lot. It was for the best," Remington said as she shrugged her shoulders.

"I'm sorry if it's a sore subject," I replied.

"Oh, no need to apologize. I was certainly the one to open that door. Everything is fine now so no big deal. Promise."

"Well, I'm always here to talk if you need me. My ex and I broke up in June, so I understand the recent breakup situation."

"Boys are dumb," replied Remington.

"So dumb," I agreed.

I noticed that we only had an hour before we needed to get to practice so we both started to get our equipment packed.

"Are you gonna drive down to the field or walk?" asked Remington.

"Myles brought me here actually, so I don't have my car here yet."

"Do you want to ride with me? My car is parked just outside in the lot."

"Yeah, if you don't mind. That would be great. Thanks," I replied.

"All right, let's go. You ready for our first college practice?" she asked.

"Hell, yes," I said as we walked out of our room.

***

I was not, in fact, ready for my first college practice. That was absolute torture. My high school coach has nothing on Coach Wimble. We did full-field sprints, suicide drills, and then repeated it all over again.

"I promise you'll thank me when the season starts," said Coach Wimble after we all had passed out on the ground after practice was over.

As everyone was stretching, I saw the men's soccer team walking over to the field. They must have practice right after us. As I stood up to get some water, I felt someone behind me. I turned around to see that I had stepped on one of the guy's feet with my cleats.

"Oh, my god. I'm so sorry. Are you okay?" I asked with concern.

"Shit. Yeah. I'm all right. No worries," he said as he started to rub his toe.

"Does it hurt? Fuck, I'm so sorry. Can I get you something?"

"Well, your name would be a nice start," he replied.

"Are you really using a pickup line in a situation like this?" I ask.

Laughing, he says, "It's not a pick-up line. I really would like to know your name. The team was watching from over there and I saw you score a really nice goal. So, I wanted to congratulate you, umm…" he trailed off.

"Prim. My name is Prim. How about you?"

"My name is Jared. Prim, nice to meet you. How was the first practice?"

"Hi, Jared. And it was brutal. High school was nothing like this. I definitely have my work cut out for me," I replied.

"Yeah, I'm not looking forward to all the running. I might just quit now," he says.

"We can quit together," I said, and I looked over to see Jared laughing to himself. "But all jokes aside, good luck out there. I'm sure we will see each other around. It was nice to meet you, Jared."

"Yeah, you too. Talk to you later."

I watched as Jared walked to rejoin the rest of his teammates. As I was watching, I felt people right next to me. I looked to my right and Remington and two girls that we ran drills with Vesper and Jax, were staring at me with wide eyes.

"Umm, what the fuck was that?" asked Vesper.

"What was what?" I replied.

"Who was that hunk?" she responded.

"Oh, umm, his name is Jared. I accidentally stepped on his foot and the conversation just kind of went from there, I guess."

"Look at you! Not even twenty-four hours on campus yet and you already have a love interest. I'm jealous!" shrieked Jax.

"Love interest? Uh, yeah, I don't think so. We literally just met."

"That is Jared Johnson. He went to my rival high school, so I've heard some stories about him," said Remington.

"Good or bad stories?" I asked.

"Both, actually. Just that he can be kind of cocky, so just be careful with that one," advised Rem.

"Got it. Thanks for the heads-up."

"Well, it is college. You live and you learn, right? No one said you can't enjoy the ride," Vesper said, winking at Prim. I didn't fail to notice her sexual innuendo. This girl is something else.

"He does have a very nice ass, I'll give him that," said Jax.

All of us laughed, packed up our things, and then headed toward the cafeteria for lunch. We all sat around one of the biggest tables so that the team could all fit. We grabbed our food, sat down, and talked about practice and what we thought about Coach Wimble so far. We all agreed that it was much harder than high school, but that was to be expected at the next level. Coach Wimble wasn't too bad.

Vesper poked me in the side. "Hey, look who it is," she said, pointing to the front door.

"Wow, have we been sitting here that long?" I asked, seeing the men's team coming down the stairs.

I looked at the team and noticed that Jared was walking right up to our table.

"Hey, ladies. What are you all up to tonight?" he asked.

I noticed that there were a lot of shoulder shrugs and "nothing" responses, so Jared continued.

"Well, we thought it would be a fun idea if our teams had a big get-together tonight on the floors. You down?"

I looked at Vesper, Jax, and Remington and they were all nodding in agreement at Jared. There were a bunch of girls who said, "yes please!" and "sounds great." Jared then looked right at me.

"Prim, are you going to be there?"

I knew my face was turning red. I was the center of attention of both teams at this point. I looked over at the girls and they kept nudging me to answer him.

"Umm, yeah, sure. I'll be there. Thanks for the invite," I replied, elbowing Ves in the side of her boob.

"Great. I'll see you tonight. Oh, and make sure to bring your pillows and blankets. This is going to be a sleepover," Jared said as he turned to walk toward the food bar.

"Uh, that boy likes you," said Ves.

"No. It's just because we met earlier on the field," I replied.

"Honey, he didn't look at us. He looked at you and only you," said Jax.

***

Later that night, Remington and I gathered our pillows and blankets and headed to the building next to ours. We met Jax and Vesper in their room first and then we were going to head down to the boys' floor.

"So, how exactly are we packing all these people into the tiny dorm rooms?" I asked.

"I guess we're gonna be extra cozy tonight. The guys obviously did this on purpose. I'm sure they aren't expecting it to be just a "bonding time," responded Remington.

"Not if I can help it," Vesper said, winking at the guy that just passed us in the hall.

"You do you, girl," replied Jax. "Our room will be free later tonight if you need to use it."

I looked past Vesper's shoulder to see Jared walking toward us. Why is he always walking toward us? It's like his thing now. Should I be concerned?

"So, are you ladies ready for a good time?" asked Jared.

"Well, that depends on how good it's going to be now, doesn't it?" I responded.

The girls were looking at me and trying to hide their grins with their hands. Remington cleared her throat.

"So, whose room are we going to?"

Jared grinned. "Mine and Tommy's. Right this way," he said as he pointed down the hallway.

We followed him and got to his room where five other people were already sitting and chatting away.

"I recognize the four guys on the team, but who are you?" asked Vesper, looking, and pointing at the guy who was sitting on the bed.

"Hey there. I'm Theo. Tommy is my cousin, so he invited me to come to school early and hang out with the team," replied Theo.

"Are you going to Silver Creek too, or are you just visiting?" I asked.

"I'll be here just like you guys," Theo replied.

"He was Valedictorian at our high school so he's been rubbing it in our faces that he could have taken his pick of any college he wanted but chose this one," Tommy said. "Am I right, Theo?"

"Hey, if you have the brains, you gotta brag about it."

"Well, I was Valedictorian of my high school too, but you don't see me bragging to anyone who will listen," Ves replied.

"Oh, well, it looks like you're going to have some competition then. Uh, sorry, I didn't catch your name?" Theo asked as he looked over at Ves.

"My name is Vesper. My friends call me Ves. Guess which one you should call me?"

"Ouch, that dug deep," Theo replied as he grabbed his chest and faked offense. "Well, it was nice to meet you, Vesper. I'm sure I'll be able to call you Ves very soon."

"Don't count on it," Ves replied, crossing her arms.

"All right, everyone, how about we set up our stuff and try to enjoy as much of the night as we can without killing anyone," I said, trying to ease the tension.

"I agree. Here, Prim, you can put your things over here," said Jared and he pointed next to what I'm going to assume was his spot.

"Yeah, sure. Thanks," I replied and put my pillows and blanket next to his.

Once everyone had made up their beds, the speakers were turned on, the music turned up, and the dancing commenced. Rem, Ves, Jax, and I followed Jared and Tommy down to the basement. There was an entire lounge area fully equipped with a kitchen and a game area, including a pool table.

"You girls up for some pool?" Jared asked as he took one of the sticks off the wall and handed it over to me.

"Sure, but I haven't played in a while. I might be a little rusty," I replied, taking the stick from him and getting myself set up. I may have lied about not playing in a while. Myles and I were pool champions throughout high school. No one could beat us in gym class. But Jared doesn't have to know that does he?

"I'll help you if you need me to."

"Yeah, actually, could you help me? I'm not quite sure how to hold the stick," I said, making sure to emphasize the sexual innuendo at the end. I watched as Jared bit his bottom lip. Oh, this was going to be fun.

Jared came up behind me and positioned the stick in my hands until I was ready to hit the ball. "Now, all you do is push the stick forward so that you push the white ball into all the others."

"Oh, you mean like this?" I replied as I hit the cue ball with my stick and broke the pool balls. Two stripes into the corner pockets.

Jared's mouth fell open.

"Oh, and Jared, that white ball you were talking about? It's called the cue ball. Maybe you should look that up," I said as I walked past him and patted his chest.

"You said you hadn't played in a while," he replied.

"I said I hadn't played in a while. I never said I wasn't good. I think you've met your match."

"Maybe I have," he said, laughing and making a motion for me to continue with the game.

After I had completely wrecked Jared in pool, we decided to go upstairs and call it a night. When we were settled in our spots, all the people in the rooms next to us screamed, "Goodnight, ya'll! Keep your hands to yourself!" Everyone started laughing and getting under the covers. Sleeping on college mattresses pushed together wasn't the most comfortable thing but it was better than the hard floor.

The lights all got turned off and I looked over to see Remington and Jax next to each other. Vesper was by the closet next to that Theo guy she was talking to earlier. I wonder how she got stuck over there. I rolled over on my side so that I was facing where Jared was laying. He turned on his side, so he was also facing me. Well, this was a little awkward. He was staring at me. I was staring at him. He reached out his arm and folded his hand over mine. I could hear my breath getting caught in my throat. We lay there like that until it seemed like everyone around us had fallen asleep. When the only sound in the room was the sound of everyone snoring, Jared leaned over to me, took my face in his hands, and kissed me.

"Goodnight, Prim," Jared said and then rolled back over to his side.

What the hell just happened? I feel like I can't move or breathe. I hope no one saw us. I had just closed my eyes and was half asleep when I saw my phone light up. I picked it up and opened a message from Myles.

Myles–Anything interesting happen yet?

Well, that was one word for it.

Chapter 3

Myles

It's been a week and a half since I dropped Prim off at school. To most people that wouldn't be a long time. For us, it's very unusual. I think the only times we've been apart for longer than a week is if one of our families went on vacation. But, even then, our families have gone on a lot of vacations together. I've called her a couple of times during the last week to see how pre-season has been doing. The other times I tried calling she said she was busy, which is understandable. She also told me that she has something to tell me when I get on campus. Some kind of surprise. I texted her at the end of her first day of practice and asked if anything interesting had happened.

Prim–Well, it's funny you ask.

Me–Oh yeah? How come?

Prim–It's a surprise. I'll show you and tell you when you get here!

I've been trying to figure out what the surprise could be ever since. Now, I need to finish packing. I swear I'm almost as bad as Prim. I shouldn't have teased her. It's just too easy. The best part about teasing her is that she always gets flustered and then runs her fingers through her blonde hair. I have her hair all over my clothes all the time. God, I miss her. I'm actually planning to get to school a little earlier than expected, so I'll be there early tomorrow morning. I'm planning on following Prim's parents to Silver Creek since they have to take Prim's car to her, so I'm going to stay at their house tonight so we can get an early start.

"We want to beat traffic," said Prim's dad, Mr. O'Brien. But I know it's just because they miss her already too so they want to see her as soon as they can. It's what happens when you're an only child, like both Prim and I are.

I get to the O'Brien house around five-thirty p.m. since they told me to come for dinner.

"Hi, sweetie," says Prim's mom.

"Nice to see you, Margaret," I replied.

Now, it might seem like I'm being rude by calling her by her first name, but she forces me to. I grew up calling her Mrs. O'Brien and she is not a big fan. She tells me that it makes her sound old. For obvious reasons, I don't want to offend her, so Margaret it is.

"Ready for the big transition?" asked Prim's dad.

"I think so, Sam," I replied. Again, same deal. I swear. They won't let me call them by anything other than their first names. It's not by choice. I would just like to stay in their good graces.

"Did you get a haircut?" asked Margaret.

"Uh, yeah. I thought I would get it cut a bit before going to school. It was getting a little long. And Prim told me it looked bad," I replied. And that was putting it nicely. *"It literally looks like you haven't washed your hair in a month. It's so scraggly."* Her exact words. So, of course, I got it cut.

"Well, it looks nice. Don't let her boss you around," said Margaret.

"I'll try my best," I answer.

We sat down to have dinner. Mr. O'Brien. Oops. *Sam* is one of my favorite cooks. Tonight, was beef stroganoff. Delicious is an understatement.

"So, Myles, I talked to Prim's school counselor today at yoga," started Margaret.

"Oh yeah?" I asked, wondering where this conversation was going.

"Yes. She knows you and Prim are close, so she asked me if you were excited to go to Lakewood," she replied.

My heart dropped into my stomach. Shit. If Prim finds out…

"Oh, umm," I started.

"You wanted to go to Lakewood, didn't you?" she asked.

"Please don't tell Prim. She was so excited when I told her that I got into Silver Creek," I pleaded.

"We figured that she didn't know," replied Sam.

"I knew that if I told her, she would make me go to Lakewood. There wouldn't have been any questions. I just couldn't…" I cut off.

"We know, honey, we know," said Margaret as she reached over and put her hand on mine. I looked over at Sam who was already nodding his head.

"Is it that obvious?" I asked, not able to look at them, feeling the tears burning behind my eyes.

"No. You're doing a good job hiding it. We're just very observant people," Sam replied.

"I don't think it runs in the family," I said trying to force a smile.

Margaret squeezed my hand a little tighter. "She'll come around."

I met her eyes and wished that were true.

***

I slept in the guest bedroom last night. I am using the word "sleep" pretty loosely here. It wasn't really sleeping. Prim's parents know. They said that I was good at hiding it, but I know they were just saying that to make me feel better. I turned off the alarm on my phone, grabbed my duffel bag, and headed out to meet Prim's parents. We got on the road around eight-thirty a.m. and headed to campus. Before we left, I sent a quick text to Prim.

Me–I have a surprise for you too.

I checked my phone again twenty minutes later at a red light. No response yet. She was probably at morning practice. We got to campus a little before eleven. We pulled up to the parking lot and Prim's mom parked her car at the front of the lot. The parking lot was in the middle of the two freshmen buildings. I was in one building and Prim was in the other. Close enough.

"I'll go see if she's in her room and have her come down to see you both. She hasn't responded to my text yet, so, hopefully, she isn't still at practice. You think she'll help me take my stuff to my room?" I teasingly asked.

"Well, she better," replied Sam.

I nodded, walked into the building on the right, and headed up to where I remembered Prim's room was. As I got to the hallway, I noticed that Prim's door wasn't shut all the way. I pushed in the door and saw two people on Prim's bed. Two people making out. And one of them was, of course, Prim.

"Prim?" I asked, not knowing what was happening. Well, I think I figured out what she meant about a surprise.

"Myles? What are you doing here? Christ, can you maybe knock?" she replied, pulling her shirt back on.

"I'm sorry. The door wasn't closed so I figured it was okay," I replied. I looked over to the guy standing next to her who had a very obvious erection.

"Umm, hi, Myles, is it?" he asked.

"Yes, that's me. And who are you?" I replied.

"Myles. Don't be rude. Myles, this is Jared, my boyfriend. Jared, this is Myles, my best friend from back home. He's going to school here too," said Prim.

"It's nice to meet you," said Jared as he extended his hand to me. I didn't take it. I looked over at Prim and she was staring daggers at me, so I caved.

I lifted my hand to Jared's and shook.

"I've heard a lot about you," Jared said.

"And I've heard absolutely nothing about you," I replied.

"That's because I was waiting until you got here. I was going to formally introduce you two when you got to campus. Why did you get here so early?" asked Prim.

"Because I wanted to see you. I sent you a text," I replied, looking between the two of them. "Clearly, you were too busy to check it."

As if purposefully sent to break the tension, a girl walked into the room behind me.

"Woah, it's a party in here," the girl said while she looked at all of us. Apparently, she noticed the tension. "Uh, everything okay?"

"Everything's great!" Prim replied, plastering on the fakest smile I had ever seen from her before. "Myles just got here a little earlier than expected. Myles, this is Remington, my roommate."

"So, this is the infamous best friend I've heard so much about. Nice to meet you, Myles, I'm Remington, but you can call me Rem. I heard you're going to school here too?"

"Nice to meet you too, Rem. And you heard correctly," I said as I shook her hand. I didn't fail to notice the annoyed look that Jared gave me when I didn't hesitate to shake Remington's hand.

"Well, welcome to campus. I see you've met Jared already," Remington said as he turned toward her bed. I could have sworn I saw her roll her eyes as she turned. I don't blame her. Okay, maybe I'm giving the guy an unfair judgment. Okay, not maybe. It's biased, I know.

"I did meet Jared, yes," I replied looking back over at Prim and Jared standing shoulder-to-shoulder. "I think I saw a little too much of him when I walked in actually."

Rem gave an understanding nod. "Yeah, it seems to happen a lot," she said as she smirked over at Prim.

"We are standing right here, you know," said Prim.

"Yes, darling, we know," Remington replied as she went over and kissed Prim on the side of the head. "So, what are everyone's plans for the rest of the day?"

"Well, I don't mean to cut in but, Prim, your parents are waiting on us in the parking lot," I said.

"Oh shit. I forgot they were coming with you. Jared, do you want to come down with us to see them? I don't know when you will be able to get to see them next," said Prim.

"Uh, sure. Yeah, let's go," said Jared.

Prim nodded. "Rem, are you going to come down with us?"

"I would love to, but I'm actually running late to meet up with my parents. Say hi to yours for me, okay?" replied Remington.

"Yeah, you too," Prim said. "All right, you two, let's go," she said as she pointed between me and Jared.

Prim, Jared, and I all headed downstairs and out to the parking lot. Prim's parents were still waiting for us by her car.

"Did you get lost up there?" asked Sam. I glanced over toward Prim and Jared.

"Uh, no, Prim's roommate was up in the room, so we were talking to her for a while. Sorry about that," I said. Sam nodded. Prim looked over at me with an apologetic smile.

"And who is this, Prim?" Margaret asked, looking over at Jared.

"Oh, Mom, Dad, this is Jared. He's, my boyfriend. I wanted to wait until you got here to introduce you all," replied Prim.

"Oh, well, hi, Jared. It's nice to meet you," said Margaret, leaning over to shake Jared's hand. "I'm Mrs. O'Brien." I noticed she didn't have him call her Margaret. Man, I love Prim's parents.

"Yes, Jared, it's very nice to meet you," said Sam, extending his hand as well.

"So, how did you two start dating? You haven't really been here that long. You guys move fast," Margaret said.

"Well, Jared is on the men's soccer team so we've been hanging out a lot since we got here," replied Prim.

"Oh, well, that sounds nice," said Margaret. "Well, Prim, we have your car here, so do you need any help with your room or need anything from the store before we head back home?"

I also didn't fail to notice that Margaret and Sam didn't linger very long on a conversation with Jared. I don't think it was them trying to be rude. Neither of them has a rude bone in their body. Maybe our conversation from last night is putting them off to the idea of other men in Prim's life. Or maybe they are just taking pity on me. That's it. It fits though. I'm taking pity on myself as we are all standing here. Cue the small violin.

"No, I think I'm okay. Thanks, though. I appreciate it," replied Prim.

"Myles, do you need help taking your things to your room?" asked Sam.

"No, I think I'll be good. I think Prim and I can handle it. Right?" I ask as I nudge Prim on the side of her arm.

"Yeah, we got it. You two can go home so you don't have to be out too long. I have another practice soon, or else I would have said we all could have grabbed lunch or something," replied Prim.

"Oh, it's okay, honey, we know you're busy," Margaret said, looking a little less lively than she had a couple of minutes ago. "Well, it was nice to meet you, Jared. I'm sure we will see each other again soon."

"It was nice to see you both too," replied Jared, waving to Prim's parents.

"All right, Myles, let's get your things to take to your room," said Prim.

"Hey, Prim, I'm going to head back to my room to get ready for practice, okay?" asked Jared.

"Oh, uh, okay, I'll see you later at the field then," replied Prim.

"'Bye, Mr. and Mrs. O'Brien!" said Jared, turning to walk back toward his dorm. Sam and Margaret waved goodbye.

"You don't have to help me if you want to hang out with him more," I said to Prim.

"No, it's okay. I'll see him later anyway," she replied.

"Okay, well, thanks," I said as Prim walked toward my car.

I walked over to Sam and Margaret to say goodbye, wanting to at least try to move past this awkward moment.

"So, did you know about Jared?" Sam asked me, making sure Prim was out of earshot.

"Nope. Just found out right before you both did. She told me last week she had a surprise to show me. Well, surprise," I replied, forcing a chuckle.

"Are you going to be all right?" Margaret asked.

"Oh, yeah, I'll be fine. I've been doing it for years. What's a couple more, right? Being close to her is enough for me."

"Well, you know where to find us if you want to talk," replied Margaret.

"Thanks," I said as she took me into a hug. I needed it more than I thought I did.

Sam and Margaret walked over to Prim to hug her and say goodbye, while I grabbed a couple of bags from my front seat.

"And you joked about me bringing too many things," said Prim as she smiled over at me. There it was. That smile.

"I mean, would you expect anything less?" I asked grabbing two more bags from my trunk. "So, I'm guessing Jared is the surprise you were talking about?"

"Yeah. I didn't think you would be walking in on us, so I wish that introduction was a bit better. Maybe I shouldn't have made him come down to meet my parents so soon. The whole thing was fucking awkward."

"I mean, it's up to you. He didn't really stick around very long though," I replied. "He seemed quiet."

"Well, you had just walked in on us and then I sprung meeting my parents on him suddenly. Wouldn't you feel a little nervous?" replied Prim, raising her voice a bit more than I was used to.

"Okay, okay, yeah, I get it. Sorry," I said, starting to walk toward my building.

"Myles, I'm sorry. Wait. Wait for me," Prim said but I kept walking. So much for my surprise. Not that I am much of a surprise to her at this point in our lives anyway. I just thought it would be nice to see her a little earlier. Now, I know that I'm more upset about this situation because I saw her and Jared kissing. But I'm just being protective. I am not, I repeat, not jealous. You know what? Never mind. I am jealous. A lot. Goddamnit.

I get to my dorm room, Prim still calling out for me as she's coming up the stairs. Okay, maybe I'm being a little overdramatic.

"Prim, the room is right here," I say.

"Jesus. Why did you just walk away like that?" she asked.

"Because you ruined my surprise," I replied.

"I didn't mean to. You can show me now. What is it?"

"Me, Prim. The surprise was me. I came to school early to see you," I said. I could see her eyes soften at that.

I put the key into my room lock and picked the bags up off the floor. The room was empty, so I figured my roommate wasn't here yet. Well, I guess I'll be like Prim and be able to pick the best side of the room. Honestly, it doesn't matter to me, so I just set my bags on the bed to my left. Prim did the same.

"Myles, look, I'm sorry. I know you wanted to surprise me. And you did. Thank you for coming early. It means a lot," she said.

"Does it though?" I asked. "It doesn't seem like it. Even with your parents. You barely talked to them while they were here. They didn't have to bring your car to school. You could have introduced them to Jared another time. This is what happens when you're dating someone. You get so obsessive and act like no one else around you matters."

I could see that tears were forming in Prim's eyes. "I'm sorry," she said. "You're right. I should have asked my parents to stay longer. I just. This is just so new, so I don't know how to act. Myles, I'm sorry. I'm glad you're here." She came over and wrapped her arms around me. Peaches. I missed that smell.

"I know. I'm sorry too. I shouldn't have said all that to you. I didn't mean to hurt your feelings," I replied, patting her back as we continued hugging. She tucked her head and chin tighter into my chest. I wonder if she can hear how fast my heart is beating. She broke off the hug. Oh, thank the universe.

"Okay, well, I should go get ready for practice. There were only a couple more bags in your car. Do you want me to help you?" Prim asked.

"No, I can get them, thanks," I said. "Have a good practice and I'll talk to you later, okay?"

"Yeah," said Prim as she started toward the door then stopped. "Oh, and Myles?"

"Yeah?" I asked, looking up at her.

"Thanks for the surprise. I missed you," she replied and then turned to walk down the hallway.

I continued unpacking my bags as I'm smiling like a damn idiot over an, "I missed you." Hopefully, coming to this school wasn't a terrible mistake that's going to completely wreck me.

And I probably just jinxed myself.

CHAPTER 4

Myles

Monday morning. First day of college classes. First day of freshmen year. I double-check my schedule and it looks like I have Introduction to Psychology first thing at eight-thirty this morning. I'm looking forward to this class. I took a psychology class in high school, which is how I figured out that I wanted to major in it. I think I might want to do some kind of therapy for kids, but I haven't figured that out yet. I still have some time. We don't have to declare our majors until sophomore year. As I head out my door, I pull out the campus map because I have no idea where I'm going, and this place is huge. I probably should be watching where I'm going because, before I know it, I bump into someone. Not just someone. Prim's roommate, Remington.

"Oh, sorry," she starts. "Oh, hi, Myles!" as she realizes who I am.

"Hey, Remington. Or wait, Rem, right?" I reply.

"You remembered! A lot of people continue to call me my full name so it's whatever. It's just more for them to say," she replied.

"Well, either one is fine with me. It's all about what you prefer," I say.

"I prefer Rem, but it doesn't catch on with most people," she replies.

"Rem it is then," I say back to her.

"Well, thanks. So, did you get all settled in your room?" she asked.

"Yeah. All moved in. Just trying to figure out where my first class is. Do you know where Stevens Hall is?"

"I sure do. Right behind that fountain over there," she said pointing.

"Thanks. That would have taken me forever. I'm not good with maps or directions," I reply.

"I'm not either. But I did read the big sign on the building that says, "Stevens Hall," Rem says, starting to laugh. "I'm just kidding. I got lost too. I went around last week during pre-season to make sure I knew where all of my classes were."

"Makes sense. Do you have any classes with Prim?" I ask.

"I'm not sure. I was going to ask her yesterday, but she was with Jared all day, so I didn't get a chance to."

"That would be why I couldn't get a hold of her then."

"Yeah, she is with him a lot of the time," she says.

"I take it you're not a fan of Jared?" I ask her.

"Why would you say that?"

"I saw you roll your eyes the day I moved in. Your response was very telling," I say.

Rem smirked. "It's not that I don't like him. It's just that he went to my rival high school, so I know a lot of stories about him."

"What kind of stories?" I ask.

"Well, from what I've heard, he seems to move on from girl to girl pretty quickly. I just don't want Prim to get hurt."

"I don't either so thanks for letting me know," I say as I look at my watch. "Well, I appreciate you showing me where the building is. We should all hang out sometime soon. Talk to you later?" I ask.

"Yeah, sure. 'Bye Myles. Talk to you later."

I walk into Stevens Hall and turn right to go down the psychology hallway. Room 120. I open the door and walk in to find that the classroom is a big lecture-style setup. Rows and rows of seats. I choose a row somewhere in the middle. There are about ten other students in the room already. Maybe I wasn't running as late as I thought. Unless college kids don't care and just show up whenever they want. Hmm, yeah, let's go with that. I pull out a notebook and pen and then mess around on my phone for a couple of minutes.

"Hey, stranger!" I hear as I lift my head. It was Prim.

"Hey! Do you have this class too?" I ask.

"Yes, sir. It's part of my education program," Prim replied as she sat down beside me. "Looks like we're stuck with each other this semester." If only she knew that was the whole reason, I came to this school in the first place. To be stuck with her.

"Looks like it. So how was the rest of your weekend?" I ask.

"It was good. Jared and I had a movie marathon, so it was nice."

"So how did you two get together anyway? I haven't been able to ask you yet," I reply.

"I stepped on his foot on the soccer field by mistake and the conversation just kind of went from there. Both teams had a get-together that same night, so it was fun," Prim said.

"A sleepover party?" I asked, trying to hold back all of the images that were popping up in my head.

"Yeah, we squeezed a whole bunch of people into the rooms. It was funny," she replied.

"And who did you sleep with?" I asked.

"Well, it was me, Rem, Vesper, and Jax in Jared's room. Another guy, Theo, was in there. And then a couple of others."

"And you slept next to…" I trailed off, waiting for Prim's response.

"I slept next to Jared and another girl on the team," she replied.

"Well, aren't you two just a match made in heaven," I added.

"Shut up," was her only reply. She took out her books and put them on her desk.

I looked up and realized that the room was mostly full by now.

"Excuse me, is this seat taken?" I looked up to my right to where the girl who just spoke was standing. She was smiling down at me.

"Oh, no, go ahead. It's yours," I replied and moved my bag off the seat.

"Thanks. Of course, I'm running late on the first day, so I had to sprint here. You're a lifesaver. I did not want to have to sit at the front. That is a college no-no," she replied. "Or so I've heard."

I laughed. "I'm Myles. Nice to meet you." I leaned over to shake her hand.

"Sabrina. Nice to meet you too."

"Oh, and this is Prim. We grew up together," I said pointing to my left at Prim.

"Nice to meet you, Prim," Sabrina said, leaning over to shake her hand too.

"Hi, Sabrina. You too," replied Prim.

"Well, look at this. We've already made some friends. I'm gonna call this day a success," said Sabrina.

The front door of the classroom opened. "All right, good morning, class! I'm Professor Gable. Who's ready for an eventful semester?"

Chapter 5

Prim

"Hey, do either of you have a pen that I could borrow?" Sabrina says as she looks over at me and Myles.

"Yeah, here. I have different colors, so you can take the one you want," I reply.

"You're awesome. Thanks," she says.

Professor Gable had just come into the classroom and introduced himself. We were in a classroom of around a hundred-and-fifty people. This class was huge. It is an introduction class, so I guess it makes sense. Professor Gable was well over six feet tall. He looked like a giant compared to my five-feet-four frame. He was even taller than Myles. I turned to Myles to comment on their heights, but he was already turned toward Sabrina, having a conversation that I couldn't make out. Okay, so he has a new friend. No big deal. Although, honestly, I don't blame him. I haven't been the best friend lately. He surprised me by coming to school early, and what did I do? I yelled at him. That's what I did. Good going, Prim. He was right. I do get obsessive when I'm dating someone. I just never know how to find a good balance between everything. I like Jared, I really do. And now that Myles is here, I just need to figure out how to spend time with both. I'm so caught up in my thoughts that I didn't realize that Professor Gable had been talking for the last ten minutes and I had no idea what he's been saying. Not the best on the first day of classes.

"Prim?" I turn my head toward Myles.

"Yeah?" I ask, realizing that he's now called my name three times.

"You, okay?" Myles asks.

"Oh yeah, sorry. I was just thinking about something. Shh, we shouldn't be talking," I reply.

"That's rich, coming from the person who's been zoned out since class started."

"I just have some things on my mind, that's all."

"Well, we can talk about it after class if you need to," said Myles.

"Yeah, maybe," I reply. There's really nothing to talk about. I just must get used to my best friend and my boyfriend being in the same place. And trying to figure out how to successfully spend time with both without one thinking I'm spending more time with the other. Easy, right?

It felt like class ended as quickly as it started. Although, it's probably because I wasn't paying attention. I'm sure Professor Gable just went over the syllabus. As I was grabbing my bag, I realized that Myles and Sabrina had already turned to walk toward the door. I followed.

"Thanks for waiting for me," I said to Myles.

"Oh, sorry. I thought you were right behind us," replied Myles.

"Hey, you look a little out of it. Is everything okay?" Sabrina asked.

"Yeah, I'm fine. I guess it's just a hectic first day already. I'm good. Thanks though," I replied to her. "So, Sabrina, which freshmen building are you in?"

"I'm in Forest Hall. What about you?" she replied.

"Oh, you're in the same dorm as Myles. That'll be nice. I'm in the other one. You know, where all the cool kids are," I jokingly said.

Sabrina laughed. "You're funny. I like you."

"Well, thanks! You're not so bad yourself," I say.

"Well, it was nice meeting both of you today. Obviously, we are going to see each other this semester, but I need to get going. I told my friend I would meet her after class," Sabrina said.

"Yeah, no problem. We'll see you on Wednesday. Or I might see you in the dorm if you're around," replied Myles.

"'Bye, Sabrina!" I say as she waved and then walked up the aisle and out the door.

"So, what exactly did I miss while I was zoning out?" I ask.

"Well, we have a group project that we need to do. It's due at the end of the semester. Sabrina asked me if we wanted to work with her, so I said yes. Is that okay?"

"Yeah, that sounds great. Sorry, I zoned," I replied.

"It's okay. I just wanted to make sure you are all right," replied Myles.

"Can I ask you something?" I ask.

"You can ask me anything. What's up?" he says.

"Do you think I'm spending too much time with Jared?"

"Well, I mean I haven't been here for that long, so I don't really know. Do you think you are?" Myles asked.

"I just don't want you to think I don't have time for you. I still feel bad about how I reacted when you got here last week."

"I told you; you don't need to worry about it. I understand. It's a new relationship and you're trying to figure everything out. Plus, you have soccer. Of course, you're going to be busy. I get it," replied Myles. "But I'm always here if you need someone to talk to. You're my best friend. Of course, I'm here."

"So does that mean you'll go shopping with me, best friend?" I asked, smiling up at him. I know he can never resist my smiles.

"Shopping for what?"

"There's a big party this weekend and I want to look for a nice outfit. I was thinking about going tonight after practice. Do you want to come with me?"

"Is Jared not going with you?" Myles asks.

"No, he and the other soccer guys are having a game night tonight. Team bonding, I guess," I replied.

"Yeah, sure I'll go. What time should I come to pick you up?" he asked.

"I get done with practice at five, so can you come to get me at like six? It'll give me time to take a quick shower before we leave."

"Sure thing. Did you want to grab dinner before we go to the mall, or did you want to go to the café?" Myles asked.

"Do you want to bring pizza back to my room after we're done shopping? We can watch a movie or something. I feel like this is the first time I'm getting to hang out with you since we got here," I say.

"Sounds good. What movie?" Myles asked.

"How about an action movie? Or a romantic comedy?" I asked.

"How about a horror movie?" Myles replied, smiling at me. He knows how much I hate getting scared.

"How about no," I replied. "Unless you want to stay with me until I fall asleep tonight because I'm scared shitless."

"We can watch whatever you would like to. It doesn't matter to me. I just miss being with you," he replied.

"I do too. Okay, I must get to my next class, but I'll see you in my room tonight at six, okay?" I asked him.

"I'll be there," he replied.

Practice went a little late today. It was almost five-thirty p.m. by the time Coach Wimble let us go. We're getting ready for our first game, so he's making sure we are in top-notch form. With how much he makes us all "get on the line," we can probably outrun any team in our division by now. We say goodbye to Vesper and Jax and then Remington and I head back up to our room.

"Myles is coming over tonight to watch a movie if that's all right with you?" I ask her.

"Yeah, of course. I saw him earlier this morning and said we should all hang out, so it's perfect," she replied.

"Oh great. We're going to bring pizza back, so I'll get enough for all of us."

It was five-fifty by the time I was out of the shower and heard a knock at our door. Of course, I was only in my towel. And, of course, Remington opened the door to let Myles in. He came in, saw me in my towel, and immediately his cheeks got red.

"I always pick the worst time to come to your room. I'll, uh, just wait outside while you get dressed," he says as he leaves the room.

"You did that on purpose," I say to Remington.

"By this time, she is cracking up. "Oh my god, you should have seen the look on both of your faces," she says as she's holding her stomach, she's laughing so hard.

"You're awful," I say chuckling to myself.

"You both are perfect," she replies.

"What do you mean?" I ask.

"Oh, nothing. Don't mind me. Now hurry up so you can go save him from embarrassment."

I throw on a pair of leggings and a Silver Creek University t-shirt, tie up my chucks, pull my hair up in a messy bun, and head out the door. Rem, of course, is still laughing to herself.

"'Bye, lovebird," she calls as I open the door.

I flip her off as I close the door behind me. As expected, Myles is standing out in the hallway still looking a little embarrassed.

"Sorry, I didn't realize you were still changing. I should have texted you," he said, cheeks still red.

"It's not your fault. Rem shouldn't have opened the door. She obviously did it on purpose," I replied.

"Well, are you ready to go? Do you want to just go to the mall, or was there a specific store you had in mind?" Myles asks.

"I think we can just start at the mall and go from there. I'm not exactly sure what I'm looking for yet," I say walking out of the dorm.

"Do you want to take your car, or do you want me to drive?" he asks.

"You can drive. You'll take over the music either way so we can just go in your car," I reply throwing him a smirk.

"Probably a good idea," he replied.

We get to the mall, and it was packed. A lot more packed than I thought it would be on a Monday night. But it did look like mostly college students and families were there. The first store that I saw was *Francesca's*. Looks promising. Maybe I'll try for a dress.

"Let's go in here first," I say to Myles.

Now, when you walk into this store, it's a little bit overwhelming. Everything is color-coordinated, so if you're into that kind of thing, it's like a wet dream. My colors of choice are either black or red. We stop near the red colors first. Red dresses. Red rompers. Red everything. I think a dress might fit a party vibe better. I hold up two red dresses. One dress had off-the-shoulder straps and the second one was long sleeves that were mesh see-through. I held both up to Myles.

"Which one do you like better?" I ask him.

"Umm, I think I like the mesh sleeve one. It looks fancier," he replies.

"Wow. You know the word mesh. I'm impressed," I say.

"Hey. Guys can know things about fashion too."

"Oh, I absolutely know guys like fashion too. I just didn't know that *you* knew things about fashion," I reply.

"You're so funny it's killing me," he says. "Now go try on the dress. I'm getting hungry."

I walk back to the changing room and find the first empty stall. I pull up the dress but realize that I can't reach the zipper in the back to pull it up. Well, this is going to be awkward.

"Hey, Myles," I call, peeking my head outside the curtain.

"What's up?" he responds.

"Umm. I can't zip the back of this dress. Could you help me please?"

"Yeah, if you want me to. Is the rest of you covered? I'd like to not make walking in on you a habit if we could," he replied.

I chuckle. "You won't. I'm all covered. You're good to come in," I say as I open the curtain for him to come in.

"Do you want me to close the curtain or keep it open?" he asks.

"You can close it. I don't want anyone else to see me half-naked," I reply. Great. Now it sounds like I want Myles to see me half-naked. He comes in and closes the curtain.

I turn around so that my back is facing him. The zipper literally starts right above my ass. I feel him take the zipper and slowly slide it upwards.

"Are your hands shaking?" I ask, feeling him tense.

He clears his throat. "No, the zipper just got caught a bit. Give me a second."

He continued zipping the dress and I felt his finger slide against my skin. I could feel goosebumps form all over my skin.

"Are you cold?" he asks.

"A little," I lie, trying to cover up my body's reaction to him touching me.

As he finished zipping the dress, I realized that I had been holding my breath. I let it out as quietly as I could so Myles wouldn't notice. I turned around and showed him the dress.

"So, what do you think?" I asked, twirling in a circle. *Why*? Why did I twirl?

"It looks nice. I like it. Are you going to buy it?" he replies.

"Nice? Just nice?" I ask. "Maybe I should get another one."

"No, no, that's not what I meant; It looks good. Really good. You should get this one," he says.

"Are you sure?" I ask.

"One hundred percent. It's perfect," he replies.

"Now that's more like it," I reply. "Uh, Myles?"

"Yeah?" he asks as he stares back at me.

"Do you mind? I need to take this off," I say.

"Oh shit. Yeah, sorry," he says as he goes out of the stall and closes the curtain behind him.

I change back into my outfit, fold the dress over my arm, and head out to the checkout counter. After I paid for the dress, we walked to the pizza shop that was by the mall exit. We picked up two cheese pizzas for the three of us and then headed back to campus. Rem had on *One Tree Hill* when we got back to the room and got right out of bed when she smelled the pizza.

"So, what are we watching tonight?" Rem asks, grabbing a slice of pizza from the box.

"My pick would be a horror movie, but Prim doesn't like them," Myles responds.

"Oh, come on, Prim! Let's watch a scary movie. Please, please, please," pleads Remington, hanging onto my arm and moving it back and forth.

I look over at Myles and he just shrugs his shoulders and smiles teasingly. Asshole.

"Ugh, fine. *Fine*. But both of you are responsible if I can't fall asleep tonight," I said, caving into both. I swear they planned this behind my back.

Rem and Myles fist bumped as I put the pizza down on the desk. Yes. They definitely planned this.

"So, should we go with a classic or a more modern movie?" Rem asked.

"Let's do a classic," replied Myles. "How about *Halloween* or *Friday the 13th*?"

"Which one has the guy with the white mask in it?" I ask.

"Both," replied Rem and Myles at the same time.

"Well, technically, the guy with the white mask doesn't show up until the second *Friday the 13th* movie, but, yeah," Rem adds.

"Ah, you know your scary movies," Myles replied. "I'm impressed. I can never get this one over here to watch any with me."

"Can we just get this over with please?" I ask, taking a slice of pizza from the box.

Rem takes the remote and opens up Prime Video on the TV. Of course, she already owns both franchises we just talked about.

"Should we start with *Halloween* and then go from there?" Rem asks.

"Sounds like a plan," replies Myles.

"Wait. We're watching more than one of these?" I ask looking between the both of them.

"You can't just watch one horror movie. It's an ongoing cycle," Rem says. Myles nods.

"I hate both of you. You know that?" I say. They just laugh.

We settle down for the night, grab more pizza, and put on the movie.

"You know what I'm so tired of?" Rem asks.

"What?" I reply.

"I'm so tired of there being sex scenes in scary movies. I just don't get it. No one is watching these movies for sex. They can watch porn for that. And why is it the woman that always must be shown with her tits out? We're not objects, you know," she says, pointing at the TV.

"I don't think they can hear you," Myles says laughing.

"Well, they should. Come on. I understand it's supposed to let the audience know who's going to automatically die, but seriously. I don't want to see naked people in my horror movies."

"Are you done now?" I ask. "Did you get it all out of your system?"

"Yes, I think so. Okay, I'm good now. Just needed to stand on my feminist soap box."

"I completely agree with you, but shh," I reply throwing a pillow at her.

"Yeah, I understand. It's really not necessary," said Myles. "I always fast-forward through those scenes when they come on. Like I'm going to do right now," he says as he goes to pick up the remote and fast-forward through the sex scene. I'm glad though. Those scenes are always really awkward to watch with other people.

"Thank you," replies Remington. "It's just too much."

I'm glad Myles and Rem are getting along. It's also nice hanging out with Myles again. I feel like we haven't had a movie night in a really long time. Hopefully, he forgives me for being so short with him last week. I also just realized that I've barely talked to Jared all day. I send him a quick text telling him that I'll see him tomorrow and to have a good night. He responds with a similar message. Maybe I'm getting better at balancing my time than I thought. But is it bad that I barely thought about him at all ever since practice? I pushed the thought away as the movie ended, and Rem started the next one. The first *Friday the 13th* movie.

"Are you gonna be, okay?" asked Myles.

"I'm not scared, I swear!" I replied.

"Whatever you say, scaredy cat," he says, poking my leg.

We got halfway through the movie, and I felt myself dozing off. Before I knew it, I had woken up to the screensaver on the TV and both Remington and Myles sleeping. Myles was sitting on my bed, head resting against the wall, arm extended toward me. I closed my eyes, falling back asleep, Myles's hand resting on top of mine. I can't remember the last time I slept better.

Chapter 6

Prim

Over the next couple of days, I was able to see Jared a little bit more. We had lunch together on Wednesday and Thursday and then went to dinner that night. It was nice to be on a date outside of campus. When we got back from dinner, Jared had a study group to get to for a project, so he dropped me off at my dorm room. That reminded me that Myles, Sabrina, and I should probably start working on our project, so I texted Myles.

Me–Hey, what are you up to?

Myles–Just working on an English assignment. You?

Myles and I have the same professor for the Freshmen English class, so I knew the assignment about which he was talking. I have that class on Tuesday and Thursday with Vesper, Jax, and Rem. We had to choose our classes based on our soccer schedule, so we had to have mostly morning and mid-afternoon classes. All of our classes ended by three every day. Myles had morning, afternoon, and night classes since he wasn't so restricted in time. He has the afternoon English class on Tuesdays and Thursdays, so I was able to do my assignment this morning right after class.

Me–Just got back from dinner with Jared. Have you talked to Sabrina any more about when we want to meet for our group project?

Myles–No, we can talk to her tomorrow morning during class if you want. I should have mentioned something at dinner earlier.

Me–Dinner?

Myles–Yeah, I had dinner with her earlier.

Me–Oh okay. I'll see you tomorrow morning then. Have a good night.

Myles–You, okay?

Me–Of course. I'm just a little tired.

Myles–Okay, see you in the morning.

The next morning, I walked to our psych classroom. When I got there, Myles and Sabrina were already chatting in the hallway. I didn't want to interrupt them, so I slipped in the door to the left of where they were. I sat down close to where we had been sitting all this week and got out my books.

"Hey, when did you get here?" Myles asked me as he and Sabrina sat down in the seats, I had saved for them.

"Oh, I just got here a couple of minutes ago. I didn't want to bother you two talking so I figured I would come in and grab us seats," I replied.

"Prim, you're never a bother. Interrupt away," Sabrina said. "I'm the one who's hogging your best friend."

"No, it's okay. We can both share him. He's not just mine," I replied.

Myles looked over at me. Shit. I think I hurt his feelings.

"I didn't mean it like that. I just meant that other people are allowed to be your friend too, that's all," I continued. Myles nodded.

"Man, you both go back and forth like an old married couple," Sabrina said. "I wish I had a friendship like that."

"When you've been friends since third grade, it's hard not to bicker," Myles added.

"So," I said trying to change the subject, "When should we meet up to work on our project?"

"Hmm, how about sometime this weekend? I know the party is tomorrow, so what about Sunday afternoon? We don't have to meet for long. It's just the first meeting and we have all semester so we can just do the basics," replied Sabrina.

"Sounds good," Myles replied. I nodded my head in agreement.

Class started so I pulled out my phone to see if I had a text message from Jared. No message from him but I did have a message from my group chat with Vesper, Jax, and Rem.

<u>Vesper</u>–Sleepover tonight? I need a girls' night.

<u>Me</u>–Yes, please!

<u>Jax</u>–Totally in!

<u>Rem</u>–As long as there are drinks and food, I'm in.

At that, I chuckle aloud, and Myles turns toward me.

"What's so funny?" he asks.

"Oh, nothing. Just a text from the girls," I reply.

After class was over, Myles and I said goodbye to Sabrina and then walked outside. Myles was heading to Introduction to Statistics class, and I was going to Introduction to Education. Our class buildings were beside each other so we were able to walk together every Monday, Wednesday, and Friday.

"Do you want to grab something to eat tonight, or do you and Jared have plans?" Myles asked.

"The girls and I are actually having a sleepover tonight. That's what we were texting about during class," I replied.

"Oh, that sounds fun," he said.

"I would invite you, but I doubt we will be talking about anything of interest to you," I said.

He laughed. "Probably not. Well, I hope you have fun tonight and I guess I'll see you at the party tomorrow night."

"Sounds good. See you tomorrow," I replied as Myles walked off to his classroom.

Later that night, Vesper, Jax, Rem, and I were all sprawled out on our bedroom floor, cuddled in blankets. Practice was brutal today. We did some running drills but then we also walked over to the gym for strength training. We complain a lot about practice but I'm having a lot of fun with this team. And I've already found a great group of friends so I'm looking forward to our college years together. True to her word, Rem supplied the drinks for tonight.

"Where did you get all of that?" I asked her.

"Some of the seniors were able to go to the liquor store so I gave them some money," she replied.

"Coach Wimble would lose his shit if he knew the seniors were giving us drinks," said Jax.

"Nah, he knows everyone drinks in college. He's not stupid," said Vesper.

"What do you all want to do tonight? I know we have practice in the morning, but we could still watch movies or something," I said.

"How about we play Truth or Dare?" asked Vesper. She would be the one to volunteer this game. Apparently, the other two thought it was a good idea because they were both nodding in agreement. Well, I guess we're playing Truth or Dare.

"Okay, Prim! You first. Truth or Dare," said Vesper.

"Truth," I replied. Usually, it's the safest of the two.

"Have you and Jared had sex yet?"

Obviously, everyone started giggling like an elementary school kid. "Yes, we have," I replied.

"How was it?" Rem asked.

"It was good. Yeah, it was good," I replied.

"Well, that doesn't sound too confident," said Jax.

"You heard wrong then. It's good. I swear," I said, trying to move the game right along. "Next person. Let's see. Remington, your turn. Truth or Dare?"

"Truth," she says.

"How many serious boyfriends have you had?" I asked.

"Just the one in high school," Rem replies.

"How long did you date?" asks Vesper.

"Three years," she replied.

"Holy shit. That's a long time."

"Why did you two break up?" asked Jax. "Sorry if that's too nosey."

"No, it's okay. Umm, we just thought it was the best decision for us at that time. We wouldn't really have a lot of time for each other, so we didn't want to be in each other's way," Rem replied.

"Oh, I'm sorry. Do you keep in touch?" asked Jax.

"Not really, no. We haven't spoken since high school graduation."

"Jeez. I think I need a drink now," said Vesper taking the top off of the bottle of Smirnoff. She poured some into her cup and then passed the bottle over to Rem. Rem did not use a cup. She chugged right from the bottle.

"That's our girl," Jax said.

Rem stopped drinking. "Vesper's turn. Truth or dare."

"Dare, of course," Vesper replied.

"I dare you to call Theo and make sex noises over the phone to him," Rem said.

Vesper met Theo at our team slumber party during pre-season. He's cousins with one of the guys on the soccer team and, apparently, he and Vesper were both valedictorians at their high schools. They have this weird rivalry going on now. Of course, they have three classes together, so it only makes things worse.

"Do you have his number?" I asked Vesper.

"Unfortunately, yes. We were assigned a group project and he just so happens to be in my group," replied Vesper. "Ugh, hang on."

She took out her phone, scrolled through her contacts, and clicked on "Theo-dick." It was ringing. I didn't think she would go through with it, but here we are. She put the call on speaker.

"Hello?" I heard Theo's voice on the other end. He was at a party. We could barely hear him. "Hello?" he said again.

Vesper. Bless her soul. She started to let out the most erotic noises I have ever heard in my life. I swear the temperature in the room raised ten degrees just by her noises.

"What the fuck?" Theo said before Vesper quickly ended the phone call.

"I'm not going to be able to look him in the face for the rest of the year," said Vesper, covering her face with her hands.

"That was the best thing I've ever witnessed. Like ever," said Jax.

"Please don't ask me to do any more dares. That was painful," Vesper replied. We all busted out laughing.

"Okay, okay, Jax's turn. Truth or dare," I said.

"Truth for me. I can't live up to that dare," Jax said, still laughing at Vesper.

"Do you have a crush on anyone right now?" I ask her.

"Nope. Not unless you count my business professor," Jax replied.

"Not even Sean?" Remington teased.

Sean has been trying to get Jax's attention ever since we all got here for pre-season. He is the goalie for the men's team.

"Not even Sean. He tries but I'm not giving in," Jax replied. "He is hot though. And that beard really does something to you."

"I'm sure it would feel good in certain places if you let him explore a little," said Vesper smirking.

"All right, all right. Let's stop embarrassing Jax," said Remington. "Prim, back to you. Truth or dare?"

"Truth," I replied.

"Have you ever had feelings for Myles?"

"No. No feelings. We're just friends," I replied.

"I see the way he looks at you," Vesper said.

"What way? He doesn't look at me in any specific way. We're best friends. Obviously, we like each other."

"Maybe one of you likes the other a little more than they are letting on," Jax replied.

"I don't. I swear. I don't look at him like that," I said.

"I wasn't talking about you," said Jax. "I was talking about Myles. But nice to know where your head's at."

"But, honestly, though, nothing has ever happened between you two to make things awkward?" asked Rem.

"Nope. Never. We both dated other people throughout high school and would always talk to each other about advice and everything, so I think we're both on the same wavelength there. There's nothing romantic going on between me and Myles and I can guarantee you there won't ever be."

"So, you wouldn't care if he went out with Sabrina?" Vesper asked. Where was this question coming from?

"No, why would I?" I replied. "Did you hear something about the two of them?" I would have thought Myles would tell me if something was going on between the two of them, considering we sit next to each other all the time in class.

"No. I was just checking. I see them together a lot, that's all," said Vesper.

"Well, we're all in class together so I'm sure they are just talking about assignments. Plus, he can have other friends besides me. I'm not his only friend."

The thought kept creeping up though. Would I care if he dated Sabrina? As our night wound down and the girls fell asleep, I couldn't help but lay in my bed with my head spinning, staring up at the ceiling, and thinking about all the times I had seen Myles and Sabrina together. They had become friends quickly. But there isn't anything wrong with that. Is there?

Chapter 7

Prim

"I think I'm gonna puke," I say to Remington as I run down the hall to the bathroom.

I overdid it last night. We all overdid it. I should not have had that much alcohol. Maybe we shouldn't have played truth or dare while drinking. We had way too many drinks and way too much to say to each other. So many things were said, and I don't remember half of them. I had to go to the bathroom three times during practice this morning because I got sick. I told Coach Wimble that I thought it was some kind of food poisoning. He believed me. Or at least I think he did. But, as Vesper said, he's not stupid. He's been to college. He knows the deal. Rem came into the bathroom and made sure I was okay.

"I thought I drank a lot last night," she commented, coming over to rub my back. "Are you good?"

"I'll be okay. I'll just have to take it easy the rest of the day before the party tonight," I said as I sat on the floor next to the toilet. "I am not missing that."

"You are the definition of boot and rally," Rem said laughing. "But are you sure you still want to go? Don't push yourself too much."

"Not funny. I feel miserable right now, but I still want to go tonight. I'm just glad we didn't have to do sprints at practice. I really think I may have passed out."

"Well, just rest for right now. You still have plenty of time to recuperate before the party. And Jared just called you. I picked up and told him you weren't feeling well so I think he's coming over soon," Rem said.

"Okay, thanks for letting me know," I said. "Do we have any crackers or ginger ale or anything like that?"

"I don't think so. I can always pick some up from the store after I meet with my parents. I'm having lunch with them in a bit."

"No, that's okay. I can ask Jared if he can get some for me. Thanks though," I reply as I get up from the floor, splash water on my face and wash my hands.

We head back to our room and find Jared already sitting on my bed.

"Hey, baby," he said as I walked into the room.

"Hey. What are you doing here so fast?" I ask him.

"Rem told me you were sick, so I wanted to stop by and check on you. I'm meeting the guys for lunch, so I have to go in a couple of minutes. Are you okay?"

"I'll be okay, thanks," I reply. "Do you know how long you're going to be out with them?"

"I'm not sure. I think they also wanted me to hang out and pregame with them before the party, so I'll probably go back to their place after lunch. The senior guys invited us," he replied.

"Would you have time to grab me some crackers and ginger ale when you're out?" I asked.

"Yeah, I'll ask them if we can stop at a store after we get lunch."

"Okay, thanks. I appreciate it," I say as I get onto my bed and under the covers. "Just text me when you get back to campus. I'll still be here."

"Got it," Jared replied.

"Do you want to meet somewhere before the party tonight so we can go together?" I ask.

"Yeah, sure. I'll text you before I head to the party, and we can meet up."

"Okay. Are you sure you can't stay here any longer?"

"I'm sorry, babe. I told the guys I would meet them and I'm already running late. I called to check on you because you didn't look so good after practice and then Rem told me what was going on," he replied.

"All right. Well, thanks for coming to check on me. Have a good time with your friends," I replied, trying to hide my disappointment as I pulled the covers up over my mouth.

Jared leaned down and kissed me on the forehead. "I'll text you later, okay? Feel better." He said 'bye to Rem and then left the room.

I turned over onto my right side so that I was facing Remington.

"You know he should be here taking care of you, right? Like, I don't want to overstep any boundaries but it's kind of shitty that he can't stay with you," said Rem. "He shouldn't keep picking his friends over you especially if you are sick."

"I know, but he already had plans. Should I just expect him to drop everything and stay with me for the rest of the day?" I asked her.

"That's *exactly* what you should expect. He's your boyfriend," she replied. "If the roles were reversed, what would you do?"

I let out a long sigh. She's right. "I would stay with him," I replied.

"My point exactly. Any good significant other would do that. Again, just tell me if I'm saying too much. I'm just looking out for you."

"I know and I appreciate it. I really do," I replied.

I picked up my phone off my stand and realized that Myles had texted me ten minutes ago.

Myles–How was your sleepover last night?

Me–The sleepover was great. My hangover not so much. I've been puking pretty much all morning so I'm in bed right now.

After I sent that reply, I saw that Myles was calling me.

"Hello?" I say as I answer the phone.

"Hey. Are you all right?" Myles asks, concern obvious in his voice.

"Yeah, I'm okay. I'm just going to stay in bed and rest today before the party."

"Do you think you'll be okay to go to the party? You don't have to go if you aren't up for it," he says.

"That's exactly what Rem said. Are you sure you both don't plan all these things out? But, yeah, I want to go, so I'm probably going to sleep for the rest of the afternoon."

"Do you need me to do anything?" he asks.

"No, I think I'm good. I just need to drink water and get some more sleep," I say.

"Okay, well text me if you need anything. I don't have any plans today before the party so I can run to the store if you need me to," Myles replied.

"What would I do without you?" I ask.

"I have no fucking idea," he replies, both of us starting to laugh. "Well, again, just text me if something comes up. Does Jared know?"

"Yeah, he stopped by a couple of minutes ago. He left to go lunch with his team," I replied.

"Did he bring you anything to eat or drink?" Myles asked.

"Uh, no, he was late going to lunch so he was only here for a couple of minutes."

There was a long pause and then I heard a sigh from the other end of the phone.

"Myles?" I say.

He cleared his throat. "I'm here. Are you in your room by yourself?" he asked.

"No, Rem is here too but she's leaving soon to go meet her parents."

"Okay, well, try to get some sleep, all right?"

"I will. Thanks for calling," I say as we end the phone conversation.

"I'm going to assume that was Myles?" Rem asked.

"You assumed correctly," I said, trying to manage a chuckle.

"You know, I'm going to test out a theory here," she replied.

"What theory?" I ask.

"You'll see, don't worry," she said.

I have no idea what she's talking about, and I don't think I have the energy to try and figure it out. I roll over onto my other side so I'm facing the wall. I pull the covers over my shoulders and tuck Mr. Tusky under the blanket with me. I had just started to fall asleep when I heard someone knocking on our door. I turned over and saw Remington look through the peephole first. She looked back at me and smiled.

"My theory has been proven. So, it's no longer a theory. It's a fact. A damn fact," she said.

She opened the door and Myles came walking in with two plastic bags.

"Hey, Myles. What are you doing here?" I ask, sitting up in my bed.

"I went to the convenience store across the street and got you crackers, ginger ale, bagels, and Gatorade. I didn't know if you needed any medicine so I figured these would be good enough," he replied.

Before I knew what I was doing, I was getting out of bed, walking over to Myles, and hugging him.

"Thank you," I said to him, squeezing him so tight.

"You're welcome. I just wanted to make sure you were okay so I'm going to hang out here with you if that's okay. I don't want you to be by yourself," Myles replied, hugging me back even tighter.

I pulled back and felt tears running down my cheeks.

"Prim, what's wrong?" Myles asked, eyes going wide.

"Nothing. Nothing's wrong. I'm just glad you're here," I replied.

Myles took his thumb and wiped away the tear that was falling down my right cheek. "Of course, I'm here. We must get you sobered up for that party tonight." He looked down at me and smiled. I heard Rem clear her throat beside us.

"Well, I was going to stay here a bit longer to take care of you before I went to see my parents, but I think you are going to be well taken care of. My mission here is done," said Remington. "Myles, lovely as usual to see you. Take care of our girl, okay?"

"Will do. Have a good time with your parents," Myles replied.

"See you tonight," Rem said as she closed the door.

"Here, you get back in bed and I'll put some crackers on a plate for you. The ginger ales are already cold so you can drink some now, if you want," Myles said putting the bags down on my desk.

I got back into bed and sat up so that I could eat the crackers without making too much of a crumby mess.

"Myles, thank you. Seriously, thanks," I said. "You didn't have to come over."

"Of course, I did. I would be stupid not to. If the roles were reversed, you would have done the same for me."

"I would have," I replied, recalling the conversation I had with Rem before Myles showed up. It wasn't even a question. I absolutely would have done the same if the roles were reversed. For Jared or Myles. It was just who I was. And also, because it was the right thing to do. But Jared didn't do any of this for me. And Rem said her theory was proven. What was her theory? Obviously, something about Myles.

"I know," Myles said lifting his hand and putting it to my cheek. "You feel a little warm. Let me get a cold cloth for you. I'll be right back." He took a cloth from my closet and walked down the hall to the bathroom. When he came back, he sat down beside me on the bed and held the damp cloth on my forehead. It felt good. I didn't even realize that I was that warm.

"Lay back and try to get some sleep. I'll be here when you wake up," he said.

"What are you going to do?" I asked.

"I brought my laptop, so I was going to work on some assignments for class. I brought headphones so I won't bother you."

"Are you sure you didn't have any other plans?" I asked.

"Nope. I was going to work on these assignments in my room anyway."

"I love you. You know that, right?" I ask him. The corners of his mouth pulled up into a small smile.

"I know you do. Now get some sleep."

I smiled at him and turned over on my side, hugged Mr. Tusky, and fell asleep. I'm not sure how long I was asleep but, when I woke up, I heard voices. Male voices. Two male voices talking to each other. I sat up in bed and saw that both Myles and Jared were standing in my room.

"What's going on?" I ask as I get out of bed.

"Maybe you should ask him," Jared said as he pointed at Myles.

"Ask him what?" I replied.

"He's trying to move in on you, Prim," said Jared.

"Move in on me? What the hell are you talking about?" I ask.

"Why has he spent the whole day here with you then?"

"Because she was sick and needed someone to be here for her. I shouldn't have even needed to be here. You should have. You're the boyfriend, right?" Myles replied.

"Yeah, I am. But you want to be," Jared said getting closer to Myles and pushing a finger into his chest.

"And I'd do a much better fucking job at it than you are right now," Myles replied.

"What?" I ask, looking up at Myles. He froze for a second but then turned to look at me.

"I just meant in general, as a boyfriend," Myles replied, cheeks flushing.

"Okay, listen, that's enough. Both of you," I said, stepping in the middle of them.

"Prim, I wasn't done with this guy," Jared replied.

"Yeah, well, you're done now," I said. "What the hell is wrong with you? You come to my room this morning, find out I'm sick, and then still leave to go hang out with your friends. Not one text was sent from you checking in on me throughout the day. Not one. Oh, and by the way, Jared, did you even try to go the store and get the things I asked you to?" I asked, already knowing the answer.

"The guys didn't want to stop at the store after lunch," he replied looking down at the ground.

"So, you're just perfectly all right with leaving your sick girlfriend alone while you're getting drunk with your friends? And don't tell me you weren't drinking. I can smell it all over you," I replied.

"I told you, my plans. You told me to have a good time."

"Read between the fucking lines, Jared. You're a grown adult, for god's sake," I said. "This is why Myles came over. Because you wouldn't. You weren't there and he was. He's allowed. He's my best friend."

"Then what do you want me to do, Prim?"

"Right now, I would like you to leave. And thanks for asking me if I'm feeling better. It really means a lot," I replied.

"But I'm here now. Let me stay," Jared said. "I want to make sure that you're okay."

"I don't care that you're here now. I'm not on your timetable. I'm on mine. So, please, get the hell out of my room," I replied.

"Am I gonna see you tonight?" he asked.

"That's what you're worried about right now? The party?" I asked.

"I was just asking," he replied.

"Please leave," I said, moving him out into the hallway and closing the door behind him.

I leaned my forehead up against the closed door and squeezed my eyes shut. It was all I could do to stop the tears I felt building up behind my eyes. I felt a hand on my shoulder and turned around to see Myles looking at me. I moved forward and tucked myself into his chest, my arms wrapping around his waist. He pulled me in tighter and started stroking my hair. He smelled like strawberries. I never noticed that before now. He moved from my hair to my back as he started making a circular motion with his hand. He knows this is what my mom used to do to me when I was younger and didn't feel well. It's so comforting.

"Prim, I'm so sorry," Myles said, still not letting go. "I didn't mean for you two to start arguing. I shouldn't have come."

"No, I'm glad you came. I didn't want to be alone. And you're my safe place," I replied.

Myles smiled down at me. "Are you feeling any better?"

"Actually, a lot better. All the adrenaline build-up helped," I replied. "Nothing like an argument with your boyfriend to get rid of a hangover."

"I'm proud of you for standing up to him. I know you don't like confrontation," Myles said.

"He was being a jackass, so I needed to say something. I'm sorry he got in your face. I will be talking to him about that later."

"Do you think you'll see him at the party?" asked Myles.

"I don't know. Maybe. Right now, all I want to do is go to the party and have a good time with everyone. If I see him there, I'll deal with it when the time comes," I replied.

Myles nodded. "Well, we only have two or so hours before the party starts. Did you want me to grab you something to eat?"

"No, I think I'm just going to stick to the bagels and Gatorade you brought. Probably the safer option," I replied.

"Do you want me to stay with you for a bit longer?" he asked.

"You don't have to. You've done enough for me today already. Rem should be back soon and then I'm sure we'll take showers and get ready for the party. Are you going to be there?" I asked.

"Yeah, I'll go for a bit. My roommate is going so I'll probably just tag along," he replied.

"I don't really see Lawrence a lot," I said.

"His girlfriend only lives like thirty minutes from campus, so he hangs out there a lot. I guess she's visiting this weekend so they'll both be there," he replied.

"Oh, well, it'll be nice to see them both then," I said.

"All right, well, I'll let you get ready and whatever else, so just text me if you need anything," he said as he turned toward the door. "I mean it, Prim. Please tell me if you need anything else. I know I'm not Jared but at least I can do some things for you."

"No, you're not Jared. You're Myles. And that's even better."

He dipped his head and smiled, looking at the ground. "Yeah, well, you know I'm always here for you."

"Thanks, Myles. And not just for bringing me all of this. For being here for me all day. I can't believe you stayed with me this whole time. I'm sorry if I'm making your college experience annoying so far. I don't mean to be a burden, especially to you."

"It's what I'm here for," he replied. "And you'll never be a burden to me. Not ever. I'll see you later, Prim."

"'Bye, Myles," I said as he turned and walked out of the room.

CHAPTER 8

Prim

It was close to nine-thirty p.m. when Rem and I finished getting ready for the party. She had on a skin-tight black sleeveless dress and her red hair was all flowy curls down her back. I had on the red dress Myles helped me pick out, a pair of tan wedges, and my hair pulled up loosely with strands pulled out of the ends. We had both done each other's makeup so we both felt like designers. The bagel and Gatorade earlier did wonders for my stomach. I didn't feel like puking anymore so that was a start. I told Rem everything that happened this afternoon, so she was caught up with the whole Jared fiasco. She was not surprised. Honestly, I wasn't either. I just didn't think that there would be a confrontation between the two of them.

"Hey, ya'll!" said Jax as she came into our room.

"Who's ready to party?" asked Ves as she came in right behind Jax.

"I think we're good to go," I say as Rem and I grab our purses and walk out the door with Jax and Vesper.

The party is at the football house right outside of campus. They just came off a big win against our rival school today so the party was going to be extra big tonight. I'm sure there is enough alcohol for the whole school in that house. The house isn't too far off campus so the girls and I decided to walk over. On our way, we saw a lot of other students walking over to the house. There were going to be a lot of people there, from the looks of it. I don't even know if I want to see Jared at the party or not. He is currently on my shit list. He's already pissing me off so much.

"Hey, Cade," Jax said as she waved at the guy who was passing us on the right.

"Hey, Jax. Are you going to the party?" Cade asked.

"Yeah. We're heading there now. Are you going to be there at all?" she replied.

"Nah, parties aren't really my thing," he said. "But I hope you have a good time. I'll see you in the dorm later."

"Okay, 'bye," Jax said as she waved again and then turned back to walk beside us.

"Who was that?" I asked.

"Oh, that's Cade. I met him this past week. He lives in our dorm. I totally smoked him in Black Ops," Jax replied.

"Uh. Black Ops?" Rem asked.

"It's a video game. Call of Duty," Vesper replied.

"Look at you knowing your video games," Jax said.

"I dabble from time to time," Ves replied.

"Good to know," said Jax.

We could hear the party before any of us saw the actual house. The front yard and porch were covered with students. I could only imagine what the inside looked like. Music filled the rooms as soon as we went into the house. Crowded was an understatement. It was nice though. Our first college party. It was overwhelming. Our first stop was to the kitchen to get drinks. The kitchen was huge. It had a different station for every kind of drink you could imagine. I started out with some kind of liquor concoction. The whole "liquor before beer, in the clear" kind of thing. Some of the other girls on the team came up to us to chat for a bit and then we moved to the dance floor. "We R Who We R" by Kesha was blasting through the speakers so we, of course, had to dance. I grabbed Rem, Ves, and Jax, and pulled them closer. We threw our heads back, let the music flow through us, and danced. By this time, everyone else had crowded onto the dance floor too. There was barely any room left but we didn't mind dancing pretty much on top of each other.

"Hello, everybody!" screamed the football captain over a microphone. "Welcome to the first party of the year. Let's drink, dance, get naked, and have a fucking good time!" He handed the microphone back over to tonight's DJ and went back to his dance partner.

We all started dancing again and I had to turn down two guys from dancing with me. I don't think Jared would like me dancing with other people. Wait. No. It's just dancing. I'm having a good time. I turned around and grabbed one of the guys who asked me to dance before.

"I thought you said no," he said.

"I changed my mind," I replied as he grabbed my hips and started dancing up against me.

"Body Bounce" by Akon and Kardinal Offishall was now playing. Ves, Rem, and Jax had all found dancing partners too. We were all smiling and having the best time. After the song was over, Rem tapped me on the shoulder.

"Myles is here. He's looking over here at you," she said pointing to the other side of the room.

I waved over to him. "I'll be right back," I say to Rem and my dancing partner. They both nodded.

I go over to where Myles is standing with his roommate and a girl, I'm going to assume is Lawrence's girlfriend.

"Hey, guys, what's up?" I ask.

"Not much. We just got here a couple of minutes ago," Myles replied.

"Hey, Prim, this is Rebecca, my girlfriend," Lawrence said as he pointed to the girl attached to his arm.

"Hey, Rebecca, it's nice to meet you," I said, leaning over to give her a hug. "Do you all want to dance? My friends are in the middle over there, I think."

"Yeah, let's go," Rebecca replied.

I grabbed her hand and started to lead the three of them to the dance floor.

"Prim!" I heard from behind me.

I looked back and realized that it was Jared calling my name. He walked over to us.

"Prim, can we talk please?" Jared asked.

"I'm busy with my friends right now," I replied.

"Please. I just want five minutes."

"Fine. Five minutes," I replied. I turned toward Myles. "Go find the girls. I'll be there soon."

"Are you going to be, okay?" Myles asked.

"I'll be fine, don't worry."

I took Jared's arm and pulled him to the hallway outside the living room.

"What do you want?" I asked.

"I just want you to forgive me. I'm sorry. I was a shitty boyfriend today. I should have been there with you and not with my friends. I know that now. I'm sorry I overreacted earlier," he replied.

"Is this going to keep happening though? You need to do better. You can't just get in Myles's face like that, Jared. He's my best friend. Please don't ever treat him like that again. I'm very protective of him," I said.

"I know I shouldn't have done that. I know. I'm sorry, baby. Can you please forgive me?" he asked, pulling me in by the waist and kissing my cheek.

"This is your last chance. I want to enjoy this year. Don't fuck it up," I replied. "Oh, and you need to apologize to Myles. Now. Don't ever do something like that. I won't be this nice if there's a next time."

"Scout's honor," he said crossing his heart. "Do you want to go dance?"

"Sure. Let's go. Myles and everyone else are there, so be nice and remember what I said, Jared. Apologize," I replied.

"I will. Promise," he said as we pushed our way back into the middle of the dance floor.

"Okay, we're back," I say as we reached the rest of the group. I could see Myles and Remington sharing a look between the two of them. I know they're not happy about Jared and neither am I. It's his last chance.

"Hey, man, I'm sorry about earlier today," Jared said, looking over at Myles.

"No worries. I was just looking out for Prim," Myles replied.

"I know. Thanks for doing that."

"I'm always going to," Myles said confidently, looking back at Jared. They held each other's gaze for an uncomfortable amount of time.

They are never going to get along.

***

The next morning, or afternoon, I should say, I get out of Jared's bed, pull on my pants and shoes, and head back to my room. I look at my phone to a text from Myles telling me to meet him and Sabrina at the library at one-thirty p.m. to work on our group project. I'm glad he texted me about it or I probably would have forgotten. I had Jared's t-shirt on and a pair of sweatpants that had holes in them, so I decided to change into something a little more presentable. T-shirt, leggings, and Chucks it is. I put a bit of foundation and mascara on my face and braided my hair. I headed out my door with five minutes to spare. I get to the library and see Sabrina and Myles sitting in the back corner of the library.

"Hey, Prim," said Sabrina as I walk up to the table. "How was your night?"

"Better than the day, that's for sure," I replied, taking a seat next to Myles.

"Oh? What happened yesterday?" she asked.

"Just boyfriend drama. Nothing too exciting," I said.

"Are you feeling better today? I think I still have some crackers in my room if you need them," said Myles.

"I'm actually feeling really good today, so I guess I just needed to get it all out of my system. Maybe I'll take it easy next weekend," I said.

"Probably for the best," replied Myles as he gave me a small smile. I nodded.

"Okay, so does anyone have ideas for our project?" I ask.

"Yeah, so since we still have the whole semester to work on the project, how about we just brainstorm topics today?" asked Sabrina.

"Sounds good. So, we must create a presentation on a specific aspect of psychology, right?" I ask. Myles and Sabrina nod.

"What about something to do with phobias? Like we could do a presentation on a specific phobia," said Sabrina.

"Oh, I like that," replied Myles. "I was going to say learning disabilities, but I like the phobia thing better. Prim, what do you think?"

"Hmm, I was going to say gender roles in society, but any topic is fine with me," I replied.

Sabrina and Myles looked at each other.

"And we have ourselves a winner!" Sabrina said, clapping her hands along with Myles.

The student at the front desk looked over at us and held his finger over his mouth.

"Sorry," Sabrina said, holding up her hand to the guy at the desk.

"Are you sure you want to do that topic? I was just kind of pulling it out of my ass," I replied, laughing a bit to myself.

"No, Prim. It's perfect. And it sends a good message," Sabrina said. "Not too many people want to dig deep into the different gender roles and how completely and utterly traditional and outdated they are."

"I agree. But, again, if you two want to do something else, please feel free to choose one of your topics. I'm just happy to be here."

"Gender roles, it is. All right, well, I'm glad we got that settled," Myles said. "Do you both want to grab some lunch somewhere?"

"Sure, let's do it," Sabrina replied. Myles looked over at me and I nodded.

We grabbed our bags and headed out to Myles's car. I started to have a weird sense that I was the third wheel in this group.

***

A little over a month later and it was already October. This semester was flying by. Our soccer team has the best record of anyone in our division, so we were all looking forward to hopefully earning a spot in the playoffs. My parents came to see my game this past weekend so, of course, they brought a huge care package of food and other goodies for both me and Myles. They took Jared and me out to dinner yesterday, so it was nice for them to see him again. He and I have been doing better these days. We don't really argue anymore. We hang out when we can. Some days I feel like I'm faking a smile, but I keep telling myself it's because I'm tired and the intensity of classes has picked up.

I meet Myles and Sabrina outside of our dorm buildings and walk to psych class. When we walk into the classroom, the topic of today's lesson was already written on the board.

Fear and Catharsis: Understanding the Horror Genre.

Well, Myles is going to love this one. We sit down just as Professor Gable comes into class.

"Good morning, everyone! If you noticed on the board, we are going to be looking at the relationship between fear, catharsis, and horror movies during today's class. Before we get started, who can give me a definition of catharsis?"

A student to the left of us raised his hand and Professor Gable called on him.

"It's basically like trying to get rid of any anxiety, fears, or negative emotions you have from life," he said.

"Yes, excellent," replied Professor Gable. "So, let's start there. We know that the horror genre is huge in today's world, right? Why do you think that is?"

Sabrina raised her hand. "Well, I know movies and TV shows can be a form of escapism for a lot of people, so maybe it's because people are trying to get rid of their own worries by watching other people go through bad things, so they don't have to? I guess it's kind of a form of release."

"Yes. Perfect explanation. Thank you," said Professor Gable. "Okay, let's put those two responses together. We're looking at how catharsis relates to the horror genre, so think about it like this. When we watch a scary movie, we are practicing catharsis. We're releasing all the negative emotions and fears that we have in the real world onto the screen. We're purging ourselves of the negativity and anxiety by watching it be played out in a movie or a TV show. Cool, huh?"

I looked around the room to most students nodding along.

"Who in here is a horror movie fan?" asked Professor Gable.

About half of the hands shot up in the air.

"What's a horror movie that you want to see?" asked Professor Gable.

"*The Black Phone!*" said both Myles and Sabrina out loud at the same time.

The whole class, including Professor Gable, started to laugh.

"I think that's out in theaters right now," Sabrina said, turning toward Myles. "We should go see it together."

"Definitely," Myles replied.

They both looked over at me.

"Don't look at me. I've had enough horror movies for a lifetime," I replied.

Well, look at that. They have a cute little date.

CHAPTER 9

Myles

"Should we do something this weekend?" Prim asked as she lay underneath the tree on the quad.

It's early October so it's the perfect weather to be outside. The "quad" is what the students call this area right in the middle of campus where there is nothing but trees and grass. There are a lot of students laying out with their blankets, books, and music. The women's soccer team has the day off today, so me, Prim, Rem, Vesper, Jax, and Cade are all laying here working on assignments. Cade lives in the same dorm building as me, Jax, and Vesper, so we've all started hanging out together. Apparently, Jax and Cade became friends after a video game battle, so she introduced us to him. He's a cool guy. More of my speed actually. We both like to be alone for the most part so I'm sure he dies a little inside whenever Jax pulls him along to all of our hangouts.

"What were you thinking?" I reply to her.

"I'm not sure. We have a morning game on Saturday but then we could all do something in the afternoon if you wanted to," said Prim.

"We could all go see a movie?" Vesper asked. "Apparently, they opened up a new theater near campus over the summer and I've heard that it's pretty nice. They have reclining seats. I'm in."

"You're in for what?" I heard from someone coming up behind us. Jared.

"Oh, hi, Jared. We were just talking about going to a movie this weekend," replied Jax.

"Sounds good. I'm in," he said. He walked over to where Prim was sitting, sat down beside her, and kissed her.

They are doing well these days. Prim forgave him way too quickly at the party. But my opinion doesn't matter. I don't think she would listen if I voiced my concerns to her about him. I just don't think he's a good guy. He doesn't take care of her. I'm not saying I think she can't take care of herself because she can. I just don't think he's right for her. He acts too much like a frat bro. I know Prim. She normally wouldn't go for someone like that. I know I'm biased in this situation; I really do. But I know Jared isn't it. Prim and Jared both lay down on the blanket together. She laid her head on his chest and he kissed the top of her head.

"Eww gross, PDA," said Vesper, moving farther away from where Prim and Jared were laying.

"Oh, you're just jealous," Prim replied.

"Not at all," said Vesper.

"So, Ves, I heard you throw out some pretty interesting sex noises," Jared said.

"What are you talking about?" Ves replied.

"Theo told Thomas that you called him a while ago and all he could hear were sex noises. He thought you butt-dialed him while you were fucking," he replied.

"Oh, fuck. I knew this was going to be awkward," she said.

Rem, Jax, and Prim are doubled over laughing, tears coming out of their eyes at this point.

"Uh, did we miss something?" I ask, looking at Prim.

"Oh, my god. We played truth or dare at one of our sleepovers earlier in the semester and we dared Ves to call Theo and make sex noises over the phone," Prim replied, still laughing at pointing at Ves. "I swear I have never heard such erotic noises before. It was awesome."

"It was certainly not awesome for me. He wouldn't leave me alone for two weeks after that happened," Ves replied.

Okay, I will admit. That's funny. I was laughing along with everyone until Prim and Jared started making out again. I need to get away from here.

"Who wants to grab lunch at the café?" I ask as I stand up and grab my bag off the ground.

"Yes, please," replied Rem and Cade at the same time.

"Great. Let's go," I said.

"We'll catch up with you in a bit," Prim said, finally not sucking face with her boyfriend. I nodded.

"You ready?" Rem asked, looking at me and Cade.

"Yeah. Let's get out of here. I'm starving," I replied, doing my best to cover up the real reason I need to get myself out of this spot.

We were later to lunch today than normal so there weren't as many people, which was good. I needed the space. But that also meant that the food options were pretty scarce. The only options left were pizza and things to make sandwiches. I opted for pizza. I just needed to grab something so that I could try and get the image of Prim and Jared kissing out of my head. Jared and I haven't spoken much since our confrontation in Prim's room and, honestly, I'd like to keep it that way. The café looked right out to the quad so I led Rem and Cade to the side of the cafeteria where we wouldn't have to see any more cuddling or kissing.

"Thanks for getting us out of there," Rem said.

"Oh, sure. I was starting to get hungry, and I wanted to make it here before lunch closed," I replied.

"Is that the real reason you got up?" Rem asked.

"Yeah. What other reason would there be?" I ask, looking between Rem and Cade. Cade took a sip of water and looked over to the right.

"Well, just know that I've already proven my theory, so you don't have to play dumb."

"Theory? What theory?" I asked.

"Come on, dude. Even I know the theory and I just started hanging out with you all," said Cade.

"What are you two talking about?" I ask, but I couldn't hear their answer. The rest of the group walked into the cafeteria and came over to our table.

"What's for lunch?" Prim asked as she put her bags on the chair next to mine.

"Pizza and sandwiches are all that's left. I think lunch closes in about thirty minutes, so you better get some before it's gone," Rem replied.

While we were eating, Jared kept putting his arm around Prim and kissing the side of her face. Since Prim was sitting right next to me, it felt like they were right on top of me. This is what I was trying to avoid by coming in here in the first place. I've moved my chair over to the right twice already. This was getting ridiculous.

"Hey, Jared, do you think you could not suck face while we're all trying to eat over here, please? Thanks," I said, a little more aggressively than I intended.

Rem and Cade both raised their eyebrows at me.

"Yeah, man, sorry. I was just trying to show my girl some love," Jared replied.

"Well, could you show her some love some other time?" I asked. I knew I was being a dick. I didn't care.

"Sorry, sorry," Prim said. "We'll stop. Jared, wait until we get back to the room." She looked over at me. "Sorry, Myles."

"So, how about that movie this weekend?" asked Jax. Thank, the universe, she changed the subject.

"Let's do it. I'll have to look up what movies are showing in the afternoon Saturday. Everyone good with a movie then?" Prim asked.

"Sure. Sounds good," I replied. Everyone else nodded.

"It's settled then. Group movie date," said Jax. "Cade, are you going to come too?"

"Yeah, sure, why not?" he replied.

"Yay. I have made it my mission to make you more sociable," said Jax.

"I was doing perfectly fine on my own," Cade replied.

"Whatever you say," Jax said, smirking at him. "I'm going to have the best influence on you."

"I highly doubt that," he replied.

Jared leaned over and whispered something in Prim's ear.

"Babe, not now. Later," Prim said trying to keep her voice down. Since everyone at the table was not staring at them, she obviously failed miserably. Her cheeks went red.

"I'm going to head back to my room and work on an English assignment," I said, standing up and grabbing my tray.

"But we don't have an English assignment this week," Prim replied.

"Sorry, I mean psych assignment."

"We don't have one of those either."

"Then it must be my statistics class," I replied, trying not to sound too annoyed.

"Okay, sorry," Prim said.

"I'll see you all on Saturday," I said as I took my tray to the stack and walked out of the cafeteria.

Now that I can breathe again and think clearly, I probably shouldn't have gotten up and walked out like that. I didn't want to seem rude, but I had to get out of there. I think I need to distance myself a bit from Prim and Jared. This is actually something that I've been thinking about for a couple of weeks now. Do I want to be away from Prim? No. But I need to, for my own sanity. Every time I want to hang out with her, Jared is always there, or he always interrupts. I swear to God he's everywhere. He's obviously figured out that I like Prim. I'm sure he's doing it on purpose. Flaunting all the PDA in front of me. Well, it's working. I'm terrible at this game and I don't want to play anymore. I can't. I know I'm not going to win this. I haven't won yet. What makes this time any different? I'm never going to be with her and I'm too scared to confess my feelings. That would only make things worse, and I don't want to lose her. As long as I'm near her, that's good enough. I've been accepting that more and more each day.

I just need to take a little step back to try and get these feelings under control. I get up to my room and Lawrence is sitting on his bed playing video games. I think he and his girlfriend may have had a fight because he hasn't left the room all week. There are Cheeto crumbs all over his bed and I can definitely smell that he hasn't taken a shower in a couple of days.

"Dude, it smells so fucking musty in here," I say, picking up one of his shirts off the ground and throwing it at him. "When's the last time you took a shower?"

"I have no idea. What day is it?" Lawrence asked.

"Thursday," I replied.

"Uh, then Sunday," he said.

"Dude. Gross. What's wrong with you?" I asked.

"Rebecca broke up with me," he replied.

"Wait, what? Why?

"I couldn't get a straight answer out of her either. She just said she didn't want to get in the way of my education and college years, so she dumped me. She didn't even let me try to stop her."

"Did something happen over the last month between the two of you?" I ask.

"No, nothing. I thought we were fine. She's a couple of years older than us, so she just graduated from here in May. We both live in the same town so I thought that would make things easier. Thirty minutes is nothing. Other couples are like hours apart and still make it work. I don't know what I did wrong."

"And that's all she said to you? Nothing else?"

"Nope. She did it over the phone, so she hung up on me," he replied.

"She broke up with you over the phone?" I ask.

"I guess she thought it would be easier. I've tried to contact her all week, but she hasn't responded," he said holding up his phone to me so that I could see all ten messages he sent.

"Damn, dude, I'm sorry. Do you want to drink tomorrow night instead of just laying here? I'm sure there are some parties we could find," I said. "It would help your broken heart. And, honestly, I could use a night out too."

"Yeah, I could go for some drinks. What's going on with you?" Lawrence replied. "Wait, let me guess. It has to do with Prim?"

"It cannot be that obvious to everyone," I said.

"Dude, you're like a walking Prim billboard. All you need now is a sign on your chest that says, *"I love Prim O'Brien"* to really nail it on the head."

"You're an asshole," I replied.

"Have you ever thought about telling her how you feel?" Lawrence asked.

"Of course, I've thought about it. But she's with Jared and I don't want to lose my best friend."

"Jared can go suck a dick, in my opinion. He's an arrogant son of a bitch. But, seriously, Myles. You have two options. You either need to tell her how you feel, or you need to try and move on and get on with your life. You can't keep pining after her unless you're going to actually do something about it," he said.

"I think I just need some space from them. I don't want to be away from her, but where there's Prim, there's Jared and it's driving me nuts," I reply.

"Okay, so do that. Join a club or something on campus. Find some new hobbies. There are flyers all over the bulletin board on the quad. Find something to take up your time and it'll help you get that space you need."

"I thought I was supposed to be the psychology major here?" I ask, smirking at him.

"Hey, I'm not just a pretty face," Lawrence replied.

"Sure, you aren't," I say as I lay back on my bed. "Now, can you please take a shower? I'm not going with you tomorrow if you smell like that."

"Fine," he replied, stopping the game, picking up his towel and heading to the showers.

"Don't forget to use soap!" I called out to him.

"Fuck you," Lawrence replied from down the hall.

Okay, space, let's see what you can do for me. I make a mental note to check the bulletin board sometime over the next couple of days. I need to do something.

Chapter 10

Myles

Prim is straddling me. She's on top of me. She's not just doing that. She's riding my cock. I'm inside her. I can hear her moaning. She leans forward right beside my ear and sucks my earlobe and kisses my neck.

"Harder, Myles, don't stop," she whispers.

It sent a shiver down my spine, so I press down and pull up her hips faster as I thrust into her harder.

"I want you on top of me," she says.

I flip us over so that she's right under me. I continue thrusting into her. God, she feels good.

"Yes, right there, Myles," Prim says, her nails scratching into my back.

"Come for me, baby. Touch yourself. I want to see it," I reply, giving her some space to circle her clit as I continue thrusting. I'm almost there, oh god, I'm going to bust.

"I'm coming! Jared, I'm coming, don't stop!" she says. "Fuck, Jared!"

I stop thrusting. "Jared?" I ask.

The dream ends. I'm left staring up at the ceiling, picturing Prim, and Jared together, laying here in wet boxers. Well, this hasn't happened in a while. I look over to my right and see that Lawrence is still sleeping. Hopefully, I wasn't making any noise. I get out of bed, take the sheet off my bed, and change into a clean pair of underwear. I guess it's laundry day. I throw my dirty boxers and sheet on top of my hamper and grab a packet of laundry detergent. As I'm heading out the door, I hear Lawrence roll over in his bed.

"Must have been a damn good dream you just had, my man," Lawrence said laughing to himself. "You got it bad, dude."

"Thanks for the reminder, ass," I reply as I close the door and head to the laundry room.

Later that night, Lawrence and I are getting ready to head out for the night. We drank a bit in our room so we're both already a bit buzzed. He seemed to feel better than this past week so I'm glad to see him cheering up. Obviously, the alcohol has something to do with his mood. This whole space thing will be good. I can put some distance between me and all the kissing and, hopefully, everything will work out for the best.

The basketball team is getting ready to gear up for their season, so they are throwing a party tonight to *"send out the wolves,"* as they have been saying. Considering our school mascot is a wolf, I find the whole thing pretty clever. And a couple of the players are in my statistics class so I already told them I would swing by. Both the men's and women's soccer teams have a game tomorrow morning, so I doubt they will be at the party. Looks like it's just me and Lawrence tonight. We get to the basketball house, and I greet Maverick and Jensen, the two players who are in my class, on the front porch. The party isn't as big as the parties the football guys throw but the football team is twice the size of the basketball team. Plus, the football team has won a couple of national championships over the last couple of years so they tend to draw in a bigger crowd.

"Hey, Jensen, Maverick, this is my roommate, Lawrence," I say as we approach the guys on the porch.

They all shake hands and then Jensen directs us into the kitchen to grab drinks.

"You excited for the season to start?" I ask.

"We're pumped," replied Maverick. "We got some really good freshmen this year and we're already impressed with seeing them play during the team throw-arounds we've been having."

"That's great. We'll have to come to some of the home games," I replied.

Lawrence and I make our way out onto the dance floor. Well, as close to it as we can get. The floor is packed with people so Lawrence and I decide to stay against the wall and watch everything around us. Lawrence seemed to be getting into the music and enjoying himself so it made me happy too. He deserved a night out. Hell, so did I. Two girls came up to us and asked us to dance.

"Why not," I replied as the girls led us out on the dance floor.

As I was dancing with the girl, I had to hold my cup up higher, trying not to spill anything on her. She had a white top on so I'm sure she wouldn't appreciate having beer spilled all over it. She was pretty and a great dancer, so we got into the music more. We kept dancing, but the whole time I kept thinking to myself, this isn't Prim. I started to feel bad, but why should I? I'm not doing anything wrong.

"Do you have a girlfriend?" she asked, leaning back so I could hear.

"No, no, girlfriend," I replied.

"Would you like one?" she asked.

I knew where that one was going. "Uh, I actually have feelings for someone else right now, but I appreciate the offer," I respond.

"Why aren't you two together?" she asks.

"It's complicated," I reply. "Will you excuse me for a second? I need to use the restroom."

I tell Lawrence that I'm headed to the bathroom and then I leave him and the two girls on the floor. There was already someone in the downstairs bathroom, so I head up the stairs to find one there. I try the first door at the top of the stairs. Nope. Not a bathroom. Bedroom. I open the door to the second room. *Fuck*. Not a bathroom either. It's another bedroom. And it's occupied. Occupied by none other than Prim and Jared taking each other's clothes off.

"What the fuck?" I shout.

"Fuck, Myles. You show up at the worst possible times, you know that?" says Jared. "Why do you have to be everywhere?"

"I'm everywhere? I can't hang out with Prim without you being there," I reply.

"Myles, I'm sorry," says Prim. "I didn't think you would be here."

"Yeah, well, that makes two of us," I say. "You have games tomorrow. Why are you here?"

"Because it's college and we can do whatever we want, dad," Jared says.

"Well, I'm sorry to barge in. I'll be going now," I say as I start to walk away. I turn back around.

"Good luck at your game, Prim."

"Aren't you going to be there?" she asked.

"I don't think so," I say and turn to walk back down the stairs.

I find Lawrence and tell him that I must go.

"Are you okay?" he asks.

"I'll be fine. Are you good here by yourself?"

"Yeah, dude, I'm good. I'll be back to the room later."

I couldn't get out of the house fast enough. I start walking back to the dorm. I can't do this anymore. I kick over the trashcan on the curb. I could punch someone right now. I won't, obviously. What am I going to do? I think it was a mistake coming to this school. Maybe it's not too late to transfer. I get back to my dorm room and really don't feel like being alone. I take out my phone.

Me–Hey, are you in your room?

Sabrina–Yeah. What's up?

Me–Do you mind if I come over and hang out for a little?

Sabrina–Of course not. Come on over.

I don't usually have a lot of friends so; besides Prim and the rest of the group, Sabrina has become one of my closest friends. And, before anyone says anything, there are no romantic feelings involved. None, like at all. Since I'm not her type, it's much easier that way. I knock on Sabrina's door and hear her getting out of bed. She opens the door and when she sees me, her eyes go wide.

"Myles, what's wrong?" Sabrina says as she pulls me into her room.

"What?" I ask.

"You've been crying. What's going on?"

I reached my hand up to my face and realized that my cheeks were wet.

"Damn. I didn't even realize I was crying. It's, uh, it's been a long night."

"Here, sit down," Sabrina said as she pulls me over to her bed. "Tell me what's wrong."

"I... I don't... I can't..." I started but couldn't finish. I broke down and hugged her. Tears were pouring down my face. I'm not going to lie, it felt good to get it all out. I didn't have a lot of people I can talk to about this. I let go of Sabrina and started wiping my face.

"Fuck, Sabrina, I'm sorry. I don't mean to bombard you with all of this."

"You don't need to apologize. Tell me what's going on."

"Umm, there's something I haven't told you yet. It's about Prim," I start.

"Okay. What is it?" she replied.

"I'm in love with her," I say.

"Yeah, I know," she replied.

"You do?"

"I mean, it's obvious. With the way you look at her and everything."

"Christ. The whole school's going to know about this before she does," I reply.

"Probably. I mean, I love the girl, but she either knows and is just pretending, or she's just completely oblivious."

I chuckle. "Yeah, she is that."

"What happened?" she asks.

Before I could answer, Sabrina's door opens and a girl with long brown hair walks into the room.

"Hey, babe. I was wondering when you were going to get back," Sabrina says, going over to kiss the girl's cheek.

"Sorry, it took me so long. There were a lot of people in the pizza line," the girl replies.

"Myles, this is Bethany, my girlfriend," Sabrina says.

"Hey, Bethany, I'm Myles. I've heard a lot about you. It's nice to finally meet you," I reply, extending my hand to her.

"Hey, Myles. I've heard a lot about you too," Bethany says. "Thanks for being friends with my girl while I'm not here."

"My pleasure. She's one of the good ones," I reply.

Over the last month or so, Sabrina has been telling me about how she came out to her parents over the summer whenever she met Bethany. They both worked at their local pool for the summer and started dating shortly after they met. So, hopefully it's obvious why there are no romantic feelings between the two of us. We're both in love with two completely different people.

"Are you okay?" Bethany asks, drawing attention to the wet streaks on my face.

"Just what I was about to get out of him before you popped in," Sabrina replies. "Spill, Aratis." She pulled out the last name.

"Bethany, I hope you don't think less of me when I tell you all of this. It's going to make me seem pathetic," I say.

"No such thing. Do tell," she replies.

I go on to tell them both about what's been happening ever since we got to school, walking in on Prim and Jared twice, arguing with Jared because he doesn't take care of Prim, and always seeing them together everywhere I go.

"Do you think you'll ever tell Prim how you feel?" asks Bethany.

"I don't know. I feel like I've done everything *but* confess to her. All my actions. Everything that I do. It's always been for her. I just haven't said the words," I reply.

"And she's still with Jared?" asks Sabrina.

"From what I saw tonight, yes," I say.

"Well, from what I can see, you have two options," starts Sabrina.

"Confess to her or try to move on?" I ask.

"That's exactly what I was going to say," she replies, looking surprised.

"My roommate told me the same thing," I say.

"Well, he sounds smart," she says. "But, seriously, though. I know you're afraid of losing her as a friend if you confess to her, so maybe the better option is to put some distance there. It might be good for both of you."

"That's what I was planning until I walked in on them tonight," I reply.

"How about this? Bethany is leaving tomorrow afternoon so why don't you and I go see *The Black Phone* like we were talking about in class? I think it's still in theaters for another week or so," says Sabrina.

"Oh, shit. I'm so sorry. I'm taking up your alone time by being here," I say, apologetically to Sabrina and Bethany.

"Gosh, no, you're fine. We see each other most weekends, so it's no biggie," replies Bethany.

"Are you sure? I can leave," I say.

"Absolutely not. So, how does that sound? Movie tomorrow night?" asks Sabrina.

"Sure. Yeah, that sounds great."

"It's settled then," she says.

I get back to my dorm room close to one-thirty in the morning. Lawrence is sleeping so I pull out my phone to plug it in for the night. I have two missed calls and a text message from Prim.

Prim–Myles, I'm sorry.

I don't want to deal with this right now, so I turn my phone off, get in bed, roll over, and go to sleep.

The next morning, I get another two texts from Prim asking me if I'm going to come to the game. I ignore it. I grab lunch at the cafeteria with Lawrence and then spend the rest of the afternoon working on our psychology project. At this point, Sabrina, Prim, and I are each working on our individual parts, and then we will put them all together during our meeting next month to finalize everything.

It was close to six o'clock when I called it quits on the project for the day. I picked up my phone and had another missed call from Prim and another two text messages.

Prim–Where are you? Why aren't you picking up?

Prim–I thought you were going to the movies with us. We're getting ready to leave. Call me.

I did not call her. Instead, I walked to Sabrina's room so we could leave for the movies. It might be shitty of me to bail on the rest of the group, but I'm doing this for me. It's too painful to see them together. I'm exhausted.

Since the theater was close to campus, we decided to catch the seven o'clock showing of the movie. We got to the theater, chose our seats, and sat down just in time for the previews.

"I swear the previews are the best part of the movie," Sabrina said, reaching over to grab some popcorn out of the bin.

"I love that we have the same brain," I replied.

The movie started playing and it was pure horror genius. An hour and forty-two minutes later and Sabrina and I are speechless.

"That's probably one of the best movies I've seen in a really long time," she says.

"They don't make them like that anymore," I reply.

"Were you purging your negative emotions by watching that movie?" Sabrina asks me.

"Why, yes, Professor Gable, I was," I reply, laughing at her.

"How cathartic," she responds, laughing right back. "Well, do you wanna get out of here?"

"Sure. Let's go," I reply grabbing the empty popcorn bin and soda.

We walk out of the theater and to the parking lot. As I'm getting into the car, I look up and see Prim, Rem, and Jared all standing by his car. Prim and I both make eye contact while the others are getting into the car. For a moment, we both just stare at each other trying to figure out who's going to make the first move. I make the first move. I take my eyes off Prim, get in my car, and drive back to campus.

When we get back, I drop Sabrina off at her room and then head out to sit on the quad because I don't feel like being in my room. I sit underneath the tree where the group usually hangs out. I don't want to ignore Prim. I just don't know what to say to her. She's living her life and I don't want to stand in the way of her happiness. I just know that I'm not happy.

"Myles," I hear beside me. Shit. "Myles, what are you doing out here by yourself?" asks Prim.

"Just sitting," I reply, dreading this conversation. I should have just gone to my room.

"Why haven't you answered any of my messages or calls?" she asks.

"I've been busy."

"But I saw you at the movie. Why didn't you go with us? We made plans together."

"Because I went with Sabrina instead. Prim, I really don't want to talk about this right now. I came out here to be alone."

"You went with Sabrina? And, honestly, I don't care. You've been ignoring me ever since yesterday and I want to know why."

"Why? You want to know why I've been ignoring you? Because I keep walking in on the two of you together, Prim. I'm tired of it," I say, raising my voice.

"I'm sorry that keeps happening to you. I don't mean for it to be like that. They're just bad coincidences," she replies.

"It can't keep happening. I don't like seeing you with him. I don't like him, and I don't think he's a good person. He doesn't deserve you. You only see the relationship from your point of view. You have your head so wrapped around him and the relationship that you can't see what everyone else sees. I've tried to be patient and I've really tried to get along with him and be okay with you two, but I just can't. I can't do it anymore, Prim."

"You can't do what?" she asks.

"If you're going to keep being around Jared all the time, then I think I need to try and keep my distance for a while," I reply.

"Keep your distance? Like, what, just not hang out with me?"

"If that's what I have to do," I say, breaking my own heart as I say those words aloud.

"I'm dating Jared, Myles. I don't know what you want me to do about that. You want me to break up with him because you don't like him?"

"I'm not saying that. If you're happy then I'm happy. I just need some space to do my own thing and figure some things out."

"So, what are you going to do then?" she asks.

"I don't know yet. Maybe join a club or something like that. I just need to be away from all of this for a little. I just can't stand seeing him with you. He doesn't take care about you," I reply.

"Myles, please don't leave," Prim says, tears falling down her cheeks.

I blink back the tears starting to form in my own eyes. "I'm not leaving and we're still going to see each other in class, but I just can't be around you two."

"If that's what you must do then do it. Obviously, there's nothing I can say to stop you."

"I'm sorry, Prim. It's just something that I need to do. You didn't do anything wrong so please don't think that it's your fault."

She was really crying now. All I want to do is go grab her and hug her, but I can't.

"Have a good night, Prim. I'll see you on Monday," I say, turning around and walking back to my building. I guess I did know what to say after all.

As soon as I get to my room, I close the door behind me and fall to the floor, putting my head in both my hands.

"Myles, I'm so sorry," Lawrence says.

"I'm losing her, man. I don't know what to do."

He came over to me, sat on the ground with me, and let me cry for the rest of the night.

CHAPTER 11

Myles

I looked up the word "distance" in the dictionary to make sure I was doing this right. *An amount of space between two things or people.* If you make the word "distance" into a very, it says *make someone or something far off or remote in position.* Well, I'm doing it right. It just sucks. Seriously. I can't remember a time when Prim and I didn't hang out for this long. I obviously see her in class, but she's started talking to a couple of other students in class now, so she doesn't sit right beside me and Sabrina anymore. It does make this a little easier, but it wouldn't be my first choice. I took Lawrence's advice. I decided to start taking guitar lessons and I'm planning to join the intramural volleyball team. I've always enjoyed volleyball. I played during middle school and the first two years of high school, but then I decided to stop.

    I was going to try playing soccer, but soccer was always Prim's thing and she's good at it. She scored two goals during their game last weekend. And she plays defense. Pretty impressive. I, at least, know some of the plays. The team was taking a corner kick and the coach had Prim go up into the other team's eighteen-yard box. I've seen her score multiple times in that box during high school. Vesper took the corner kick. It soared into the box and found Prim's head. Right into the back of the net. The second goal was similar. It was another corner kick but, after the kick was taken, the ball landed in the box without anyone touching it. It volleyed in the air and then Prim kicked it out of the air into the right side of the net. How do I know that she scored if I'm supposed to be distancing myself from her? Well, I may have gone to her game and hid at the side of the bleachers to watch. I'm still supporting her and she's still my best friend. I can never give that up.

I hated the look on Prim's face when I walked away from her that day. It looked like she had just had her heart broken, and I don't like that the look was put there by me. From what I can tell, everything is fine between Prim and Jared. But, then again, how would I know? And it's not like she would tell me if something was wrong. I told her I needed space from them so I would be the last person she would come to if they were having issues. I do still talk to Rem and the other girls now and then. It's a little more awkward trying to talk to them when Prim's around. It's not that I don't want to talk to her; I just don't know what to say. I know things aren't good between us right now, but she's at least respecting the space and distance I asked for. I don't know how I would get along if the roles were reversed so I wouldn't blame her if she caved. She's stubborn though so I know she's not talking to me to make a point. It's one of the things I love about her.

On my way to class the other day, I saw Prim walking toward the cafeteria. She was looking down at her phone, so she didn't see the football players throwing the ball back and forth. One of the players threw the ball a little too far. It was about to land right on her.

"Prim, look out!" I said as I moved to block the ball. I tried to catch it because that would make me look cool. I did not catch the ball. It hit the top part of my wrist and bounced off. It may have hurt a bit.

"Shit. Myles are you okay? Where the hell did you come from?" Prim asked.

"I saw the guys throwing the football and then I saw you weren't looking, so here I am," I replied.

"Well, thank you. I didn't really want to get a concussion today so I'm glad at least one of us is paying attention."

"Glad I could help," I said. "Well, now that you are okay, I better be going. Have a good day, Prim." I started turning back around.

"Wait, Myles. How have you been?" Prim asked.

"I'm all right. Promise. You don't have to worry about me."

"I just don't want you to be lonely, that's all," she replied.

"I'm not lonely. I've been hanging out a lot with Sabrina the last couple of weeks, so that's been nice."

"Oh," she said looking down at the ground. "That's nice. I'm happy for you. Did you join any of the clubs you were talking about?"

"Yeah. I actually have my first guitar lesson today and then, next week, I'm starting to play for the intramural volleyball team. I think it'll be fun," I replied.

"Ah, so you didn't want to play soccer and try to beat me, huh?"

"Nah. I would never be able to do that. I've already had my ass handed to me by you plenty of times to even attempt to beat you. You flattened me to the ground one time; do you remember that?"

"I do remember that," she said.

"After that, I vowed to never try and beat you again."

"Well, as long as you know," Prim said. We both laughed.

"Well, I gotta get to class but I'll see you later," I said.

"Okay, yeah. It was nice talking to you," she replied.

"You too, Prim."

I walked away from her toward my class building and continued to tell myself repeatedly that I was doing the right thing. She seemed so sad like she wanted to tell me something.

I talked to my mom last night and updated her on everything that's been happening She told me that she thinks I'm doing the right thing.

"Honey, I just don't want to see you get hurt, that's all," she said after I told her that I was taking a step back for a while.

"Mom, I'm already hurt. That's why I'm doing this. To try and not get hurt any more than I already am. It's hard seeing them together."

"And you explained all of this to her?"

"I did. Well, I didn't necessarily come out and tell her my feelings, but I told her most of what I was thinking. She wants us to all get along and hang out together, but I can't do that if I want to punch the guy every time I see him. He's not good to her," I replied.

"Then it's good you are getting a breather. You can't force her to make a decision. She's going to have to figure it out on her own. It's her life, Myles. You can only just be there for her."

"I know, and I am here for her. It's just hard being here for her when she's with someone else."

"I know, sweety, I know."

Of course, my mom called Prim's parents to talk about everything after our conversation. Which, of course, made Prim's parents call me to make sure that I was okay.

"Hi, Myles. Your mom just called us. What's going on? Is everything okay with you and Prim?" asked Margaret.

"I wouldn't have expected anything less from her," I said.

My mom and Prim's mom have been best friends for about as long as Prim and I have.

"I'm okay, though. Nothing to worry about."

"So, you don't like Jared, huh?" she asked.

"I don't. And it's not just for the obvious reason. He treats her like an afterthought, and she always comes second to everything, especially his friends."

"Yeah, well, she doesn't really talk to us much about him."

"I'm not surprised. You wouldn't like how he treats her so I'm sure she just thinks it's easier to pretend everything is okay," I replied.

"That's what I'm gathering," said Margaret. "Are you at least taking care of yourself?"

"Yes, I am. Don't worry. I'm starting to learn how to play guitar so I'm looking forward to that. Trying to fill up my time as much as possible. I'm starting to think that transferring is the best option," I replied.

I've also never said that aloud to anyone yet. It's something that I've been thinking about. I contacted Lakewood last week to see what my options were in terms of transferring for the second semester. My courses would transfer easily. I still don't know what I'm doing to do yet. When I talk to Prim about it, she'll find out that Silver Creek was never my first choice.

"Myles, you need to do whatever is best for you. If you think transferring will help the situation, then do it. But if you can put up with everything for the next three-and-a-half years, then stay," said Margaret. "We just want you to be happy."

That was the million-dollar question. Was I willing to put up with everything? If she continues to date Jared, probably not. I keep having thoughts that this is going to ruin our friendship.

I make my way to the music hall to meet Casey. Casey is my new guitar teacher. I saw a flyer on the bulletin board for guitar lessons last week and I figured it wouldn't hurt to try. If I suck, I suck. At least the lessons will get my mind off things. It feels good stepping out and doing things on my own.

Casey was sitting in the classroom when I walked in. The room was packed with all things musical. Guitars, pianos, trumpets, violins, you name it.

"Hi, you must be Casey," I say as I walk up to her and shake her hand.

"That would be me. Myles, right?" she replies.

"Nice to meet you. So, uh, do you teach people how to play all these instruments or do you just like to have all of them as trophies?" I ask.

"I teach guitar, piano, and the violin," she replied. "I come from a very musically inclined family, so I was raised around all of it."

"That's pretty impressive," I say, putting my bag down on the chair beside hers. "I don't have a story that's half as cool as that one."

"Well, what brings you in here?" she asks.

That's a great question.

"Uh, I guess just branching out to try new things. I'm going through some personal things, so a friend recommended I join a club or something. So, here I am. I signed up for intramural volleyball too actually. Just throwing myself into things, I guess," I reply.

"I actually started giving lessons for something to do after my ex and I broke up, so I understand the need to keep busy," she says. "Plus, it pays pretty well, so I've been doing it for the last three years. I'll be sad to stop after I graduate in May."

"Oh, I didn't realize you were a senior. Have you enjoyed your time here? I need some hope that it gets a little better. Lowly freshman here," I reply.

"You're not having a good time here?" she asks.

"No, it's not that exactly. I've made some good friends here and all that but, lately, I've been thinking about transferring next semester."

"Well, one of the best ways to let out some frustration is through music So, let's get started. What do you know about playing guitar?" Casey asks.

"Uh, I know that the thing you're holding is the guitar you're referring to and it plays music," I say. We both start laughing and she nodded her head.

"Yes, yes. This is a guitar. A+ for the day. Well, we start from the basics then. Okay, here. Hold this," she says as she hands me the guitar.

The guitar was much lighter than I expected.

"Okay, so first, let's go over the basic anatomy of the guitar. Probably the best first step," she says.

"I at least know what the strings are and what they do," I reply.

"Yes, those are the strings. We'll go over the chords a little later. Today, let's just focus on what everything is and does. Then, we'll start playing."

I nod my head.

"What are these silver oval things called at the top of this long stick thing?" I ask.

Casey closed her eyes and laughed.

"Well, first, that long stick thing is called the fretboard. The strings start at the bridge," she says as she points to the piece going horizontally along the bottom part of the guitar, "go all the way up the fretboard, and then end up at the tuning pegs, which are the silver oval things you were talking about."

"And the tuning pegs help you to tune the guitar?" I look up at her and smirk.

"Wow, you are one of my best students. I'm sure you could figure out the rest all on your own," Casey says, smiling.

"Okay, so fretboard, bridge, strings, and tuning pegs. Got it," I reply. "I think I'm ready for my recital now, coach."

"What do you think this does?" Casey asks as she points to a big hole in the middle of the guitar.

"Is it a place to keep your wallet and keys?" I ask looking up at her.

"Very funny. That is called the sound hole. Basically, it helps the sound echo out to produce all that pretty music we hear," she replies.

"Well, hopefully, I can get to that point soon," I say.

"You will. Let's take it slowly though. No need to rush. It takes a while to learn if you're not used to it."

I start strumming the strings with my fingers.

"Oh, here take this," she says as she hands me a pick. "This will make things much better. And, by the way, I think you're holding the guitar wrong. Let me help you."

Casey flips the guitar in my hands.

"You're right-handed?" she asks.

"Yeah," I reply.

"That's what I thought. Okay, so you're going to want to be able to strum and pick the strings with your dominant hand. Then, you'll use your left hand to press down the strings on the fretboard. Got it?" she asks.

"Yes. Got it."

"Okay, we will go over the chords and everything during the next couple of lessons. Then, I'll get you started with an easy song," Casey says.

"Sounds good."

Over the next couple of weeks, Casey taught me all the chords, showed me how to correctly pick the strings, and started me out playing the song *Wonderwall* by Oasis. I'm not going to lie; I was catching on quickly. I was spending all my free time picking up the guitar and continuing to learn beginner songs. Casey lent me one of her guitars from the music hall, so I found myself carrying it around with me everywhere on campus. I was on my way to another lesson with Casey when I ran into Remington. I do feel bad sometimes because my distance from Prim also meant not seeing our friend group as much either. For the most part, I've been hanging out more with Sabrina and Lawrence.

"Hey, Myles," Rem said.

"Hey, Rem," I replied. "How have you been?"

"I've been really good, thanks A couple of papers to write coming up, but nothing else exciting."

"I saw you all made it into the playoffs."

"We did! Yeah, it's pretty exciting. We have three games coming up here over the next week or two and, if we win those, we'll play in the championship game at the end of November. We won't get much of a holiday break, but it'll be worth it," she replied.

"That's great, Rem. I'm happy for you all."

"So, how have you really been?" she asked.

"What do you mean?" I replied.

"I know you're keeping your distance from Prim. She told me a little about it, but she didn't want to go into too much detail. I know she missed hanging out with you. It's weird not seeing you two together."

"I miss her too, but I think this is good. We both need time to grow outside of being with each other. I also despise Jared and can't watch him with her," I replied.

"So, you didn't hear. I thought as much," Rem said.

"Hear what?"

"Prim and Jared broke up," she said.

"What? When?" I asked. My heart started racing in my chest.

"This past week. I guess they had a big fight because he doesn't spend time with her and is always with his friends. He's canceled their last three dates because he's either with his teammates or at a study group. It's bullshit if you ask me," Rem replied.

"Is Prim, okay?" I asked.

"Honestly, I thought she would have said something to you. The breakup was her idea. I guess she's getting tired of coming second to everything else."

I didn't really know what to think. Should I go see her and make sure she's, okay?

"Are they broken up for good?" I asked.

"I don't know. I think she broke up with him until he can learn to appreciate her. I don't think she should be giving him this many chances but it's none of my business," Rem replied.

"Does she at least seem okay?" I asked.

"I think so. She is acting normal, and it is nice to see her without Jared. I don't know how long the breakup is going to last though."

I nodded.

"Well, thanks for telling me," I said.

"Where are you off to?" she asked.

"I've been learning how to play guitar so I'm on my way to my lesson," I replied, almost forgetting that I was on my way to do something.

"Are you enjoying it?" she asked.

"Yeah. I have a couple of songs down now so I think today, I might try writing my own."

"I'm happy for you and I'm glad you're staying busy. You know I'm always here for you if you need me."

"I know. Thanks, Rem," I replied.

"Are we going to see you soon?" she asked.

"Maybe. I'll let you know. Take it easy, Rem."

"Yeah, you too, Myles."

I headed back toward the music hall. I didn't know what to think about Prim and Jared breaking up. I'm also not sure if I should reach out to her.

We talk to each other about everything. Or at least we used to. I guess I shouldn't expect her to contact me.

Casey is waiting for me in the usual classroom. We do a refresher on the chords, play a couple of songs that I've been practicing, and then I tell her I've been wanting to try writing my own song. There's been a melody in my head for a couple of days now, so I don't want to lose it.

"Go for it," Casey replied. "Do you know any of the lyrics or do you just have the melody so far?"

"I have some of the lyrics. Not much though."

I grabbed paper and a pencil from my bag and wrote out the first line, *From that day when we were kids, until now, it's always been you.*

***

I left the lesson with the first verse of the song done. Lawrence and I were supposed to have dinner, so I pulled out my phone to text him. I had two text messages. One from Lawrence and the other from Prim.

Lawrence–Hey, man. I won't be able to do dinner tonight. Rebecca wants to talk about something.

Me–No worries. Have a good time.

Maybe they were going to make up. Or maybe Rebecca was just going to tell him to stop texting her all the time. The last I heard, they were still broken up and Lawrence was still sending her texts multiple times a week. I have no idea if she returned any of them.

The second message was from Prim.

Prim–Hey, Myles. I hope you are enjoying your guitar lessons. Just wanted to let you know I was thinking about you.

If she only knew how many times a day, I thought about her.

Me–Hey there. I do like the lessons! I already started writing my own song.

Prim–Holy shit! That's awesome. Rem told me she saw you earlier, so I wanted to say hi. I hope you're doing well other than the guitar lessons.

Me–I am! Is everything okay with you?

Clearly, I'm fishing for answers here. Maybe she'll open and tell me about Jared.

Prim–Could be better. But I'm fine, don't worry.

I am really going to regret what I'm about to do.

Me–Are you free for dinner?

What am I doing?

Her text comes literally five seconds later.

Prim–Yes! Of course!

Me–Want to meet in the café in like twenty minutes?

Prim–I'll see you there!

That was stupid, I know. I'm not expecting anything. I just want to make sure that she's okay. It's my job.

Twenty minutes later and I'm sitting at a table waiting for Prim. I sit there for a couple more minutes and then she walked in the front door looking around the room until she noticed me. She gave me a big smile and my heart turned over in my chest. Okay, this was a terrible idea. The absolute worst.

I stood up when she got to the table, and she came over to my side and hugged me. Peaches. I haven't smelled that in a long time. I hugged her tighter.

"Hey, Myles," Prim said. "I missed you."

"I missed you too," I replied.

"I'm surprised you asked me to meet you, honestly," Prim said.

"Well, I couldn't stay away for too long now, could I?" I replied.

"I hoped you wouldn't."

"So, what's going on with you?" I asked. "You didn't seem too confident in your message."

"As a matter of fact, I do have something to tell you."

"What is it?" I replied.

"I broke up with Jared."

I tried to make it seem like I didn't already know all of this. I kept a straight face as much as possible.

"When did this happen?" I asked.

"Last week," she replied.

"Are you okay?"

"Well, I'm much better now that you're here," she said. "You make me feel better about everything, Myles. I hope you know that."

"I'm glad I can do that for you," I replied.

There was a long pause where we just looked at each other. I was holding so many words back. So many emotions. So many longings.

Prim broke the silence.

"So, other than guitar lessons, what else have you been doing?"

"I start the volleyball thing soon. Our first get-together is in a couple of days. It's just a bunch of games. Something fun to do," I replied.

"Would you mind if I came to watch sometime?" she asked.

"You're more than welcome," I replied.

"I figured I should return the favor since you've been coming to all of my home games."

"What do you mean? I haven't been..." I started. Prim held up her hand to stop me.

"Don't even try that. I saw you hiding by the bleachers the whole time. You suck at hiding," she said.

"I could never get anything past you," I replied. "I know I told you I needed distance, but I still wanted to support you. And I didn't have to see Jared around you since you were preoccupied."

"Yeah, well, the men's team is usually practicing when we have home games, so he hasn't seen me play a lot."

"I'm sorry, Prim."

"It's okay. I'm not going to him. He's going to have to come to me and apologize."

"You think you'll get back together?" I asked.

"Honestly, I don't know. He would have to do something big to win me back."

I didn't know what to say so I just nodded.

"Are you going to the Halloween party next weekend?" she asked.

"I haven't really thought about it actually."

"Well, just think about it."

I nodded again. We finished our dinner, said our goodbyes, and then went our separate ways.

CHAPTER 12

Myles

The following Wednesday night, I went to pick up Sabrina in her room. She told me she wanted to come to watch us play volleyball and that she was going to make me a sign and everything.

"You should feel like a real athlete now," Sabrina said after holding up her sign.

Myles Aratis is my idol. Go, Myles!

I've never had someone make a sign for me, so it was actually really nice. We got to the gym at seven-thirty and the game started at eight. The team and I all introduced we and I also introduced them to Sabrina. They were all, of course, jealous of my sign. The team and I had met one time before when we all went to sign up, but we didn't do any introductions until now We decided to name ourselves *The Newb Squad*. It's really mature, I know. No one on the team except me has really played volleyball before; at least not on a team or anything. So, we thought the name was fitting. Okay, I shouldn't include myself in this. I voted against the name, but the majority rules. Our opponent is a team called *Go for the Dig*. They probably know what they're doing.

"I'll be over on the side watching, okay?" Sabrina asked.

"Sounds good," I replied.

"Good luck."

"Yeah, thanks. I'm going to need it."

The game started and we actually weren't doing as bad as I thought we were going to. We had eight people on the team, so we substituted the other two every so often. We were playing that the first to twenty-one points wins. I was able to spike the ball and get two kills early on in the game, so I was pretty proud of myself. This was fun. After our team had scored and we were getting ready to serve the ball, I heard the side door open and looked over to see Prim coming into the gym. She spotted me and gave me a wave. I smiled and waved back. I thought that she would go over and sit with Sabrina, but Prim stayed by the door and watched.

The score was twenty to fourteen. If we make this last point, we win. The other team was serving. They served the ball over to our side and we sent it back over to theirs. I saw that they were trying to set up a spike. Me and the guy Terrence on our team jumped up by the net just as the other team spiked the ball. We blocked it and it bounced over to their side and hit the ground. That makes twenty-one. We win. We cheered, clapped, and hugged. We went over to shake hands with the other team, and then I saw Sabrina running toward me with her sign. She threw her arms around me and pulled me in for a hug.

"Wow. You were great, Myles! This is awesome. I'm coming to all of your games from now on," Sabrina said.

"Well, thanks for coming. And thanks for the sign," I replied.

Sabrina was still hugging me and, as I looked over to Prim to wave her over, she had already turned around and was walking out the door.

"Sabrina, hold on a second. I'll be right back," I said as I ran over to the door and went outside.

Prim was walking back to the dorms ahead of me.

"Prim. Wait, where are you going? Why didn't you say anything?" I asked as I ran up to her.

"I didn't want to bother you. You were having a moment with everyone so I figured I would just leave," she replied.

"You should have come over. I would have introduced you to everyone."

"It's okay. Maybe next time. Good job tonight, Myles. Tell Sabrina I said hi. I'll talk to you later," she said as she turned and walked away from me.

Wait. What the hell just happened?

**

I decided at the very last minute that I was going to the Halloween party. I wasn't going to but then Lawrence convinced me to. He and Rebecca just got back together, apparently, so I didn't want to ruin his good mood. He's been moping around for the last month. Tonight's Halloween party theme is *"Masked or Maimed."* Basically, you had to wear a costume with a mask, or you weren't allowed in. Lawrence was going as Ghostface from the *Scream* movies. I approved, of course, I chose Batman. Now, usually, I would go for something scary, but Prim and I have always talked about dressing up as Batman and Catwoman together for a Halloween party. Lawrence and I had to make a quick stop at the store to grab my costume but, thankfully, I found what I was looking for.

Today is actually Halloween so it makes the night even spookier. We stop by Sabrina's room to pick up her and her girlfriend. Bethany was visiting for the weekend so they decided to go to the party together. Bethany was dressed as the Phantom of the Opera and Sabrina was dressed as Christine Daae with a masquerade mask. We walked out of the dorm and headed to the party. One of the fraternities was hosting the party We got to the house and walked in. It sounded like someone created a Halloween playlist. *Thriller* was playing as we walked into the kitchen.

"What's your drink of choice tonight?" Lawrence asked.

"I think I'm just going to stick to beer," I replied. I go to pour a glass of beer and realized that the fraternity brothers must have put green and orange food coloring into the drinks. I grabbed the green beer.

There were decorations all over the house and, from what I could see, I couldn't recognize anyone with their costumes on. It kind of made it more fun that way. Everyone was in masks. There were also some people who just threw on a mask so that they would be able to get into the party.

"Let's go dance," Sabrina said as she led us into the living room.

The Monster Mash was up next. But I realized that all the songs had some kind of remix to them. I guess to fit the party scene more. Sabrina and Bethany started dancing and then Lawrence and I followed along. I bumped into someone behind me and, when I turned around, I realized that it was Prim. I hadn't seen her since she walked away from me after my volleyball game. *Oh my god.* She was wearing a Catwoman costume.

"Oh, sorry," Prim said as she turned back around and continued to dance with, who I'm going to guess were, Rem, Vesper, and Jax.

Could she really not recognize me with this costume? I actually almost forgot I had a costume on. I started to wonder if I should tell her that it was me. I chose not to. She looked so good in that costume. It was the Catwoman costume from *The Dark Knight* so she was more recognizable than the other people here. I can't believe she remembered our deal. She had the face mask and then her long blonde hair flowing over her shoulders. Damn, I missed her. I looked back over my shoulder and saw that Prim wasn't there anymore. I look around the room and saw her going up the stairs.

"I'll be right back," I say to Lawrence.

I make my way up the stairs and see Prim opening the door to the bathroom. Okay, I'm going to do something really stupid. I am absolutely going to regret this but it's something that I've wanted to do ever since high school. I follow her into the bathroom, shut the door behind us, lift her up onto the sink and kiss her. I press my body into her, and she wraps her arms and legs around me. I grind my hips into her, and she lets out a little moan. She kissed me back as our tongues danced around each other. Oh god, she tastes so good I pull away, tilt her head back, and kiss her neck. I don't know what's going through her head right now and I'm not even sure if I know what's going through my head. Does she think it's me or someone else? She and Jared broke up. Does she think it's him? No, I need to stop. Jesus! I'm kissing Prim right now. The only light that's on in here is a skeleton decoration that's lit up orange. We can see each other but it's too dark to recognize anything. I pull back from the kiss.

"I'm sorry," I say quietly as I turn to grab the door handle.

"Strawberries," Prim says touching her lips.

"What?" I ask as I turn back around to her.

"You taste like strawberries. When did you start smelling like that?" she asks.

"I don't know," I reply in a low tone as I open the door. "I'm so sorry."

I closed the door behind me and ran downstairs and out the front door. I took off my mask and wondered if I had just made the biggest mistake of my life.

Chapter 13

Prim

"Do you even understand why I'm doing this?" I ask Jared.

"No, I don't Prim. This is stupid. You can't just break up with me for no reason," replied Jared.

"I do have a reason. Clearly, you're not listening to me. No surprise there."

"Just because I like to hang out with my friends once in a while?" he asked.

"I don't care if you hang out with your friends. But you're with them all the time. I feel like I haven't seen you for weeks because you keep canceling our dates. You don't appreciate me at all. You always push me aside when something better comes along."

"I just have a lot of people that I hang out with. I'm trying to make everything even, but it's hard."

"I also have people I hang out with but you don't see me canceling three of our dates in a row, do you?" I asked.

"I said I was sorry about that. What else do you want from me?" Jared replied.

"You know what, Jared? I don't want a fucking thing from you. Not anymore. Why don't you come talk to me when you can learn how to appreciate me," I said as I stormed out of his room.

Jared and I haven't been doing well, obviously. Over the last three weeks, he's canceled pretty much all of our scheduled dates. Since we're both playing soccer and have tight schedules, we planned out times to go on these dates. It was supposed to be something special, and I was really looking forward to them. He either decided that he wanted to be with his friends or that he forgot that he had some kind of study group. Honestly, how many fucking study groups does one college student need. Rem told me that she had seen Jared at his "study groups" a couple of times and she said that it was always him and two other girls or just him and one other girl. She said that it didn't really look like there was a lot of studying going on. He told me that his one class has mostly girls in it, so he had to work with them. I've just always wondered to myself if he was telling the truth. Like Rem said, how much studying was actually getting done? Rem has always told me stories about him since they went to rival high schools, but I just don't know what to believe. Everyone thinks he's a tool and, honestly, he just might be.

Not talking to Myles has been hard. He's always been my go-to person for all of this. I'm starting to realize that maybe I don't appreciate him enough. Maybe I'm guilty of the same thing that Jared is doing to me. When Myles told me that he needed distance, I honestly felt like he was breaking up with me. I just felt so different from our other arguments. He looked like he was in so much pain. I just wanted to give him a hug, but I knew I shouldn't. I feel his absence so much that it feels like a part of me is missing. I still see him in class but it's not the same. There are a couple of other students that I've started talking to, so I moved my seat closer to them. I'm trying to respect Myles as much as I can without letting him know how sad I am. Every day I pick up my phone to text him, but I always delete my message. It's always the same one I type out. *Hey, Myles. How are you?* If he went into our message conversations, I'm sure he would see the little typing bubbles appear on his screen at least once a day. But, again, I refrain. He's also with Sabrina a lot, so I don't want to mess anything up. He seems happy when he's with her, so I'll leave them be. He deserves to be happy. She's there for him. I just haven't figured out how I feel about that yet.

It's a week later and I'm debating, yet again, whether I should text Myles and let him know everything. I have also gotten a couple of messages from Jared saying that he is sorry and all that garbage. I really don't know what to do. I feel like I've already given him too many chances as it is.

Rem walks into our room, comes over, and throws herself on my bed with me.

"Hey, roomie," she says as she gives me a smirk.

I don't trust this look at all. She's up to something.

"Hey, back. Uh, why are you looking at me like that?" I ask.

"Oh, nothing. I just saw Myles on my way back from class. He looks just as sad as you are," she says.

"Did you talk to him?"

"I did. He's on his way to a guitar lesson right now."

"I guess he did start those lessons after all. I hope it's going well for him," I say. "Do you think that I should text him?"

"That's up to you, babe. It's not like he would be devastated to hear from you," Rem replies.

"I know but I'm just trying to respect his wishes."

"And I'm glad you're doing that but sending one text message isn't going to hurt anything. Prim, he's your best friend and I hate seeing you two like this. It's not the same with us all not hanging out together. And, plus, my theory, remember?"

"Ugh, what is it with you and this damn theory?" I ask.

"Well, technically, it's a fact since I've already proven it."

"Are you ever going to tell me what this theory, oh, I'm sorry, *fact* is?" I ask.

"I'm going to take a guess and say that you might already know it," she replies.

I do. I do know it. I just don't want to say it out loud.

I pick up my phone and send a text to Myles.

Me–Hey, Myles. I hope you're enjoying your guitar lessons. Just wanted to let you know I was thinking about you.

I shouldn't be surprised that he responded, but I am. We send a couple of messages back and forth and then he asks me if I am free for dinner. Maybe this is a good sign? I hope so. I miss him in my life, and I don't like how things are right now between us.

When I walked into the cafeteria, I saw him sitting at a corner table and I'm sure my face lit up. It took everything in me not to sprint over to him. I hugged him. I pulled together into his chest. Strawberries. He still smelled like strawberries. I was so happy during dinner, but it did definitely feel a little awkward. We caught up on everything that we had been doing since the last time we spoke and, yes, I told him about Jared. I wasn't sure if Rem had told him anything or not. He asked me if I thought Jared and I would get back together and I wasn't entirely sure what to say because I honestly didn't know. I explained the situation and told him that Jared would have to do something pretty big to make my final decision. Myles went on to tell me about taking guitar lessons and starting on the intramural volleyball team next week. Of course, I asked him if I could come. His first game was next Wednesday. I would be there.

The following Wednesday, I was getting ready to go to Myles's volleyball game when my phone started ringing. It was Jared. I knew I was going to regret this, but I picked up.

"What do you want, Jared?"

"Can you please just talk to me?" asks Jared.

"I'm pretty sure that's what we're doing right now," I reply, knowing I was being petty.

"Can you at least let me explain?"

"No, Jared. Not right now. We'll talk later. I'm busy."

"What are you doing?" he asks.

"It's really none of your business," I add.

"You're seeing Myles, aren't you?"

"Again, it's none of your business. I'll talk to you later. Goodbye," I say as I hang up before he can reply.

Great, I'm now late for the game. I grab my purse, put on a sweatshirt, and head to the gym. When I get there, I go in through the side door. The game had already started so no one was paying attention to me. No one except Myles. He saw me come in and looked over at me. I waved to him, and he did the same back. The game continued. I saw Sabrina sitting over beside the rest of the crowd who came to watch, but I decided to stay closer to the door by myself. Myles's team was winning from what I could see on the scoreboard.

"Excuse me," I say to the person standing beside me. "How many points do they go up to?"

"Twenty-one," she replies.

"Thanks."

I had never seen Myles play like this before. He looked like he was having so much fun. I don't really know all the rules and regulations for volleyball but, whatever Myles's team was doing, was working. I looked back over at the scoreboard and realized that their team had only one more point to go until they won the game. The team lined up, getting ready for the other team to serve the ball. They served the ball, the game continued, and then Myles and another of his teammates jumped up to block the ball. If I'm understanding volleyball correctly, I do believe that Myles's team wins the game. I was right. They all cheered and celebrated with each other. The spectators were clapping and so was I. After the team stopped hugging each other, I started to make my way over to Myles to congratulate him but, as I took a couple of steps toward him, Sabrina ran out onto the court.

She ran up to Myles and hugged him. My stomach did this weird thing where it felt like it turned over inside itself. Of course, he hugged her back. Why wouldn't he? Well, I'm not going up to them now. That would be more awkward than I want. I would feel like I was getting in the way of something. They were sharing a moment. As they were still hugging, I turned back around and walked out of the gym door. I started walking back to my dorm and felt a tear fall out of the corner of my eye. I heard my name being called behind me and knew exactly who it was. I wiped away the tear that had fallen down my cheek and then turned around to face him. He looked really hurt. He told me that I should have come over to him so that he could have made introductions to the team, but I told him that he was sharing a moment with the team and Sabrina, so I figured that it was better to not go over. I couldn't get out of there fast enough.

"It's okay. Maybe next time. Good job tonight, Myles. Tell Sabrina I said hi. I'll talk to you later," I said as I turned and walked as fast as I could back to my dorm room.

I felt like the roles had been switched here. The last time, it was Myles who was walking away from me like this. It does feel good being the one turning and walking away but I hate that this keeps happening with Myles. Where did we go so wrong? What's happened to us? It's like we're completely out of sync with each other these days and I really have no idea how to fix the situation. When I got back to my room, I opened the door, lay down on my bed, and started crying.

"Prim, what's wrong?" asked Remington as she got out of her bed to come over to me.

"I don't know," I replied.

"Weren't you just at Myles's volleyball game? Did something happen?"

"Nothing happened. I just hate not being with him, Rem. Sabrina was there, and she ran up to him and gave him a hug after the game. I didn't want to interrupt so I just left."

"Did Myles say anything to you after the game?" she asked.

"He came up to me as I walked out of the gym to try and get me to come back inside, but I said that he needed to go back in and that I would see him later."

"You didn't want to talk to him at all?"

"Of course, I wanted to talk to him but I'm just getting in the way. He's made new friends and he has his team and Sabrina now," I replied.

"Oh, honey, you don't think that he's dating Sabrina, do you?" asked Rem.

"I don't know what I think anymore. If they were dating, don't you think he would have told me?"

"I'm going to be perfectly honest with you and tell you that I don't think he and Sabrina are dating. It's not like what it seems to me," Rem said. She sighed. "You both are like two peas in a pod, and you don't even realize it."

"Realize what?" I asked.

"You'll figure it out soon enough."

***

Today is Saturday. It also happens to be Halloween and the night of our school Halloween party. The last two days have been rough. I haven't really been in the partying mood, so I wasn't entirely looking forward to going to this party tonight. I even skipped psychology class yesterday morning so that I didn't have to see Myles. After what happened Wednesday, I just wasn't in the right head space. I also didn't know if Myles was going to the party. I had asked him about it before during dinner, but he said he wasn't sure and that he hadn't thought about it. I'm also fairly sure that Jared is going to be there so this night is either going to be really fun or be a complete shitshow. Please don't be a shit show. I feel like this whole semester has been a shit show so far. This is not really what I thought college was going to be like. For starters, I thought that Myles and I would be hanging out a lot more than we are now. I also never thought that I would have a boyfriend and then break up with him already. It hasn't even been a full semester yet.

I have been having these realizations lately. Jared and I never once said that we loved each other. I never told him; he never told me. Was that normal? I know we have only been dating since the end of August, but we never even had a conversation about what we meant to each other. We would always just hang out either just the two of us or with my friends. We would always be busy doing something, so conversations never got any deeper than surface level. My parents have been texting me over the last month asking me how things are with Jared. I always reply with a "things are good!" I'm not sure how much they believed me when I said that. I didn't talk to them a lot about Jared. There wasn't really a lot that I could say. Nothing exciting happened so there was nothing to say. I don't blame Myles for not liking him. Now that I think about it, I don't think any of my friends really like him.

Speaking of friends, Vesper and Jax walk into our room with their costumes on. Both had masks on since the party was called "Masked or maimed." We didn't feel like getting kicked out, so we all decided on costumes that already had masks as part of the outfit. I spent a lot of time trying to figure out what I was going to be. Back in the summer, Myles and I talked about what we would be for our first Halloween at college. We decided that we would have a matching costume or at least something that is related to each other. We came up with the perfect duo. He would be Batman and I would be Catwoman. We would do it up *Dark Knight* style. That was back in the summer though. Things weren't the greatest right now so I'm not sure if he would even remember what we talked about, let alone, if he would even go to the party in the first place.

Vesper was a devil. Very fitting for her personality. Jax was dressed up as Mrs. Incredible from *The Incredibles*. She was into all of the nerdy stuff, so I'm not surprised she went with this option. Both girls were wearing red, and they were definitely pulling it off. I did end up deciding on Catwoman. If Myles were there dressed as Batman maybe, he would see that I was at least trying. Rem went with a bank robber costume. She stuffed her bag with the fake money that we had bought at the store yesterday and then we headed out the door.

We headed to the fraternity house and made our way into the crowd. The house had a very spook aesthetic to it, including all kinds of Halloween decorations and music. It even looked like the brothers bought fog machines because we walked through fog up to our shins all the way through the house. It definitely set the mood, so I was starting to cheer up a bit more than I was earlier. Maybe this night won't be so dull after all.

"Hey, I'm gonna get us some drinks. What do you want?" asked Rem.

"Just beer please," I replied. I'm going to keep it simple tonight. I also don't want to drink too much. I've been doing way too much of that lately and I don't want that to be my method of coping with everything that's been happening the last couple of weeks. Also, we are getting ready to go into our playoff games so I need to make sure that I'm in good enough shape for those.

Ves, Jax, and I made our way onto the dance floor because where else do you go when you're at a party? We moved our way past all kinds of different costumes. It looked like a Halloween store threw up in here. In the best way possible, of course. There was a DJ at the front of the room. Green and orange lights were hanging all around the rooms. It did kind of resembles a haunted house in here.

We all started dancing to *The Monster Mash* and then Rem came up behind us and gave us our drinks. Everyone's hands and drinks were in the air as we all grabbed dance partners and tried to successfully maneuver around everyone with all of our costumes in the way. As I danced, I accidentally bumped into someone standing behind me.

"Oh, sorry," I said, noticing that the person I hit was wearing a Batman costume.

It couldn't be Myles, could it? No. I'm sure there are going to be plenty of people here tonight wearing Batman costumes. I shook my head and then turned back around to dance with the group. We continued to drink and then I realized that it was time to break the seal. I hated always being the first one to break the seal, but I swear I have the smallest bladder in the world. I told the rest of the group that I would be right back and headed out to the stairs.

There's a whole fraternity house and the only bathrooms are on the second floor. I walk up the stairs and turned left toward where the bathroom is. Yes. No one waiting in line. I open the door but, before I could flip on the light switch, someone came up behind me, closed the door, and then picked me up and put me on top of the sink. There was only one light on in the bathroom and it was coming from a glow-in-the-dark skeleton figurine. It was hard to see who the person was because they were in a dark costume but, before I could figure that out, he was kissing me. Jared? He kept kissing me. I tasted his lips. They smelled like strawberries. A realization dawned on me. I kissed him back. I wrapped my arms around his neck and then wrapped my legs around his waist. I pulled him in closer to me and felt his erection pressed against my core. I let out a small moan. *Oh my god*. Did I really just moan?

I deepened the kiss, but it didn't last very long. The mysterious stranger pulled away from the kiss and backed away from me.

"I'm sorry," he says as he turned back toward the bathroom door.

"Strawberries," I say touching my fingers to my lips.

"What?" he asks.

"You taste like strawberries. When did you start smelling like that?" I ask.

"I don't know," he replies as he turns and walks out of the bathroom, closing the door behind him.

I thought it was Jared at first trying to make up for what's happened between us lately. But no. That wasn't Jared. Not with that scent. I only smell strawberries around one person.

Myles.

Chapter 14

Prim

It was Myles. I know it was Myles. The question that I'm trying to answer now is *why* was it, Myles? He kissed me. I know he did. And I kissed him back. I liked it. It was honestly the hottest thing that has happened to me in a really long time. Things were okay with Jared, but it doesn't even compare. The way he lifted me up on the sink and pushed into me… Is it just me or did it get hotter in here? I'm sitting on my bed trying to figure out what is going on in my life. After the kiss in the bathroom at the Halloween party, Myles left. He just left. And this past week? Extremely awkward. Myles won't even look at me in class. He's not doing a very good job of trying to hide that it was him. Jared doesn't smell like strawberries. Myles does. That was the dead giveaway. And now he thinks that he can pretend that nothing happened and get away with it. I should confront him. I really should. But I have no fucking idea what I would say to him.

What's happening to us? For Christ's sake, this is Myles we're talking about. But lately, I've been feeling differently. I've missed him. I guess it's one of those things where you don't start to miss it until it's gone. That's certainly the case here. I just don't know what to do about what happened. If I try talking to him about it, he's going to say that it wasn't him and that maybe it was Jared trying to get back with me. Myles isn't a very confrontational person, but I still do think that this is something that needs to be addressed.

Although, I will say, I think I've figured out Rem's theory she was talking about. I feel stupid for not having realized it sooner. I mean, I know I was feeling differently the last month or so about things. And it also would explain why Myles told me that he needed some distance. It was right in front of my fucking face this entire time. Myles has feelings for me. Why else would he need space? Of course, he didn't like seeing me and Jared together. Now I feel like an asshole.

It was the following Monday and I had just gotten back from practice. I lay down on my bed and looked at my phone. One new text from Sabrina. Sabrina? Why was she texting me?

Sabrina–Hey, Prim. Are you still meeting us at the library for the project?

Oh, shit. I completely forgot I was supposed to meet them. I sent a quick reply.

Me–Yes, so sorry. On my way now.

Well, hopefully I don't smell too bad. I throw on some deodorant and body spray, hoping that would mask any sweat odor. I'm almost twenty minutes late, so I jog over to the library. I had a feeling that this was going to be awkward. I didn't know how I was going to act around Myles. I wonder how he would react around me. Obviously, he doesn't know that I know it was him who kissed me, but I'm sure he still might feel uncomfortable. *I'm nervous.*

I walk in the front door and spot Sabrina and Myles at our usual corner spot. I keep my head down for most of the way to the table, not wanting to look straight at Myles.

"Hey, Prim!" said Sabrina.

"Hey, Sabrina. I'm so sorry I'm late. I completely forgot after practice," I replied.

"No worries. We won't be here very long since we each already have what we need. We just need to put everything together into one presentation and then it should be ready to go."

"Sounds good," I said. I turned to look at Myles, but he was looking down at his notebook. "Hey, Myles."

"Hey," he replied. I could see a tint of red form on his cheeks. He didn't say anything else after that.

I forced a smile and then sat down across from Sabrina. I took out my laptop and pulled up my part of the presentation. There was a very noticeable tension in the air, and it was so uncomfortable. I was trying to look for something to do on my screen so that it would distract me and be less awkward.

"Uh, did I miss something between you two?" asked Sabrina looking between me and Myles.

"What do you mean?" I replied.

"Well, the awkwardness is so thick in here we could cut it with a knife, so spill. What's going on with you guys?"

"Nothing's going on," I said.

"Yeah, everything is fine," Myles chimed in.

"Did you two have a fight or something?" Sabrina asked. "Myles told me he couldn't text you because his phone was dead but I'm starting to think it's because he's avoiding you." She looked over at Myles and raised her eyebrows.

"I'm not avoiding anything," Myles replied. "Can we get on with this project please?"

"Someone's grouchy today," Sabrina replied.

"I'm not grouchy."

"Says the person with a scowl on his face."

Sabrina and Myles both opened their laptops.

"So, why don't you two just send me your files and then I'll put everything together into the presentation," I said, desperately wanting something to occupy my time so I didn't have to sense the tension radiating off Myles right now.

"Sure, sounds good. Thanks for doing that," Sabrina said. She then elbowed Myles in the side.

"Ouch," he said, rubbing the sore spot, then looking at me. "Yeah, Prim, thanks. We appreciate it." He glared at Sabrina. I'm glad to see they're getting along well. *Maybe.*

I opened the files they just sent me and copied their information into the presentation that I had already created. For our project, we chose to focus on how different gender roles in society are creating ideas of inequality. We analyzed different gender norms, gender roles, and stereotypes that have been placed upon the different genders for years. My part of the presentation was to focus on how gender roles are harmful to society. We were giving this presentation right before Thanksgiving break, so we still had a couple of weeks before it was due.

"So, Prim, did you have fun at the Halloween party?" asked Sabrina.

Myles then started choking and coughing up the water that he had just been drinking. Sabrina pulled tissues out of her bag and helped him clean up the spilled water all over the table.

"Uh, yes, I had a great time. Very eventful," I said looking straight at Myles.

"Oh, yeah? How so?" asked Sabrina.

I was trying to figure out how much I should tell her. Myles looked like he was about to pass out, so I decided to spare him any more humiliation on this topic.

"Oh, you know, there's nothing that screams a college party more than your roommate throwing up all over our bathroom."

I wasn't lying. When we all made our way back to the dorms after the party, Rem got sick all over the bathroom. The floor, the sink, the toilet. I know it's not the most appealing thing in the world, but I welcomed the cleanup. It took my mind off other things that I wasn't really ready to confront quite yet.

"Sounds about right," Sabrina replied.

"I'm gonna use the bathroom. I'll be right back," Myles said as he shot up out of his seat and headed toward the library door.

Sabrina chuckled and shook her head.

"That kid is a piece of work, isn't he?" she asked.

"Don't I know it," I replied.

"So, what's been going on between you two? I know he was getting some space, but how are you holding up? I feel like we don't talk enough. I only know what Myles tells me about you."

"I don't know, Sabrina. I thought coming to this school with him would be good for us. We've never been like this before. Sure, we've had arguments growing up, but it was just kid's stuff. I guess it just comes with getting older."

"I know that he cares a lot about you. You're both going through a tough time right now and that's understandable. I heard you broke up with your boyfriend?" Sabrina asked.

"Did Myles tell you?"

"No, I overheard Jared talking about it in one of our classes. No offense or anything, but he seems like a real dickhead."

"Yeah, well, that's one word for him."

"I also know that Myles really hated seeing the two of you together. The only question that you need to figure out is why he got so worked up over you two."

"He told me he didn't like seeing how he treated me, which I'm assuming is true. But I'm also going to assume that it was for another reason. One that I am slowly starting to realize."

"Listen, I'm the last one that should be giving you relationship advice and, please, tell me if I have no business being in this, but I don't like seeing you and Myles fight like this. He hasn't been himself lately, and it doesn't seem like you have been either."

"I haven't," I reply.

"How long have you two been friends?" Sabrina asks.

"Since the third grade."

"Exactly. Don't let this little hiccup break all of that up. You two have already come this far."

"I know you said you shouldn't be giving relationship advice but you're pretty good at it," I say smiling over at her.

"Well, it's one of those things where I can give advice, but I'm terrible at taking my own."

I nodded. "I'm glad Myles has you, Sabrina. I just want him to be happy."

"Wait, you don't think..." she started. "You don't think that Myles and I are going to get together, do you?"

"I just thought since you two have been spending a lot of time together, it seemed like he liked you," I reply a little confused.

"Oh, he does like me, just not in the way that you're thinking."

"What do you mean?" I ask.

"I can absolutely guarantee you that nothing romantic is going on between us. He's not really my type," she replies.

"Not your type?"

"Yeah. He has a little too much dick for my taste."

"Wait. What?" I ask. Oh. *OH*. I waved my hand. "I get it now. Don't mind me. Just completely oblivious over here," I say as I put my face in my hands.

"No, no, it's okay, really. I never really put it on blast, so how could you know?" Sabrina asks.

"So, the girl with you at the Halloween party?"

"She's, my girlfriend. Bethany. We met over the summer and started dating soon after that."

"I'm so happy for you. Damn! I wish I would have known. I'm not going to lie, Sabrina; I haven't been the warmest toward you. I thought. I thought," I start.

"You thought that I was trying to get with Myles?" she asks.

I give a slight nod. The embarrassment I feel right now is making me dizzy.

"Hopefully, that eases your mind then. I'm glad I met Myles and he's been a great friend. I actually don't have a lot of friends so it's nice to have a couple close ones. But I also hope that you and I can be friends too. Especially now that you know that I'm not going to be in the way of anything."

"Be in the way?" I ask.

"I know you're smart. You'll figure it out. No offense, but both you and Myles are so dense when it comes to this stuff."

I sigh. "I've been trying to avoid it. Lately, I've just been feeling a bit different than I used to."

"Believe me, I know the feeling. Look, you're not wrong to feel what you're feeling. And I'm not even saying you must do anything about it. I just don't want to see either of you continue to be hurt by these things, you know?"

"I know. And I appreciate it," I say as Myles walks up to the table.

"Well, you were gone for like an hour," Sabrina says.

"There was a line," he replied.

"A line? For the men's bathroom? In the library, of all places? Never heard of it."

Myles sat back down, and we spent the next thirty minutes finishing the presentation. After we were done, I made sure to save everything on my flash drive and then we packed up and left the library. We headed back to the dorms and split off between the two freshmen buildings. Before I went into my building, I turned my head and saw Myles looking at me. When he realized I was looking over at him, he quickly turned his head and walked into his building.

I thought back to what Sabrina said to me and I really hoped that our friendship could withstand anything.

Chapter 15

Myles

Thank God that was over. Being in the library with Prim was fucking torture. She kept looking at me and, of course, Sabrina kept asking questions. If I didn't go to the bathroom when I did, I probably would have combusted. I never should have kissed her at the party. I hadn't told Sabrina what happened at the party so I can't blame her for asking all those questions. Sabrina, Lawrence, and I decided to go for a late dinner, so we went back to my room to pick up Lawrence. I figured now was as good a time as any to confess. I couldn't keep this in anymore.

"Sabrina, Lawrence, I need to tell you guys something," I said as Sabrina sat down on my bed and Lawrence sat up on his.

"Uh, is everything okay?" Sabrina asked.

"I'm not sure how to answer that question. Let me just get this out first and then both of you will understand what I mean," I replied.

Sabrina and Lawrence both looked at each other with nervous glances.

"I kissed Prim at the Halloween party," I said closing my eyes so that I couldn't see their reactions. I slowly opened my right eye and looked at both of their faces.

"You did *what?*" asked Sabrina, shooting up off of the bed.

"I kissed her," I replied. "Look, before either of you say anything else, I didn't go to the party with the intention of kissing her. It just kind of happened."

"You let me rattle on and on about that party at the library and you didn't think to clue me in on what happened? Jesus. No wonder you were uncomfortable and left," said Sabrina.

"Is that why you left the party early?" asked Lawrence.

"Yeah. I, uh, followed her upstairs at the frat house and then I kissed her in the bathroom."

"And how did she react to you kissing her?" Sabrina asked.

"Well, here's the thing, and I know you're both going to get pissed at me."

"Spill," replied Lawrence.

"She didn't know it was me," I said.

"What do you mean she didn't know it was you?" asked Sabrina.

"I mean, we were all dressed up in our costumes and our faces were covered and the bathroom was dark, so there was no way that she could know that it was me who kissed her."

"So, you kissed her and didn't say anything to her?" asked Lawrence.

"I said a couple of things to her, but it was just answering her questions, but I kind of changed my voice a bit so that she wouldn't recognize that it was me. Listen, I know it wasn't the best idea, but I wasn't thinking."

"And you know for sure that she doesn't know that it was you?" asked Lawrence.

"I just kind of figured that she would think it was Jared trying to get back together with her or something."

"So, if she didn't think that it was Jared, you just let her think that it was some random person coming up to her, locking her in the bathroom, and kissing her?" replied Lawrence.

"I told you it wasn't the best idea and, yeah, now that you bring that up, it does sound really sketchy and weird. Fuck, what am I going to do?"

"Okay, just hold on a second. Everything is going to be fine. What all did she say to you when you kissed her?" asked Sabrina.

"Well, she didn't really say much. She just kept kissing me back," I replied.

"She didn't try to stop you or anything?"

Realization dawned on me. She didn't try to stop me.

"No, she didn't. So, if she thinks that it was Jared, does that mean that she wants to get back together with him?"

"I don't know. What else did she say?" asked Sabrina.

"When I was leaving the bathroom, she told me that I tasted like strawberries and asked me when I started using that scent."

"Strawberries?" asked Lawrence.

"Yeah, I use a strawberry-scented body wash. I've been using it since high school."

"Does Prim know that you use strawberry-scented body wash?" asked Lawrence.

"I would think so. She's the one who bought it for me in the first place. We got each other stupid gifts for Christmas during high school and, in freshman year, she got me that body wash. I've been using it ever since."

Lawrence and Sabrina both started to laugh.

"Dude, I can almost guarantee you that Prim knows it was you who kissed her. I don't think Jared was the one who ever crossed her mind," Lawrence said.

"What? How?"

"Come on, man. Use your big head, not your small one. You just said that Prim was the one who bought you that body wash, right?"

"Yeah."

"And then she told you that you smelled like strawberries when you kissed her, right?"

"That's what she said."

"Do you still not see where I'm going with this?" asked Lawrence.

"So, you're saying that she knows that I kissed her?" I asked.

"I mean, it would explain why she looked so uncomfortable at the library. To be fair, you both looked uncomfortable in the library but, if that kiss was lingering all over in the air, then I would say that she might know," Sabrina said.

"I knew this was going to be a mistake," I replied.

"Yeah, it probably wasn't the best idea, but I wouldn't say that it was a mistake, necessarily. What are you going to do next?"

"I don't know. I know she's broken up with Jared but that doesn't mean it's the perfect time for me to just swoop in and confess everything to her. Besides, I've been feeling this way for years. I'm tired of being the one who gets hurt. What's going to happen if I put myself out there and she rejects me? It's going to completely fuck up our friendship. I don't think we would be able to come back from that."

"I understand that. But, Myles, we just talked about her potentially knowing that it was you who kissed her. And you also said that she kissed you back. It doesn't seem to me like she hated the idea of you two being together," replied Sabrina.

"Yes, but I can't be positive that she knows it was me."

"What kind of kiss was it?" asked Lawrence. Sabrina leaned over and slapped him on the arm.

"Ouch. What? I'm just curious," said Lawrence.

"I don't think this is the best time to ask that kind of a question," Sabrina replied.

"I picked her up and put her on the bathroom sink kind of a kiss," I replied, leaning over, and putting my elbows on my thighs and my face in my hands.

"Well, holy shit," said Lawrence.

"Damn, Myles," said Sabrina.

"I told you I wasn't thinking, and I missed her, and it all just happened in the moment. This has been building since high school for me, guys. I just wanted to kiss her."

"Well, you can't just leave it at that. Tell us what else happened," said Lawrence.

"Nothing else happened. It was just kissing. She wrapped her legs around me and it was just one of those kisses. It ended quickly because I realized how fucking stupid I was being, so I broke it apart. That's when the whole strawberry thing came up."

"Are you still trying to distance yourself from Prim at this point or is that over now?" asked Sabrina.

"I can't keep distancing myself from her forever. I need her in my life even if it's just going to be in secret like this."

"I feel like we're at another dilemma. It's kind of like we talked about before. You still have two choices but this time they're different. One, you can either confess to her or, two, you can continue being best friends with her. But, if you choose that route, you must be okay with her meeting other people. I'm not trying to be harsh with you, but I just want you to be aware of the reality. If you say nothing to her, you have to be okay with the outcome."

"I know. I just can't make up my mind which way I'm going to go."

"I think it would still be a good idea to continue guitar and volleyball. I know you weren't happy to be away from Prim but, honestly, I think it was good and healthy for you to branch out to other things. You seem to really enjoy both of those activities and we love coming to watch you play," Sabrina replied. Lawrence nodded.

Lawrence and Sabrina haven't missed a single volleyball game that I've had ever since I started. Well, Lawrence didn't go to the first one because he was with Rebecca but, ever since then, they've been my biggest cheerleaders.

"Do you think you're going to go to Prim's soccer games still? Their playoff games start soon. I think they have their first game this weekend actually," Sabrina said.

"Yeah, I'm still going to go. It means a lot to her, and I want to see her play," I replied.

"It's your life, Myles. Take hold of it," Lawrence said.

I knew he was right. The only question was if I was ready to handle the consequences.

Chapter 16

Prim

It's a little over a week since the Halloween Party and I still haven't talked to Myles about what happened. I know he doesn't want me to know that it was him since he was dressed up and it was dark in the bathroom, but did he really expect that I wouldn't smell him or remember that he was supposed to be dressed as Batman? Meeting him and Sabrina in the library this past week also didn't help a lot. It was super awkward, and Sabrina definitely knew that something was up between us. I wasn't sure of just how much though. All her little hints kind of made it seem like she knew everything. Who knows? Maybe she did. Although, I was glad to find out that nothing was going on between her and Myles. Not that I don't want Myles to be happy, but it made me uncomfortable thinking about Myles with a girl. I guess that's exactly how he felt when I was with Jared. I shouldn't have been so hard on him.

    The team was in the locker room getting ready for our first playoff game. There are three playoff games that we are scheduled for in November. The first one is today, the second is two weeks from now, and then the last and final championship game is scheduled during our Thanksgiving holiday break. If we win these next two games, we are in the championship. We've gotten this far; I think we can keep going. The girls have done great this season. Coach Wimble has trained us and whipped us into top-notch shape, and it has shown over this season. Rem is on fire this season. She's scored twelve goals alone, and that's not even counting all the assists she's had. I've scored a couple of goals which I'm super proud of. My parents haven't been able to come to many of the games because of their work schedules. The hospital doesn't make exceptions for anyone.

    We are playing against Laurelville University tonight, and they have the same exact record as we do. They are the team to beat this season, so we just must go out there and do what we've been doing all season. Playing with determination and heart. Our team has a lot of chemistry and depth, and Coach Wimble told all of us that it was really hard picking a startling line-up because he could have picked any one of us for each spot. I was the center back for the team. We play three defenders in the back line, so I was in the middle, Vesper was on my right, and Jax on my left. It's funny how that worked out. We were a solid backline. Rem was one of the forwards. We all worked well together, and me, Ves, and Jax would always try to find the open through ball for Rem to run onto. It worked. *Most* of the time, that is. Rem is one of the fastest players I've ever seen, and her footwork is like no other.

It was forty minutes until game time, so we jogged out onto the field to start our warm-ups. Ves came up with a killer playlist for the season, so remixed music was coming out of the speakers in the top booth. It was a game under the lights on a Saturday, so the stadium was packed with students and most likely their family members. There was no way that I could tell if Myles was here or not, so I just didn't even bother to look. Jared obviously wasn't going to be here. They had practiced earlier this afternoon so I'm sure he's spending time together with his teammates getting trashed tonight. I don't blame him for not being here though. I haven't talked to him a lot since I broke up with him, so clearly it didn't really affect him as I thought it would. Although, I guess I shouldn't be surprised. It's for the best that we won't get back together.

The referee blew her whistle signaling for the captains to meet so that we could find out who had kick-off and which side of the field we would be on. Two of the seniors on our team ran over to meet the ref and shake hands with the other team's captains. After the coin toss, they jogged back over to us and told us that we would be starting off the game with kick-off. We made our way back over to Coach Wimble before we headed out onto the field to take our spots. Ves, Jax, and I have a backline handshake that we always do before games, and today was no different.

"Kick ass tonight, right?" I ask.

"Hell, yeah," says Jax.

"You're fucking right we will," Ves replies.

We take our three spots in the backline and wait for the ref to blow her whistle. The game begins. We go through the entire first half of the game without any score. Our two teams are an even match. They are tough, but so are we. We almost scored off a corner kick, but one of the seniors shot just wide of the net. The ref signaled that it was halftime, so both of our teams ran over to the sidelines to get a ten-minute break.

"All right, listen up. You're doing well out there. Seriously, some of the best soccer I've seen. Now, we just gotta put one in the net," Coach Wimble says as we all grab our water and circle around him.

"We have to watch out for number 15. She's starting to chip at our ankles, so she's definitely getting frustrated. Don't let her do that to you," Rem says looking around to the whole team. "Be aggressive."

"Agreed," replies Coach Wimble. "They're not better than you, so don't think that. It's a tie game right now. It's anyone's game at this point. But it's going to be ours. Who's gonna win?"

"WE ARE!" shouts the team.

"Who's gonna win?" repeats Coach Wimble.

"WE ARE!" we shout back.

"What team are we?"

"The wolves!" we shout as we all start howling in the air. This was a little game ritual that Ves came up with during our first week of practice and it has always stuck. A little embarrassing to do in front of all the fans in the stand, but it gets the job done, nonetheless.

We take our places on the field again to kick off the second half of the game. We get about twenty minutes into the game and Rem gets a breakaway headed straight to the other team's net. Our outside midfielder follows her up the field. Rem passes the ball to the winger as she speeds past the defender in front of her. The winger passes the ball right back to her as Rem runs right in front of the net. She taps the ball into the corner of the net, sailing past the goalie on the right. *GOAL.* Twenty-five more minutes. All we had to do was hold the other team off for twenty-five more minutes and the game would be ours.

The ball was kicked over to our end of the field. I started running for the ball before the other team caught up to it, but I felt someone sliding into me from behind. She took both of my ankles out from underneath me as I flattened to the ground. I heard the referee blow the whistle and signal a yellow card for the other team. I tried to get up onto my feet but, as soon as I put pressure on my right ankle, I stumbled and fell back down to the ground.

"Prim, are you okay?" Ves asked as she ran over to me.

"No, I don't think so. I can't walk on my ankle," I replied.

"Do you need the trainer?" she asked.

"Fuck. No, I don't want the trainer. I want to play," I said.

"Prim, you can't walk. Just let the trainer look at it. I promise you, we got this. We won't let you down," Ves replied.

Ves called the trainer out onto the field. Of course, I would get hurt during a fucking playoff game. It couldn't have been at the beginning of the season. The trainer held me up by my waist and helped me hobble off the field. Jax came up beside me and let me lean on her shoulder for more support. We got to the side of the field and then Jax ran back out to rejoin the game. Coach sent in a substitute. *Please win this game. Please.*

I sat down on the bench and the trainer carefully pulled off my cleat and sock so that she could look at my ankle. Well, it was definitely going to leave a nasty bruise. My ankle was already turning a nice shade of blue and purple.

"I don't think it's a sprain or anything like that. I think you may have just rolled it when the girl tackled you," said Rose. This was Rose's first year as a trainer for the school, but we've gotten close to her over the course of the season. She graduated from Silver Creek two years ago but wanted to come back as soon as she'd finished her master's degree.

"Are you positive I can't go back out?" I asked, already knowing the answer.

"Dude, there's no way. You can barely walk," Rose replied.

As she continued to look at my ankle, I felt a hand on my right shoulder. I looked up and saw that it was Myles.

"Myles? What are you doing here?" I asked.

"I was standing over by the fence and saw you get hurt. I wanted to make sure that you were okay. What happened?" asked Myles.

"She just rolled her ankle. Nothing too serious. We need to get it iced and wrapped though before the swelling gets any worse. The truck has a flat tire right now, so we'll have to try carrying you back to the office," Rose replied.

"I got her," Myles said as he kneeled in front of me.

"What are you doing?" I asked.

"I'm gonna carry you to the athletic office," Myles replied. "Here, get on my back."

"Myles, no, you don't have to carry me. I'll be fine," I said.

"Prim, just get on my back, please. You can't walk like that."

Rose helps me up off the bench so that I can get onto Myles's back. We start walking, well, not me, but we start walking toward the athletic office. The game continues without me. I hope I'm not letting my team down. No. They've got this. *Think positive, Prim.*

Myles walks me into the trainer's office and then sits me down on the table. Rose pulls out a plastic bag from the drawer and fills it with ice. I put my leg up on the table and put the bag of ice on my ankle.

"Keep it on there for about fifteen minutes and then I'll go ahead and wrap it for you. It's a good thing you don't have another game for two weeks. Your ankle is going to need all the rest you can give it," Rose says.

"Thanks, Rose," I say as lay back on the table. I almost forgot that Myles was still here, so I sit back up and look over at him. He is sitting on the chair next to the table looking at me with concern in his eyes.

"Thank you for bringing me here," I say to him as he continues to look at me.

"Yeah, no problem. Like I said, I just wanted to make sure that you were okay," he replies.

"Were you there for the whole game?" I ask.

"Uh, yeah. I was standing by the fence for most of it. And then I saw you go down, so I wanted to be there in case you needed anything."

"Thank you, Myles. Really, I mean it."

"You don't have to thank me," he replies.

"Yes, I do. You're here for me."

Rose came back into the room with a bandage, so our conversation was cut short. She wrapped the bandage around my ankle and then pinned it closed.

"All right, you'll have to keep this on for the next couple of days. You're going to have to sit practice out too," Rose says.

I nodded and obliged. I didn't want to miss practice, but if we were going to continue playing until the championship game, I didn't want to risk getting any more injured than I already am.

"How are you getting back to your dorm?" Rose asks.

"Uh, I'm not sure. I want to go back out to the field again before I leave though to see how the game ended," I reply.

"I'll carry you back out," Myles says.

"No, Myles, I can't ask you to do that again."

"Prim, please. Just let me do this, okay?"

Myles bent down again in front of me so that I could get on his back. He carried me back out to the field. I slowly peeked my eyes up to the scoreboard, not knowing what to expect. The game had been over for about ten minutes already. Silver Creek: 2, Laurelville: 0. *We won.* We fucking won.

"Myles, we won!" I screamed.

"I see that. See, you had nothing to worry about. Your girls have your back."

The team was still huddled around Coach Wimble having the usual after-game talk. Myles took me over to the group and put me down beside Rem, Ves, and Jax.

"Prim, nice to have you back with us," said Coach Wimble.

"Thanks, Coach. Congrats, everyone," I said looking around at all of the team.

"How are you feeling?" asked Coach.

"I'm okay. Rose said that it's just a rolled ankle. I need to take it easy over the next couple of days, so the swelling goes down," I replied.

"Good. Rest up. We're gonna need you in two weeks against Piedmont."

"You got it, Coach."

"All right, team, great job tonight. You should be proud of yourselves. Now go back to the dorms and get some rest, nothing else," Coach Wimble said as he glared daggers over at Ves.

"What?" asked Ves as the team all looked back at her and started laughing. "Oh, come on, you guys. I don't party that much."

"If you say so," Jax replied. "I do live with you."

"All right, back to your dorms everyone. Have a good night. Take care of yourself, Prim," said Coach Wimble.

I came to find out that Ves was actually the one who scored the second goal. Since I wasn't on the field, apparently Coach sent her up whenever our team took the corner kicks. She headed that ball into the back of the net.

"I think my work here is done. Since Ves scored, I'm stepping back. My head is no longer needed," I said.

"You better not fucking step back," Ves replied. "We need you out there. If I see you walking on your ankle over the next week, I'm going to throat-punch you."

"I will guard my throat as much as possible then," I said.

Rem came over to us and looked at Myles since I was bracing myself on him so I wouldn't fall over.

"Hey there, Myles," Rem said. "Long time no see."

"Hey, Rem. Nice to see you," Myles replied.

"And what are you doing here?" Rem said, smirking up over at Myles.

"Oh, uh, well I was watching the game and saw Prim get hurt, so I figured I would lend a helping hand."

"Uh huh," Rem replied. She smiled, looking between the two of us. I shook my head because I knew that she was embarrassing Myles on purpose.

As expected, I looked up at Myles and the redness was spreading to his cheeks and up his neck. Poor guy.

Myles cleared his throat. "Prim, are you ready?"

"Yeah. Are you sure you can carry me? I can get a ride back with Rem or someone?" I asked.

"You two go along now. I'll see you in the room, Prim. Have a good night, Myles," Rem said, picking up her bag and heading to her car.

I got back on Myles's back and he started walking back toward the dorm. It was silent for a couple of minutes, and I wasn't sure if I should say something or continue in the awkward silence. I decided to break the silence.

"Thank you for doing this," I say.

"You're welcome," Myles replied. "Do you want me to take you straight back to your dorm or were you supposed to meet Jared somewhere? I wasn't sure if he saw you at the game or anything."

"We haven't really talked since the breakup. He's texted me a couple of times so I'm not really sure what's going on with us."

"So, he wasn't at the game?"

"No. They had practice earlier today, so I'm sure he's out with his friends."

"Shouldn't he be checking on you?" Myles asked.

"I don't know. He obviously wouldn't know and I'm sure no one is going to tell him. It's not a big deal. We're broken up."

"But, Prim, come on. He hasn't tried to get back with you at all since. Is he fucking stupid?"

"Myles, I don't know, okay? I don't know," I say, raising my voice and getting down off of his back. "I don't know what you want me to tell you. We're broken up. Shouldn't you be glad that we're broken up?"

"What's that supposed to mean?" Myles asks.

"You know exactly what I mean," I reply. Myles didn't say anything. He put his face in his hands and shook his head. I could see that he was getting emotional.

"I'm just trying to look out for you, Prim. Why can't you ever understand that? Everything that I've been doing is for you. To make sure that you're okay," Myles finally said.

"I understand that. I'm sorry I raised my voice at you. I know you're just trying to help me," I replied.

"Can I ask you something?" Myles asked, looking back up at me.

"Sure."

"Do you really think you'll get back together with Jared? I want the honest answer."

"Honestly, I don't know. He hasn't shown me if I meant anything to him since we've broken up, so I really think it's over between us."

"He's not good for you, Prim. You deserve someone who's going to treat you like the sun sets around you every morning he wakes up. You deserve someone who's going to tell you how much he loves you every single day and never forgets. You don't need his immature shit. I know there's someone out there who would do that for you. You just haven't been looking hard enough."

"And who is that?" I asked, my heart starting to race.

Myles just looked at me. There were so many emotions trying to be conveyed between us. I felt like so many years were catching up to us and it felt so overwhelming I didn't really know what to do.

"You'll find him one of these days," Myles replied quietly.

"I appreciate you looking out for me. I'm sure Jared isn't the person I'm going to end up with. I never thought that he was. But I did have a good time with him, at least for some of the time I was with him," I said.

"He should have been better with you. He should have been here tonight and made sure that you were okay. But it's always me doing this stuff. And I'm not saying I don't like being here for you, but it just gets so exhausting watching you get hurt repeatedly. I hated watching it happen in high school and now, I'm seeing it all over again. Don't you ever get tired of it, Prim?"

"I do. Which is why I broke up with Jared in the first place. I know he didn't treat me well. I promise, Myles. I do know that. I may not have realized it at first, but I know it now. I have you, Rem, Jax, and Ves to thank for that. You mean so much to me. Sometimes it's embarrassing having you protect me all the time. I feel like I can't do it on my own."

"I know you can do it on your own, but I *want* to be here for you. I *need* to be here for you. You're the best thing in my life right now."

"I miss this," I replied. "You getting all worked up and emotional."

"I'm not getting emotional," he said, rubbing the back of his head.

"If you say so." I felt my phone vibrating in my pocket. "Hold on a second," I said as I opened the text message. It was from Jared.

Jared–Can I take you out to dinner soon? Please, Prim. Let me do this.

"What's wrong?" asked Myles.

"It's a text from Jared. He wants to know if he can take me out to dinner," I replied.

"What are you going to say?" Myles replied, concern etching on his face.

"I know exactly what I'm going to say," I replied. I started typing out my response on my phone.

Me–Yes. I'll text you later.

Chapter 17

Prim

"You said *what*?" asked Rem as I told her about my conversation with Jared when I got back to my room that night.

I had a plan. I obviously let Myles in on the plan. I was going to the dinner with Jared, no doubt. But I was planning to confront him about everything. He was a terrible boyfriend; I know that now. I don't deserve to be treated like that. Myles, and everyone else were right. And Jared thinks that he can get away with everything over a simple dinner. No way.

"I said yes, but hear me out," I replied, as I went into detail about my plan. I know the plan might sound a little harsh, but he deserved it. If he was going to treat me like an afterthought, then I would treat him like he wasn't worth any of my time.

"Okay, you are my favorite person, like ever!" Rem replied, clearly pleased with my plan.

"I'm going to need my confidence to be at an all-time high for this night to play out well. How about we get the girls together that night and dress me up?" I ask.

"Perfect. Just tell me when!" Rem replied.

Two weeks later, I finally schedule a dinner with Jared. It was the afternoon of our "date" and Ves and Jax both came over to our room to make me look as confident as I felt. I really felt good about doing this. Jared can't just walk all over me like this. Over the last two weeks, he has continued to text me sweet little things that he thinks are going to get me to get back together with him. He's the dumbest fucking person on the planet if he thinks this is going to work after nights and nights of me being left alone in my dorm room because he canceled all our dates.

"All right, Prim, let's get you all beautified!" Ves emphasized as she pulled out her curling iron and makeup bag. Jax brought all her stuff as well, so we had a lot to choose from. I decided to go with one of Rem's black dresses with a jean jacket over top. It was almost mid-November now, so it was pretty cold outside, especially at night. I also chose flats to wear because my ankle was still bothering me a bit. Jared had said that he was going to pick me up in my room at six, so we had about an hour to get ready.

I did a have a drink or two while getting ready because I needed all the liquid luck and help that I could get tonight. I was finally going to put an absolute end to me and Jared. No more playing around. No more games. I was done. *Done.*

It was around six-forty-five, and I was just about ready when Rem's phone started buzzing on her desk. She went over to pick it up and immediately covered her mouth with her hand.

"What? Rem, what's wrong?" I asked, making my way over to her.

"Prim, I don't know if you want to see this," she replied.

"What are you talking about?" I asked.

"One of the seniors just texted me a picture," she said handing me her phone.

I took the phone and looked at the message from Tanya. Tanya was one of the senior captains on our team. There was a picture of two people kissing attached with a message saying, *"Isn't this Prim's boyfriend?"* I recognized where the picture was taken. It was taken in the parking garage across the street from my dorm building.

"Prim, that's the girl that I saw him with in the library for his study groups," Rem said, worry all over her face.

"You've got to be kidding. Let me see that," Jax said as she took the phone out of my hands. "Son of a bitch. That little fucker!"

I didn't know what to say. My plan was to upend his night, not the other way around. He cheated on me. I walked over slowly and sat on my bed.

"Prim, are you okay?" Rem asked.

"Uh, I don't know," I replied. *Son of a bitch.*

There was a knock on our door and all of us spun our heads toward the door. Rem started toward it.

"No. I got this," I said as I got up out of bed and walked up to the door. I opened it and there was Jared, with a smile on his face that I wanted to punch off him.

"Hey, babe. You ready to go?" he asked.

I let out a laugh. No, it couldn't have been a laugh. It sounded like a full-on cackle. I sounded possessed. I had never made that sound before in my life.

"Am I ready? Ready to do what? Go make out with someone else in a parking garage? Oh, no, I'm sorry. That's you who does that," I replied as I took my phone back from Jax and held up the picture so that Jared could see it.

His face flushed instantly. That's right, fucker. You're caught now.

"I, uh, it's not what it looks like," he replied.

"Are you fucking kidding me right now? What else does it look like to you, Jared? To me, it looks like you're putting your tongue down a girl's throat."

"Listen, Prim. I'm sorry, okay? We weren't doing well, and she and I have been studying together and things just kind of happened," he said.

"If you don't punch him, I will," Jax said leaning in beside me.

"Jared, here's what's going to happen. For one, you are never going to contact me ever again. Number two, you are going to fuck all the way off. And number three? Hmm, let me see. What should number three be?" I ask. "Oh yeah. This is number three," I say as I punch him square in the face.

He lets out a scream and puts his hand up to his face as blood drains out of his nose.

"You broke my fucking nose!" Jared screamed.

"Oh, listen, you sorry piece of shit. I'm going to break a whole lot more than your fucking nose if you don't get the hell out of this building," I replied.

He mumbled something that I couldn't hear, which was for the best, and then turned and walked back down the hall. I slammed the door behind me and sat down on my bed.

"Prim, honey, are you okay?" Rem asked.

I nodded my head up and down, but the tears were already falling down my face.

"Oh, sweety, I'm so sorry," Rem said as all three of the girls came to sit on the bed beside me.

This is not what I thought was going to happen tonight.

"I have to get out of here," I said as I went to the freezer, grabbed the bottle of vodka, and headed to the door.

"Prim, where are you going?" Rem asked, trying to pull my arm back.

"I don't know. I'll be back soon. I just need to be by myself right now. Don't worry about me," I said as I left the room.

I walked around campus for twenty minutes before I stopped crying. I kept drinking the vodka so, by this time, I felt a little dizzy and I was stumbling on the sidewalk. I pulled out my phone and missed calls from all three of the girls. I know that I should be with them right now, but I just needed to figure all of this out. I made my way back to the dorm buildings and walked into the building to the left of the parking lot. I made my way up the stairs and into the hallway. Honestly, there was only one person that I wanted to see right now. I knocked on the door and waited for an answer.

CHAPTER 18

Myles

Tonight, was Prim's date. Or I guess I should say fake date. When she told me her plan of getting back at Jared, I can't say that I wasn't a little happy. I just hope that she was going to be okay. She sounded confident about what she wanted to do but going through with it is a completely different situation. She doesn't like confrontation as much as I do, so I'm really surprised this was even her idea in the first place. I could see Vesper coming up with something like this, but not Prim. I'm glad though. She's finally standing up for herself. I hope Jared knows what he lost. He had her and he fucked it up. That's on him. I've seen him around campus over the last couple of weeks ever since he texted Prim asking her to dinner. He doesn't look like a person who is trying to win anyone back, with his arrogant and smug look every time he's talking to someone. Who the hell does he think he is? I was even more glad that Prim was doing this when I saw him.

There was a knock on my door, so I put my game controller down and went to answer it. I thought it would have been Sabrina. I was wrong. It was Prim.

"Prim, what? What are you doing here?" I asked. She had obviously been crying.

"Can I come in?" Prim said, slurring her words. She tried putting her hand up on the door to brace herself, but her hand slipped, and she stumbled forward instead.

"Jesus, Prim. Are you okay?"

I held her up by the waist and led her over to my bed.

"Where's Lawrence?" she asked as she started to take off her jacket.

"He went home for the weekend to see Rebecca," I replied. "Now, tell me what's wrong. I thought you said you were meeting Jared tonight."

"I was supposed to meet Jared. My plans changed a bit."

"What do you mean?"

Prim took out her phone, opened a picture, and handed it over to me. It was Jared and another girl kissing.

"Prim, what is this?" I ask.

"It's Jared and his fucking study group buddy putting their tongues down each other's throats. That's what it fucking is."

"He cheated on you?"

"Looks that way, doesn't it?"

"Wait. He's been cheating on you this whole time?"

"I don't know for how long. He came over to my room just before I got here and tried to explain, but I didn't really let him. He said that one thing led to another, and it just happened. The most cliché story ever."

"How did you get this picture?"

"One of the girls on the team sent the picture to Rem. I guess she had seen them together in the parking garage. I'm not mad at her or anything. I'm glad I found out."

"And what did you do when he came to the room? Were the girls there with you?"

"They were all there with me. They were helping me get ready and then we got the text message. Jared showed up soon after that with a smug look on his face. Like shit. He tried giving me that lame excuse and he wouldn't leave so I punched him in the face."

"You *punched* him?" I asked, feeling a lot of pride. That's my girl.

"I did. It fucking hurt too. My hand is going to be sore tomorrow morning."

"What have you been doing all this time? Just drinking?"

"I walked around campus a bit before I came here."

"Prim, I wish you would have called me or something. Why did you just walk all over by yourself like this? You shouldn't be alone right now."

"This is the only place I wanted to be tonight, so I came over."

"Why is that, Prim?"

"I don't know. It was the first place that I thought of. I'm sorry. I probably shouldn't be here. I should leave," she said as she started to get up off the bed.

"No, that's not what I meant. I don't want you to leave and I'm sure as hell not leaving you by yourself in this condition," I replied.

She started crying and pulled her knees up to her chest. Her black dress was all wrinkled and I'm going to assume that she spilled some because the whole front of the dress was soaked.

"Prim, please don't cry."

"I'm sorry. I didn't come here to cry. I came here because I wanted it to make me feel better."

"Come here," I said as I pulled her into me so that she could lay on my shoulder.

"Everything is going to be okay, Prim. I promise." My heart was breaking for her and I could feel her pain radiating off her body.

"I just thought he was different at first, you know? He was so charming, and he always knew what to say."

"I know," I replied.

"He was so good to me at first. I don't know where everything went wrong. I was so excited. I thought it was going to be a great college experience but it's nothing like what I thought. I should have listened to everyone sooner."

"It's okay that you didn't realize it. You're not perfect and you wanted it to be a good experience. Everyone else realized because we were all on the outside looking in. We were unbiased. I know that it's hard."

"I should have known that it wasn't a good relationship since I never wanted to tell my parents anything about him," she replied.

"I know that too," I said.

"You do?"

"I may have talked to your parents about some things a while back, and they told me that you barely talked to them about Jared."

"I haven't been keeping in contact with them as much as I should be. This stupid fucking relationship. It's all my fault."

"Stop, Prim. It's not your fault. You had no part in him cheating on you. None at all. That has nothing to do with you and everything to do with him and his fucked-up character."

"But he took me away from so much. Some of it has to be my fault because I let it happen. Myles, I let him take me away from you. You, of all people. You couldn't even be around me because I was with him. That should have told me something, but I was too stupid to see it."

"It's not your fault," I replied. "It was just something that I needed to do. I didn't want to force you to make any decisions because that wouldn't have been fair to you. So, I backed off for a little."

"But, Myles, you don't get it. I chose him over my best friend. Do you know how that makes me feel?"

"Prim, I'm not going to lie to you. It did hurt me, but I understood. You needed to make your own decisions and figure everything out. You thought you were having a good time. No one can blame you for that."

"I blame me for that. I know no one else does. But it hurts me to think about the other people I hurt just because of a stupid ass boy. I wasn't even spending as much time with the girls as I wanted to because Jared always wanted me to come over to his room. He took me away from everything I love. I must take some ownership of that, right?"

"Yes, but at least now you know, okay? Don't be too hard on yourself. Everything is a learning experience. Now you'll know for the next guy who comes along."

"Myles, I'm so sorry," Prim says as she starts crying into my shoulder.

"You don't need to apologize."

"Yes, I do."

She looks up at me and I can see a lot of pain behind her eyes that I wished I could take away for her. We stared at each other, and I hoped that she couldn't hear my heart start to beat faster. It felt like it was going to beat out of my chest.

"Myles," she whispers and then starts to kiss up my arm.

"Prim, what are you doing?"

She got up onto her knees and kept kissing me, making her way from the top of my shoulder up the length of my neck. I was frozen in place.

"Prim," I said as my breath hitched in my throat. I knew this wasn't supposed to happen, but I couldn't stop it.

"Myles, kiss me, please," she said as she ran her finger over both of my cheeks.

"Prim, I don't think we should."

"Please. I need this."

Fuck it. I pulled her on top of me and parted her legs so that she was straddling me. I pushed us both back on the bed so that my back was up against the wall. I wrapped my hand around the back of her neck, grabbed her hair, and crushed my mouth to hers. I ran my hands up and down her back, and she grinded herself down on me hard. I'm sure she could feel my erection when she pressed down. She continued to rub herself against me and I felt like I was already going to explode.

"Touch me, Myles," Prim said sounding breathless.

"I am touching you," I said.

"No, that's not what I mean," she said as she took my hand and put it in between her thighs.

"*Oh, god,*" I whimpered. I could feel how wet she was, and my cock was straining behind my pants. My dream was playing out in front of me, and it was taking everything I could do to restrain myself.

She started to ride my hand and I knew that she was looking for release. The friction from her riding both my hand and my cock at the same time was getting me close to the edge.

No. I need to stop this.

"Prim, no. We need to stop," I said as I took her off me and sat her down beside me.

"Please, just kiss me," she said as she tried to get back on top.

"No, Prim, not like this. You're drunk and you're upset. Do you really think this is a good idea?"

"I don't care. I don't want to be alone tonight. I need this."

"Well, I'm not someone you can just use. I don't want to be just someone, Prim. I want to be *the* one."

"What do you mean?" she asked.

"Why did you come here tonight, Prim? Did you come here tonight because you needed me or because you just needed someone?"

"You were the first person that I thought of, so I wanted to come see you," she replied.

"What are we doing right now, Prim? You probably won't even remember this tomorrow."

"I'm not that drunk," she replied.

"Yes, but you're drunk enough for me to realize that this isn't a good idea. We can't do this now. Not when you're like this. You came here so that I could console you after what happened with Jared. I don't have a problem doing that but what we were doing means a lot more to me than it does to you. I can't put myself in that situation."

"You don't think this means anything to me?"

"I really don't know what you're thinking right now. You just found out about Jared, so I think that is still way too fresh and new for us to be doing something like this without thinking it through first."

"Well, then let's think it through. How does this make you feel?" Prim asked.

"Let's not go into that right now, okay? I don't want to have this conversation with you when you're intoxicated."

"Myles, stop with that, okay? I'm fine. I'm more sober now than I was before I even started drinking. Certain things have sobered me up." Heat flared up the side of my neck.

"What do you want me to say, Prim?"

"I want you to tell me the truth. I want you to tell me how you feel about me," she replied.

"How do you think I feel about you? I think that's pretty fucking obvious from what we just did."

"No, I need to hear you say it. I know it was you."

"What are you talking about?"

"I know it was you at the party. I know it was you who kissed me. Did you think I wouldn't recognize you?"

I started to deny it, but Prim put her hand up to me. "Don't you dare try to say it wasn't you. I smelled strawberries." So, Sabrina and Lawrence were right. *Fuck.*

"I'm sorry. I should have never done that to you," I replied.

"Did I try to stop you?"

"What?"

"That night. Did I ever try to stop you from kissing me in the bathroom?"

"No, but I just figured you thought it was Jared."

"Myles, you were wearing a Batman costume. Of course, I knew it was you. How could I not? We were the ones that came up with the idea of dressing as Catwoman and Batman."

"Yeah, I probably didn't think that one through as much as I should have."

"You wouldn't have done that if you didn't feel something for me," she said. "Tell me how you feel about me."

"Tell you how I feel about you? Okay, let's start here. You're always on my mind, Prim. No matter what the fuck I do. You're always there and I can't get you out. Do you know what it took for me to tell you that I needed to not see you for a while! It took every fucking ounce of courage that I had. Thinking about not seeing you every day killed me and it still hurts me. And don't even get me started on what it felt like seeing you with Jared, having his fucking hands all over you all the time. I couldn't deal with it."

"Why didn't you tell me about Sabrina?" she asked.

"What do you mean?"

"You never told me that Sabrina had a girlfriend. You made me think…"

"I made you think what?" I asked.

"I thought that you two were dating or something."

"How did you find out about Sabrina?"

"She told me the day we were in the library working on the project and you went to the bathroom."

"That figures. You should have just asked me if you thought that we were together. I would have told you. Is that why you never wanted to hang out with us? Wait, is that why you left my volleyball game? Because you saw me with Sabrina?"

"I just felt uncomfortable, that's all."

I heard a phone buzz and we looked at our phones. Honestly, I was thankful for the interruption. I couldn't deal with this right now. Especially because of how upset she was. This wasn't the best time to confess all my feelings.

"It's mine," Prim said. "The girls are looking for me. I, uh, I should head back to my room now."

"That's probably a good idea," I replied. "Do you want me to walk you next door?"

"No, it's okay. I can go on my own. Thanks. I'll talk to you later, Myles. I'm sorry about tonight. I shouldn't have come over. I shouldn't have kissed you. I don't know what's gotten into me lately. Are we okay?"

"I hope we will be. There's just a lot that we both must think about and now isn't the time. I refuse to be a rebound, Prim. You need to sort everything out," I replied.

She nodded and walked over to the door. "Goodbye, Myles."

"Goodbye, Prim."

I closed the door behind her and cursed myself for having a heart. Stupid, I know. I could have met any other girl in the world and fallen for her. But, no, I had to fall for my best friend. This whole unrequited love shit was getting really tiring. But, after tonight, I'm not sure if it's an unrequited love anymore. Prim said that she thought Sabrina and I were dating, and it made her uncomfortable. Something has changed between us. That part is obvious considering that we both just almost gave each other orgasms. I can say with absolute certainty that our friendship has been ruined.

Chapter 19

Prim

I texted Rem that I was on my way back to the room. I had sobered up. I knew full well what I was doing with Myles, and I meant every word that I said to him. If he wouldn't have stopped us, I would have orgasmed all over his hand. I knew what I was doing, but I'm mortified now. How was I ever going to face Myles again? I went to his room because I knew that he could cheer me up. I never intended to start kissing or straddling him. It just felt right in the moment but now, not so much. I wanted him to tell me how he felt because it was going to confirm what I had already known. But it was also going to help me figure out my own feelings. I told him that, lately, I was feeling differently, and I wasn't lying.

I opened up the door to our room and saw Rem sitting on her bed. It was late and I wouldn't have blamed her if she was already sleeping. Obviously, she was worried. I just didn't know if I wanted to get into anything deep tonight.

"Dude, where the hell have you been? You can't just disappear like that! We had no idea where you were," Rem said getting out of bed and coming over to me.

"I'm okay, I promise. I walked around campus for a little and then I wound up at Myles's room for the rest of the night," I replied.

"You should have texted us or something, Prim. Ves and Jax wanted to wait here for you, but I sent them back to their room and told them I would text them when you got back. Give me a second," she said as she got her phone from her desk and sent a text to them both.

"They told me to tell you that they're sorry and to let them know if you need anything," she said. "They're glad you're safe. Please don't disappear like that again, okay? We're all here for you. We know you're going through a really shitty time right now. Don't shut us out."

"I'm sorry," I said, starting to get choked up. "I just didn't know what to do and I panicked."

"Please don't cry," Rem replied.

"People keep telling me that tonight," I said.

"Because no one who cares about you wants to see you hurt anymore. We're just trying to look out for you."

"I know. I just feel so pathetic right now. How could I not have known that Jared was cheating on me? Of course, all those study groups weren't actual study groups. I should have listened to my gut and you. You kept warning me about him and I didn't listen to you. I'm so sorry."

"Prim, you have nothing to be sorry about. You liked him. That's not a crime."

I start sobbing on my bed and Rem hugs me tighter. She pulls a blanket over me and rubs my back.

"What happened with Myles?" she asks.

I shook my head and cried harder.

"I don't know, Rem. I think I fucked everything up," I reply.

"Take a deep breath and try to tell me what happened."

"Please don't tell anyone, okay? This needs to stay just between you and me for now."

"I promise."

"I kissed him," I say.

"You kissed him?" Rem asked.

"Well, it was actually a little more than kissing. I don't know what came over me, but I got so horny, and he was right there, so I started kissing his neck, and then one thing led to another."

"And?" asked Rem.

"And I straddled him and basically dry-humped him. Rem, I almost fucking had an orgasm on top of him. I'm pretty sure he was close too."

"And then what happened?" she asked.

"Then he stopped it."

"Good guy, that Myles, isn't he?"

"What do you mean?"

"Prim, you were drunk and clearly upset. I'm glad he didn't go through with anything. Do you think Jared would have stopped that?"

"No. He doesn't care about that kind of thing," I reply.

"That's because he's a jackass and a waste of time," she said. "Let me ask you something. I understand you had been drinking, but it sounds like you still knew what you were doing?"

"I did, yeah," I replied.

"Would you have done what you did if it were someone other than Myles? Like if it were just some random person?"

"I don't think so, no. I would have been uncomfortable."

"That's what I thought," she replied.

"Hang on a second. You don't sound too surprised by any of this?" I said.

"I'm not and you want to know why?"

I nodded.

"I'm not surprised because, from the first day that he came to campus and I came into our room when Jared was in here, I could tell how he felt about you. It was something in the way he looked at you. Like you were his whole world. You obviously can't see it from your perspective, but from someone on the outside looking in, it's so obvious."

"You've known this whole time?" I asked.

"Of course, I've known this whole time. Prim, that man worships the ground you walk on. He would do absolutely anything for you. Why do you think he needed space from you and Jared?"

"I understand that now."

"It wasn't that he didn't want to be with you. He just couldn't see the two of you together and, honestly, I don't blame him. I wouldn't be able to do that either."

"I hated being away from him," I reply.

"I know he hated being away from you, so it looks like you were both feeling the same thing."

I start crying again and Rem reached over to the desk and passed me a couple of tissues.

"Rem, I'm so scared that I'm going to lose him."

"Why do you think you're going to lose him?"

"Because we've never done anything like this before. We've just been friends for the longest time and now all these feelings and emotions are being put into the middle of it, and I'm a little overwhelmed. Part of me wants to go back to what we were in high school, but the other part of me could potentially see myself with him. I just don't know which part of me is going to win out."

"Babe, I'm pretty sure his feelings for you didn't just start here in college. That boy seems like he's been head over heels in love with you for a very, very long time. Anyone can see that. Don't you realize how protective of you he is? I'm sure if you told him that it was okay, he would go beat the shit out of Jared with his bare hands."

"Well, I don't want him to do that. He doesn't need to be in any part of this," I replied.

"Yes, I don't want him to do that either, but you're missing my point. My point is that Myles is always there for you, no matter what you're going through. He told you he needed to step away and get some distance, but he still came to every single one of our home games because he wanted to support you. That takes some guts. And when you were sick earlier in the semester, Myles was here, not Jared, not anyone else. It was Myles. He might not be able to voice the words out loud to you, but that man is showing you how much he loves you through all of his actions. I'm sure he's just as scared as you to tell you how he feels."

"What should I do? We left off on a very awkward note and I really have no idea how to handle this. I've always been able to talk to him but now it seems different. There's this weird tension and distance between us now and I'm not sure how to fix it."

"Let me ask you another question. How do you feel about Myles? Not as your best friend. As something more."

"It's hard because I've never had to think of him as anything more than a friend before, so I'm really not sure how to answer your question."

"Just try. If you were to think about being with Myles as a romantic partner, how does that make you feel?"

"Well, I don't think I would necessarily be opposed to it. I mean, all the chemistry is there. We've just never crossed that line. Seriously, like never. I never even thought of it until we got here to school. Things have just been so weird and it's turning my life upside-down."

"What would you rather do? Tell him how you feel or risk losing him as your friend?"

"That's not a fair question. There are consequences to both of those things. They also go hand-in-hand. If I tell him how I feel, or think I feel, I could risk losing him as a friend either way."

"But what's stopping you though? You can obviously tell how he feels about you, and here you are telling me how you feel about him. I know this is all new for you, but it seems like you're at least potentially thinking about your future with him, am I right?"

"I guess so. But what if we were to start dating and then something goes wrong, we break up, and then never speak to each other again? That can't happen. That would hurt worse than the actual breakup."

"You're thinking way too far in the future right now. And who is saying that you two would break up? Listen, I'm not trying to tell you to do something you're not ready for. I know this is scary because it's a whole new territory for the two of you. I just think that you two would make each other happy. And you know for one hundred percent certainty that he would treat you like a queen."

"I think I just need time to process everything. I know we are going to have to talk about all of this at some point, I just don't know when that should happen. He told me when I was leaving his room that I needed to sort everything out, so maybe this is the part where I take a step back to figure out things, like he did. I just know that it's going to be very hard, if not impossible, to go back to how we were before. I mean, we've already made out for Christ's sake. That crossed all the friendship boundaries and threw them out the window."

"Well, yeah, I would think so," Rem replied.

"I know we've talked a little bit about this before, but have you ever been in love before?" I asked.

I could see Rem tense a little before she answered my question.

"I have, yeah," she replied.

"Was it with the boy from high school that you were telling me about?"

"It was. He was the first guy I've ever fallen in love with. He's the only guy I've ever really dated so I guess it was more special."

"Are you still in love with him?"

"Yeah, unfortunately, I am. Which is why I think this space is good. We're at two different schools doing our own thing. I'll have plenty of time to get over him and find someone else. Or maybe I just won't find anyone at all and that will be perfectly fine with me. All of my family members are big workaholics so maybe that will also run in the family like accounting," she replied, laughing a little.

"Sorry, I didn't mean to bring down the mood," I said.

"Well, it wasn't like the mood was great, to begin with," she said as we both laughed together. "So, what are you going to do about this Jared situation?"

"I don't want to talk to him again. Seriously though. Looking back on our relationship, it was so childish and immature, and I really should have known better."

"Can I ask you another question? I know I keep asking you a lot of questions about this, but I think it might help you figure things out more if you got it out in the open."

"Yeah, of course. What's up?" I asked.

"Were you in love with Jared?" Rem replied.

I had been thinking about this question for pretty much our entire relationship. It makes sense as to why we never said "I love you" to each other. It's because we didn't.

"No, I wasn't. I thought I was, but I think I just got a rush because it was a new relationship. But, honestly, I'm okay with that. I didn't love him. I liked him for a time, but then everything got complicated, so I felt myself pulling away from the relationship. Maybe he felt the same. Maybe that's why he went to find someone else."

"Prim, don't blame yourself for what happened. He was the piece of shit who was cheating on you. You can't force someone to cheat on their significant other. That was completely his choice and his action. How could you blame yourself for something like that?"

"I don't blame myself. I just kind of wish that we hadn't even started the relationship in the first place. I mean, we barely knew each other before we started dating. We just kissed one night and then started hanging out and everything else. I shouldn't have rushed into that with him."

"Everything is a learning experience. Everything you go through in life is going to shape who you are and who you become. You had this bad experience. So, now, you know what you don't want in a relationship and a man, right?"

"Right. Who knows who I'll end up with," I said.

"I could take a guess based on my theory," Rem replied.

"Of course, you and your theory," I smirked.

"I told you that my theory was proven. I proved it the moment Myles showed up at our door with food and medicine for you when you were sick. That boy is puppy dog eyes in love with you. I sniffed it from a mile away. Hence, theory proven. A fact is a fact."

"I'll tell you what to do with your dumb theories," I say as I chuck a pillow at her head.

"But, in all seriousness, though. Are you going to be, okay?" Rem asked me.

"Yeah, I think so. I'm just going to take my time and try to heal from all of this and see where it takes me," I replied.

"I like your way of thinking," she said. "Now, how about we end this night on a high note and watch some movies?"

"Deal."

As I got up to go to the bathroom before we started our movie marathon, I heard two knocks at the door.

"Hurry up, let us in!" cried a voice which I could only assume was Vesper. She was a loud one.

"We brought ice cream!" Jax said.

I looked over at Rem and she just shook her head and laughed. I opened the door to two bright and smiling faces. I'm so glad I met these girls. They have no idea how much they mean to me.

"I hope no one in here is lactose intolerant. I brought like two gallons of ice cream," Ves said as she kissed me on the side of the head.

Rem, Ves, and Jax all circled around me and gave me the biggest hug I've ever had in my life. They washed away all the sadness that I had from the night in that one embrace. Everything was going to be all right. It had to be.

Chapter 20

Prim

On Monday morning, I'm sitting in my advisor's office choosing which internship I will be starting. Usually, freshman year is a little early to start an internship, but Silver Creek has specific internship programs that they use for education majors. A lot of them start earlier than your junior year, which will look really good on future resumés. Since soccer season is almost over, I'll have more free time to devote to other activities, including furthering my career. I'm going to focus on myself for once. I haven't spoken to Myles since Saturday night, but I did almost pass him in the hall on my way to this office. I ducked inside the bathroom before he could see me. Okay, yes, I'm avoiding him. But honestly, I think anyone would in this situation. When the girls came over on Saturday, we talked more about what happened with Jared and they made me feel a lot better about everything. I didn't mention the whole kissing Myles thing to them. And Rem promised she wouldn't say anything, so she didn't. I don't think I'm ready for that cat to be out of the bag quite yet.

"Okay, Miss O'Brien, what area of education were you interested in pursuing a career out of?" asked Ms. Pembrook, my freshman advisor. She would most likely continue to be my advisor throughout my time here at school because she is specifically assigned to education majors. We don't have to declare our major until the end of our sophomore year but, since I already know what I want to do, I declared it during the registration process.

"I'm leaning more toward elementary education," I replied.

"Any particular reason for that choice?"

"I really enjoy that age group. They're still at the age where they listen to you, but not at the age yet where they will give you a bunch of that hormonal middle school attitude," I said. We both start to chuckle.

"That's very true. I used to teach elementary school myself, so I'm always here to ask questions if you ever have them."

"That would be great. Thanks."

"So, you said that your soccer season is coming to a close soon?"

"Yes, we have our championship game next week during the holiday break."

"Oh, well, good luck to you all."

"Thank you! We're excited about it."

"I'm sure. That's a great accomplishment," Ms. Pembrook said, smiling back at me. "Okay, so let's discuss the internship options you have. The actual internship won't start until next semester, but would you be free sometime this week to go to the school and help just to get your foot in the door?"

"Yes, absolutely," I replied as I nodded my head.

"Okay, great. There's an internship that is available at an elementary school about fifteen minutes from here. You would be working with a second-grade class and helping the teacher with different activities and teaching. Does that sound like something you would be interested in? If not, we have an internship in a fifth grade and kindergarten classroom."

"The second-grade classroom will be great. That sounds like fun."

"Great. I will contact the school and let them know. I believe the teacher you will be working with is Mr. Simmons. He's been teaching there for six years, so he'll be able to show you all the ropes and answer your questions."

"I'm looking forward to it. Thank you so much for setting this up," I replied.

"Of course. That's my job. Would you be available this Thursday morning to go to the school and introduce yourself and get acclimated to the class?"

"Yes, of course. I have a break from classes in the morning before my afternoon classes."

"Okay, great. I will get you the address and then just let me know if you have any other questions. Here, let me give you the registration papers. Make sure you fill these out so that we can process it through the university."

She handed me the registration papers and I tucked them into my bag.

"Make sure you get Mr. Simmons to sign off on those papers whenever you go to the school. Each day you're there, you'll do a little write-up of how the day went and then Mr. Simmons can sign off, saying, yes, you were there and did what you were supposed to do."

"Sounds good. Thank you. Do you know how many students are in the classroom?" I asked.

"I believe there are eighteen. Apparently, they are great kids so you shouldn't have any issues. Mr. Simmons seems to have great classroom management, so the kids and he have really bonded. You'll learn a lot from him as a mentor."

"Well, that's great to hear. Thanks, Ms. Pembrook. I really appreciate it. Have a great day," I said as I got up out of my seat and left her office.

As I was walking back to my dorm, I couldn't help but get excited at the thought of my future. Hopefully, these kids were half as good as Ms. Pembrook said. Things are finally starting to look up. Even though things are going my way for once, I can't help but shake the feeling that something was still missing.

***

After English class on Thursday morning, Rem, Jax, Ves, and I grabbed a quick coffee before I had to head off to Pheasant Hill Elementary School. I can't say that I wasn't a little nervous, but I was still excited at the same time. It was only a fifteen-minute drive, and I had to be there by ten, so I left around nine-thirty a.m. to make sure I had enough time. I arrived at the school and decided to sit in the parking lot for a couple of minutes before I went into the front office to get my school badge. I checked my phone and saw that I had a text message from Jared. What the hell does he want?

Jared–Prim, can we please talk?

Me–No. I don't want to see you after what you did.

Jared–I'm not going to give up. I'm sorry for what I did. You know I didn't mean to.

Didn't mean to? You know, I really hate when guys play that card like they think the entire female population is a stupid pushover idiot.

Me–You are a fantastic liar. I already talked to Shelby, and she told me everything. Stay away from me.

And I did. I did end up talking to Shelby. She approached me outside my dorm building on Tuesday because she felt sorry for breaking the two of us up. I almost punched her too because she knew exactly what she was doing, and she knew that I was his girlfriend. She must have been looking for me because she was waiting right outside the door when I was on my way to class. As soon as I walked out of the building, she stopped me.

"Prim, I need to talk to you," Shelby said.

I looked up and realized that she was the girl from the photo of her and Jared kissing in the parking garage.

"I don't really want to talk right now, sorry. I must get to class," I replied.

"Prim, please. Just hear me out," she replied.

"And why should I do that?"

"Because I know how much of an asshole Jared is."

"Oh, is that why you had your tongue down his throat this whole time?"

"I'm sorry, okay?" she said.

"Let me ask you something. Did you know that he was in a relationship? You had to know, right?"

"Yes, I did, and, again, I'm sorry. It really did start out innocently, I swear. We were placed into the same group for a project so we would meet up in the library to work on it. I had just broken up with my ex, so I was feeling vulnerable. One thing just led to another and, by the time I realized what we were doing, the damage was already done."

"And you didn't think to stop it?" I asked.

"I tried but, as you know, he can be pretty charming and persuasive."

I sighed. I knew that only too well and I hated it.

"I know that, but it still doesn't excuse what you did. You knew damn well what was happening. I'm not saying he isn't the asshole, but you also played a part. Own up to your actions."

"I know and that's why I wanted to come talk to you because I wanted to clear the air and get everything out in the open."

"How long has this been going on between you two?" I asked.

"Since the beginning of October. I promise you; I didn't mean for any of this to happen. I really didn't."

"You're lucky we aren't friends or anything because I would be a whole lot harsher with you than I'm being now. And listen to me, woman to woman, you need to start standing up for yourself. Stop bending over backwards for men who don't appreciate you," I replied.

"I know that and I'm working on it."

"And the next time you're with a guy and you know he has a girlfriend, learn to handle yourself better. I understand you were feeling vulnerable but that's not a reason to fuck over someone else in the process. This isn't how women should treat each other. Fuck the men, okay? We need to look out for each other."

"You're right. I'm so sorry, Prim. But I just wanted to let you know that I stopped seeing him. He keeps texting me, but I haven't responded to any of the messages. I can show you if you don't believe me," she said as she started to take out her phone.

"I don't need to see them. And, honestly, I don't care about the messages. He and I are done, and it sounds like you both are done as well, so he loses everything in this situation. Which he deserves."

She nodded. "Can I buy you coffee or something?"

"I don't think I'm quite there yet, but I appreciate the offer," I said as I started to walk away toward class. I turned back to look at Shelby. "Thank you for telling me everything. It's more than Jared will ever do, so you've at least earned a little bit of my respect back."

"You're welcome. I figured you deserved to know after what I had done to you."

I nodded. "Take care, Shelby." I walked away to class and held my head up high, proud of myself for finally realizing just how much Jared had walked all over me and knowing that I didn't need that kind of drama in my life.

The elementary school bell brought me out of my thoughts, and I turned my car off and headed into the building. I walked into the front office and was met by a smiling woman who looked to be in her forties. She had shoulder-length red hair, and I actually had to look twice because she almost looked exactly like Rem. Just a bit older.

"Good morning, how can I help you?" she asked, smiling up at me from her desk.

"Hi, good morning. My name is Prim. I'm from Silver Creek University and I'm supposed to start my internship today with Mr. Simmon's class," I replied.

"Prim? You go to Silver Creek University?" she asked.

"Yes, I do."

"You wouldn't happen to know a Remington Allen, would you?"

"I, uh, yes, I do. She's my roommate actually," I replied as I continued looking at her face and her red hair. *Oh my god.*

"Oh, so you're Prim!" she exclaimed. "I'm Remington's mom, Lila. She's told us so much about you."

I thought back to when Remington was first introducing herself in our dorm room on the first day. Now that I'm thinking about it, she did mention that her mom worked as a secretary at an elementary school close to campus. Why didn't I think of that when I was going for the internship?

"Oh, Mrs. Allen, it's so nice to meet you! I've heard a lot about you as well. Rem dotes on you," I replied. "I'm sorry we never got to meet at any of the home games. It would have been nice."

"Please, call me Lila. Mrs. Allen sounds so old. I thought you looked familiar when you came into the office, so I've at least seen you play. You're a great player."

"Thank you," I replied as my cheeks flushed red.

"Okay, so let's get you all set up. Let me get you a visitor's badge and then I'll walk you down to Mr. Simmon's classroom. I believe they are just starting out with their writing time."

"Okay, great. Thank you," I said as Lila printed out my badge and handed it over to me.

"All right, follow me," Lila said as she led me out of the front office and into the main hallway.

We walked down the main hallway which was decorated with pictures, sketches, and paintings from all of the students. As we walked up to Mr. Simmon's classroom, I could hear him going over the directions for their writing assignment. Lila knocked on the door and Mr. Simmons waved his hand for her to come in.

"Mr. Simmons, this is Miss O'Brien from Silver Creek University. You were notified that she was coming today, right?" asked Lila.

"Yes, the school contacted me. Welcome to Pheasant Hill," Mr. Simmons replied. "Okay, class, let's all give our attention over to Miss O'Brien and give her a big welcome."

"Hi, Miss O'Brien!" the class said in unison.

"Well, thank you. I'm excited to work with you all," I replied.

Mr. Simmons got the students started on their writing assignment and then came over to where I was sitting at the desk at the side of the classroom.

"It's nice to meet you, Miss O'Brien," Mr. Simmons said as he shook my hand.

"It's nice to meet you as well, Mr. Simmons. You seem to have a very good class here," I replied.

"They're great. And I'm not just saying that because they're my students. They really are a great bunch of kids. I got lucky this year."

"I'm excited to get to know everyone more."

"So, you'll be interning with us next semester, right?" he asked.

"Yes. My advisor told me that I'll be doing the internship next semester and today was just to get acclimated to the school and the class a bit before we go on break."

"Okay, great. I'm looking forward to working with you. So, today, if you just want to walk around and chat with the students, that would be good. They have to draw some kind of a picture and then write two paragraphs about what's going on in the picture."

"Sounds great, thanks."

"Are you looking to be an elementary teacher as well or haven't you figured that out yet?" Mr. Simmons asked.

"I think I'm leaning more toward elementary. I like this age," I replied.

"I love it. Hopefully, you will too," he said. "Okay, well, feel free to walk around and talk with the kids. Let me know if you have any questions."

"Will do. Thank you."

I start walking around the classroom and peek over the students' shoulders to see their pictures. As I approached one of the students and looked at her picture, I noticed that it was a picture of, what I'm going to assume was, her family.

"That's a really nice picture," I said as I knelt beside her desk.

"Thank you," she replied.

"What's your name?"

"Madelyn."

"Well, it's nice to meet you, Madelyn. I'm Miss O'Brien."

"Hi, Miss O'Brien. Are you going to be staying with us for a while?"

"I'll be with you two days a week starting right at the end of January. How does that sound?" I asked.

"Sounds good to me. I like meeting new people," Madelyn said.

"Me too. But, sometimes, it makes me nervous, so don't feel bad if you're nervous too."

"I'm not nervous at all. Do you want to see my picture?"

"Of course, I do. Who are all those people?"

"Well, this is my mom and dad," she said as she pointed to the two people on the left. "This is my brother Derek, my baby sister, Jenny, and then this is me. I'm the middle child. Derek is two years older than me, and then Jenny was just born a couple of months ago."

"You have a beautiful family," I said.

"Thank you. My mom and dad are the best."

"Do you know how long your parents have been together?"

"Their anniversary was last week so they told me that they've been married for twelve years. That's a long time. That's longer than I've been alive."

I laughed at what she said. She was a funny kid.

"That is a long time. That's pretty impressive."

"Do you have a husband, Miss O'Brien?" Madelyn asked.

"I don't have a husband, no. I'm still in college," I replied.

"Then do you have a boyfriend?"

"No boyfriend either."

"Do you want one?"

"I'm not really sure anymore actually," I replied.

"What's that mean?" she asked.

"Well, I used to have a boyfriend. But he wasn't very nice, so we aren't together anymore."

"Yeah, don't be with someone who's mean."

"That's what my best friend says to me," I replied.

"Is your best friend nice to you?"

"He is, yeah. His name is Myles. We go to school together."

"Well, why don't you date Myles then?" Madelyn asked, looking up at me with a questioning look on her face.

It's like this girl knew everything that's been happening in my life. Maybe she's a mind reader.

"Are you a mind reader, Madelyn?" I asked.

"I don't think so," she replied.

"My friend at school asked me the same question."

"Does Myles like you?"

"I, umm, I think so. But we're just best friends for right now."

"Maybe it'll change one day."

"Yeah, maybe.

Madelyn and I continued talking about everything but school for the remainder of writing class and, by the end of my time there, I felt like I had sat through an entire therapy session. Of course, it would be a little second-grader who made me question and think about everything that was going on in my life. I had been continuing to avoid Myles which probably wasn't the best decision. We really did need to talk at some point soon. But the reason I'm avoiding him is because I really don't know what I would say to him. We have all these unspoken feelings between the two of us, and now it's like a game to see which one of us is going to bring them to the surface first.

I pull my phone out of my pocket.

Me–Hey. We should probably talk sometime soon about what happened. How about after you get back from Thanksgiving break?

He texted me five minutes later.

Myles–Yeah, we can do that. Are you able to go home for break at all?

Me–No, we have practices and then our championship game is next week during the break, so most of us are just planning to stay here the whole time.

Myles–Okay, I'll text you when I get back from break.

Me–Tell your parents I say hi.

Myles–Will do. Good luck with your game.

Well, I guess that was the least awkward conversation that we could have after what had happened in his room. Ever since that night, I keep asking myself if I regret what happened. But the more I think about it, the more I realize that I don't regret it. Not at all.

CHAPTER 21

Prim

Well, here it was. The championship game. The end of our season. My first season of college soccer, done. By this time, most of the students had already cleared out of campus because of Thanksgiving break, so we weren't expecting a lot of fans to be at the game. I did have a lot of classmates that said that they were going to come back to see the game. Break started this last Friday afternoon, so we weren't expecting a lot of people to show up two days before Thanksgiving. Understandable, but it was just unfortunate that the game had to fall during a school break. But all I cared about was that my parents were going to be here. They haven't been able to attend a lot of games this season because of their hospital work schedules, so this was going to be nice.

All of us are sitting in the locker room. There is an hour before the game starts so we will make our way out to the field to warm-up in about twenty minutes. Coach Wimble put the starting line-up on the board and went over some of the plays that we would be using during today's game. Then he started his speech.

"Well, team, we've made it this far. I'm so proud of all of you. It's been a while since our team has gotten into the playoffs, let alone the championship game, but here we are. You've all worked hard this season and you should all be proud of yourselves as well. I've loved every minute working with you ladies this season. You have all made my job a lot easier. I've never seen a team with so much chemistry and camaraderie before. I think that's also why we've made it this far in the season. You all work so well together and it feels like you can all read each other really well."

"Coach, this is getting really emotional really quickly," Vesper replied. "I think I see a tear forming in your eye."

"Vesper, it would be you who interrupts the speech. But I wouldn't have it any other way," Coach said. "Now, back to business. Stonybrook is going to be a tough team, but you're tougher. They have great forwards on their team, but we have a better backline that is unstoppable. They have speed but we're faster. You got that?"

As I looked around the room, I saw all the girls nodding back to Coach Wimble. We all joke around with Coach pretty much all the time but, when it was game time, we all knew how to take things seriously. It's what had gotten us this far into the season.

"Now, listen to me. I know this is the championship game and our last chance to kick some ass this season. But I don't want you to put all this pressure on yourselves, okay? That's going to mess up your game. Just go out there, have fun, and play like I know you all can. Yes, being in the championship game is a big deal, but I want you all to have fun. This is a great moment for all of you, and I want you to cherish it. This stuff doesn't come around very often so make the best of it that you can."

There were hoots and hollers all throughout the locker room. The team managers were even joining in the cheering.

"Let's go out there and kick some ass!" cheered Coach Wimble.

"Let's go, ya'll!" Rem screamed as we all jogged out of the locker room and out onto the field.

When we got on the field, I looked up at the stands. I was wrong before. The stadium was packed with people. The other girls on the team looked just as surprised as I felt. This was going to be a good night. As we jogged around the field, I could see each player had an extra pep in their step. I'm sure it had to do with seeing all the fans here supporting us. It was heartwarming. After the warmup and after the captains had gathered with the referee, we gathered around Coach one last time before we started the game.

"Give them hell. You got this," Coach said.

We took the field and got into our positions. The referee blew her whistle and the game started. We could all feel the tension of this game. We all knew that there was so much at stake here. We would either win the trophy or not. We would either have bragging rights or we wouldn't. The other team was dribbling the ball toward our end of the field. Jax, who was on the left side, kept up with their forward and took her to the back corner of the field. The other teams forward tried to kick it over to the net, but Jax blocked it, and the ball went out of bounds. Stonybrook had a corner kick. They took the kick, but I headed it out of the area. One of our center midfielders, Bridgett, got the ball at her feet and sent it up field to one of our forwards, Hanna. She beat the last two defenders, wound up and shot the ball to the right of the goalie. *Goal*! Silver Creek: 1, Stonybrook: 0. We can do this.

The rest of the first half stayed scoreless but we were still excited going into halftime. We were winning but we knew that we couldn't let our guard down. Unfortunately, the other team had the same thoughts. Five minutes into the second half, Stonybrook scored. It was chaos in our box, and everyone was trying to clear the ball out, but one of their players got a foot in on the ball and tapped it into the goal. Silver Creek: 1, Stonybrook: 1. *Shit*. We had multiple opportunities for the next twenty minutes, but the ball was either shot wide, over the net, or it hit the goalpost and bounced back into play where the goalie got her hands on the ball.

There were ten minutes left in the game, and one of their forwards was dribbling down to our side of the field. She dribbled into the left-hand corner, and I started to realize what she was about to do. She was about to send the ball across to the forward waiting in the box. I saw it in her eyes. *Not today*. I caught up with her, tackled her, and won the ball. I started dribbling up the side of the field when I got a glance of Rem running to the right-hand corner. She was waving at me. This was her signature move. She would always run to the corner of the field and get through balls from one of our midfielders. And she nailed it every single time. *Do your thing, Rem*. I sent the ball up the field and she collected it at her feet. She turned and dribbled toward the net. She beat the last defender, so it was just her and the goalie. The goalie came out of her net and tried to rush at Rem, but Rem faked the ball right and spun around the goalie. She kicked the ball into the back of the net. *Goal*! Silver Creek: 2, Stonybrook: 1. The crowd erupted into cheers, and we all crowded around Rem as we congratulated her.

The game ended eight minutes later and, when the referee blew her whistle, I think we all let out a long breath of relief. We won! We did it. The trophy was ours. Everyone by the bench sprinted out onto the field, including Coach Wimble. I could have sworn I saw a tear run down his face when he came out to hug all of us. He wanted this just as much as we did.

And now we had it. All the fans from the stands came off of the benches and ran down to the fields to hug their family members on the team. My parents being two of those fans. They ran over to me and picked me up in a huge hug. I'm so glad they were able to make it. I've missed them so much. Especially after everything that has been happening, they were my comfort. I squeezed them back even tighter.

"Baby, you did so well!" my mom said after she released me from the hug.

"Thanks, Mom. I'm so glad you both could come. I missed you both," I replied.

"We wouldn't have missed it for the world," my dad said.

"Any fun celebration plans tonight?" asked my mom.

"I'm sure the team is going to get together and do something. I'm sure it will be loud in the dorms since we're the only ones here."

"Did Jared stick around to watch the game?"

I hadn't told them yet that we broke up. Honestly, I didn't really think it was all that important.

"Uh, we actually broke up a couple of weeks ago, so I'm sure he went home."

"Oh, I'm sorry, Prim, I didn't know," my mom replied.

"It's okay, really. I didn't tell you, so how were you supposed to know?"

"Are you okay?" my dad asked.

"I'm more than okay. He wasn't the best."

"Honestly, I'm glad you two broke up. My first impression of him wasn't the greatest," said my mom.

"Yeah, I'm sorry about that. It was chaotic."

"Is Myles here?" my dad asked, looking around the crowd for him.

"No, he told me that he went home."

"Oh, well, I'm sure he will hear about the game when he gets back."

I nodded, a little hint of guilt forming in my stomach. Maybe if things were a little less awkward between us, he would have felt comfortable enough to stay and watch the game. I did feel weird not having him at the game, though. I'm not used to him not being here.

***

My parents decided to stay in a hotel and then drive back in the morning since it was so late. After I said goodbye to them, I walked over to where Rem was standing with her parents. This was the first time that I was able to see them during a game, so I decided to go over and say hi.

"Hey there, Mr. and Mrs. Allen. How are you?" I asked as I walked up to them.

"Now, Prim, what did I tell you about calling me Mrs. Allen," Rem's mom said.

"Sorry, *Lila*, how are you?" I replied. Since I first went to Pheasant Hill Elementary School last week, Lila has been calling Rem at night so that we could all talk. She always asked me how I liked the school and what I thought of Mr. Simmons and the kids. Obviously, all my reviews were glowing with positivity. I was really looking forward to the internship next semester.

"That's much better. We're doing great. You girls played so awesome tonight. We're so proud of you," Lila said.

"Thanks. Well, we owe it all to Rem here. She knocked it out of the park."

"No, it was a team effort. We all played well tonight. I'm just sad that the season is already over. I feel like it was yesterday when we had the first day of pre-season. We thought we were going to die because of how much running we had to do during those first couple of weeks. But Coach was right. It paid off in the end and now we have a trophy to put in the school showcase," Rem said.

"We'll have to do the same thing next year too," I replied.

We spent the next couple of minutes talking with Rem's parents and they headed out, since the stadium was starting to empty, and more people were leaving. The nice thing for Rem was that her hometown was only about thirty minutes away from campus, so she was able to see her family a lot.

Ves and Jax came over to us after saying goodbye to their parents and we all walked out of the stadium. It was going to be a night to celebrate. As we started walking back toward campus, I turned my head and saw Jared approaching us.

"Prim, can we talk please?" he asked.

The girls looked over at me and I just nodded my head.

"I'll be fine. You go on ahead. I'll catch up with you in a little bit. I'll text you when I'm on my way back to the dorm," I said to Rem as she squeezed my hand. Ves and Jax nodded and then headed off with Rem back to campus.

At this point, I just wanted to get this conversation over with so that I could move on with my life and leave Jared behind. It's the only reason I agreed to stay behind and talk to him.

"What do you want, Jared?"

"I want to talk to you. You only responded to one of my text messages and now you're ignoring all the others," he replied.

"And why do you think that is?"

"You at least owe me this conversation."

"I'm sorry, what the fuck do I owe you? It sounds to me like it should be the other way around."

"We were together for a couple of months. Don't you think we should talk this out like adults?"

"Adults. That's laughable coming from you. If you were, as you say, an "adult" we wouldn't be in this mess to begin with. You're the one who broke us apart, and now you're saying I owe you something. Do you even hear yourself right now?"

"Please, just let me explain what happened. I've been doing a lot of thinking recently and I know that I fucked up. But I want to try and at least get in your good graces again. Maybe somewhere down the line, we could get back together."

"Jared, the only reason you are saying this to me is because Shelby won't respond to your messages either. Are you just going around hopping on from one girl to the next?"

"How do you know Shelby isn't texting me back?"

"I told you, dumbass. We talked."

"What all did you talk about?"

"Why do you even fucking care what we talked about? You obviously already know that I know she's not texting you back, so you know I'm not lying about talking to her. She has also realized how much of a pathetic human being you are."

"Because she's probably trying to make me look really bad."

"She doesn't need to try. You are doing that all by yourself. Why are you blaming her for the shit that you did?"

"I'm not trying to blame her," he started. "Shit. Damnit, I know it's my fault. Is there any way that you can forgive me? I'll do anything to make it up to you."

"No, Jared. I already gave you enough chances when we were dating, and you wasted every fucking one of them."

"I know I did."

"Can I ask you something? Was any of it real this entire time? Did you actually like me or was I just someone that you could fuck in college and be done with me?"

"Why would you ask that?"

"Answering a question with a question is never a good sign, Jared. Give me an actual answer and stop avoiding the issues."

"It was real, Prim."

"I don't think it was. Do you know what I realized after we broke up? We never once really told each other how we felt. We never once said that we loved each other. Do you realize that?"

"I didn't realize that."

"Well, I did. We didn't even tell each other that we liked each other. We just started hooking up and the relationship went from there. I've come to realize that this relationship was just physical. We looked good together, we were attracted to each other, and we liked fucking, but other than that, there was no emotional connection whatsoever. And do you know what's even worse, Jared? When we weren't together, I didn't really miss you. I was perfectly fine hanging out with my friends and not being with you. That means something, Jared."

"So, you're telling me all of that, but yet you're making me out to be the bad person in this relationship?"

"Yes, and do you want to know why? Because I never would have cheated on you regardless of if I didn't want to be with you. People who love each other don't cheat on one another. If you cheat on someone, it means that you don't like that person as much as you thought."

"But, Prim, I told you that I didn't intend to cheat on you. I was perfectly fine being with you," he replied.

"And that's the issue. What you just said. 'I was perfectly fine being with you.' The word fine isn't the word you should be using with someone you really care about. If you really liked me as much as you are saying, you never would have even thought about cheating on me. You know I'm right."

"Were you ever in love with me?"

"No, I wasn't. I liked the idea of being in love with you, but I never actually was and, honestly, I'm happy about that. There's someone out there who I'm going to meet and I'm going to fall in love with him. That person isn't you, nor do I want it to be. I don't think you're a good person. You're cocky, arrogant, and a terrible boyfriend. I know that friends are important, but if I ignored my significant other as much as you ignored and neglected me during our relationship, I would feel terrible. But the difference between you and me, Jared, is that I never would have treated you that way, and I didn't. You canceled so many dates and plans that we had just because you wanted to hang out with your friends, or you had a stupid study group. Well, I guess I know now what you were doing during those study groups of yours."

"Jesus Christ, Prim. I'm sorry. How many goddamned times do I have to say that to you for you to forgive me. Who else are you going to go to, huh?"

I let out a laugh and I must have scared him because I saw him flinch and back away from me a little.

"Are you fucking kidding me? You listen to me," I replied as I stepped two steps toward him so that I was looking at him dead in the face. "Don't you dare try to make me feel bad about this! I'm not in the wrong here, you are. You have no right to comment on who I'm with or not with, got it? You never had that right. And here you are trying to make me get back together with you by insulting me?"

"I just want us to try. You need to drop the whole cheating thing. It's in the past and I can't change what happened. Stop giving me shit for it."

"In the past? Jared, it was only a couple of weeks ago. That's a very recent past for me to just forgive you like that. But, honestly, maybe I should forgive you because it's not me who's going to have to live with what I did. That's going to be you. I won't give you the satisfaction of knowing that I'm hurt over this because I'm not. Not anymore. I've moved on pretty quickly from this, and I'm proud of myself. But it also tells me that I didn't like you as much as I thought I did, and that makes me so relieved. I can now move on and find someone who is actually going to appreciate me."

"And who is that going to be? Myles?" he asked.

"Don't you dare talk about him! Myles is nothing like you. You don't even deserve to be compared to him at all."

"I know he has feelings for you," he replied.

"And what if he does? Why is that so wrong? Maybe I have feelings for him back."

"I fucking knew it. See, this is one of the reasons that I pulled myself away from you and went to someone else. Because of him. You and he are too close to just be best friends. Anyone you date would be annoyed by how close you two are. He's always around you. What guy would be willing to put up with that?"

"Well, I guess it's good that I don't care about the opinions of those men, especially yours. I make my own decisions and I will choose who I want to be with. If it ends up being with Myles, so be it. But I can guarantee you that he would treat me one hundred times better than you ever did. I feel sorry for the person who ends up with you. Maybe I should warn her if I see her."

"And maybe I should warn Myles how boring you are to be with. At least Shelby gave me a little bit of excitement in my life," he replied with a smug look on his face. It's a good thing that look didn't last for very long. I stepped forward and punched him.

"Prim, what the fuck! This is the second time you've punched me in the face. What's your problem?" Jared asked.

"My problem is that I've put up with your bullshit for way too long, but that all ends tonight. I want you to listen to me and listen to me closely. If you ever try to contact me or come up to me again, I will continue this tradition of knocking those arrogant ass looks off your face. If you don't believe me, then try me. I don't mind. It's good practice for female empowerment."

"You're a crazy bitch, you know that?"

"And you are just a small-minded dickhead of a human being. Call me a bitch all you want. You're just upset because your poor little ego was bruised, and your face was flattened by someone who isn't a guy. See, that's the problem with the male population. You look down on women because you think we're weak. I could show you crazy if you would really like me to. But, on the other hand, you're not worth my time or energy. So, please, leave, Jared. I'm done with you. Go find someone else to walk all over."

"Whatever. This is your last chance. I'm not coming back again," he replied.

"Well, then that's a relief. Now, please, kindly fuck off."

Jared stomped off back toward campus and, when I turned my head to the right, I saw Myles standing by his car in the parking lot. Why was he here? He told me that he went home for break.

"Myles!" I yelled over at him.

I was hoping he would come over so that we could talk but, when I called after him, he got back into his car and drove off.

I picked my bag up off the ground and started to walk away from the stadium, but then I changed my mind and turned back around and walked to the field. The lights were still on, so I decided to go sit on one of the benches. I wasn't quite ready to leave yet. I needed to process everything. One, our season was over. Everyone was probably back at the dorms celebrating and I hated Jared for making my mood like this. I didn't want to celebrate at all. Or I should. I actually have two things to celebrate. I get to celebrate my freedom from Jared. And now, I get to celebrate the fact that we fucking won the championship game. That's something to be proud of. But I couldn't quite shake the second thing that was on my mind. Why was Myles here, and why did he completely ignore me when I called for him?

I decided to text him. We still needed to talk and, if I could muster up the courage to talk to him after what I did in his room, he could talk to me too.

<u>Me</u>–I thought you were going home for break.

He texted me back a couple of seconds later. Oh, so he can return the message, but he can't come up to me and talk.

<u>Myles</u>–I did go home, but I wanted to come back to see you play.

<u>Me</u>–And why did you get in your car and drive away when I was calling you over?

<u>Myles</u>–Because you were with Jared. I saw you two talking, so I figured I wouldn't interrupt.

<u>Me</u>–Did you hear our conversation?

<u>Myles</u>–No, but it looked like you two were getting close.

Oh, so he thinks Jared and I are getting back together. That's why he drove away like that.

Me–Do you think we're getting back together?

Myles–I don't know what to think anymore, Prim. You told me you weren't sure what you were going to do about him, so the thought had crossed my mind.

Me–Then you must have missed the part where he stormed off. You also must have missed me punch him in the face.

Myles–Wait. You punched him?

Me–Yes. So, you can take back what you just said.

Myles–I must have just caught the end of it then. I'm sorry.

Me–We're not getting back together, Myles. I made it perfectly clear to him that we weren't.

Myles–Well, I'm glad. He's an idiot.

Me–I agree with you.

Myles–What are you doing for the rest of the night?

Me–Probably just going back to the room. I'm sure the girls want to celebrate after tonight.

Myles–Sounds good. Have a good night, Prim.

Me–We still need to talk, you know.

Myles–I know, but not tonight. Go enjoy your win. You deserve it.

Me–Thanks, Myles. And thanks for coming to watch. You didn't have to drive all the way back here.

Myles–Yes, I did. I haven't missed a home game yet, and I don't plan to start now. You're stuck with me, O'Brien.

I couldn't help the smile that formed on my face when I read that last line. Myles was a part of me. He was a part of my life that I never wanted to get rid of. I just need to gain the courage to tell him.

CHAPTER 22

Myles

Okay, things were really fucking awkward between me and Prim. Ever since the night in my room, we've barely talked. And I swear that she's been avoiding me. I'll see her out on campus somewhere, but then she completely disappears, and I have no idea where she went. I guess I can't blame her though. I'm embarrassed too. But I'm also a little concerned. I mean, there's no chance of us trying to mend the friendship back to the way it was. That door has long been closed. But we do need to figure this out. I know I should probably do more to try and contact her and talk to her, but then I remember what I told her before she left my room that night. I told her that she needed to figure it out and reach out to me. Honestly, I mean it. I feel like I'm always the one going after her. It's been that way ever since high school, and it's so exhausting. I'm not sure if I was too harsh on her that night, but it felt good getting all of that off my chest.

There's all this weird tension between us, and I swear that she feels it too. I mean, that's obvious considering everything that we did the other night. I know I should have stopped it before it even started but, when she was on top of me and I was kissing her, it just felt so right. Her in my arms. It's the only thing I've ever wanted. Granted, I wanted her to be sober while doing it, so I stopped it. I couldn't do that to her. I knew she was already regretting it. It seemed like she sobered up quickly after that though. I didn't want her to leave, but I also didn't want her to feel more awkward than it already was.

A couple of days before the school let out on break, I got a text message from Prim.

Prim–Hey. We should probably talk sometime soon about what happened. How about after you get back from Thanksgiving break?

I did want to talk to her about everything, but I also thought it was best that we waited until after break. And this was her taking a step in the right direction and figuring things out. But I also know that they have a championship game coming up, and I didn't really want her to worry about this on top of everything else that was going on. I told her that after Thanksgiving break would be good. I also found out that she wouldn't be going home at all during the break because of practices and the game schedule.

It was Friday afternoon and classes had ended for the day. As I was on my way back to the dorm, I saw everyone packing up their cars to head home for Thanksgiving break. I would also be leaving soon but I hadn't packed anything yet. Honestly, I've spent the last couple of days trying to figure out if I should stay or not, but my mom wanted me to come home. So, that's what I'm going to do. The only reason I wanted to stay was to make sure I was there to watch Prim during the game. By the time I got up to my room, Lawrence had already left, which was fine because he texted me earlier telling me to have a good break and that he would see me when we got back. Sabrina also left earlier today since she didn't have any afternoon classes, so I was by myself.

After I packed up my duffel bag, I got in my car and made the two-hour drive home. I hadn't seen my parents since the beginning of the semester so it was nice to see them, and they welcomed me with a freshly-baked pumpkin pie as soon as I walked in the door.

"Myles! Welcome home, sweety," my mom said before I barely made it in the front door.

"Hey, Mom. It's good to see you," I replied.

My dad came up behind her, also wearing an apron. They must have tag-teamed with the pumpkin pie.

"Your mom and I just got finished baking this pumpkin pie if you want some," he said, white powder very noticeable on his cheek. Every year my parents decide to put powdered sugar on top of the pumpkin pie. As if the thing needed more sugar to begin with.

I had to chuckle to myself. My parents have never acted like real parents throughout my life. They were more like my friends. I mean, they did discipline me whenever I needed it growing up, but that was a rare occasion.

"Thanks, Dad. I'll have some a little later after I get settled. How have you both been?" I asked.

"We've been great. We were thinking about going Christmas shopping this weekend. Are you in?" my mom asked.

Our family didn't do Black Friday shopping. It was always a nightmare, and no one wanted to get up early enough to go out. It's nice that the stores extend their Black Friday shopping, but we always found that it was less crowded if we went the weekend before.

"Sure. I need to get a couple of gifts," I replied.

"Is one of those gifts for Prim? Speaking of, is she not coming home for break?" my mom asked.

"No, she can't make it home this break. Their season got extended because they made it into the playoffs and now, they have the championship game on Tuesday. They'll be busy with practices and games, but I'm sure some of the girls will at least go home on Thanksgiving to be with their families. I'm not sure if that's what Prim is doing or not."

"Are things any better between the two of you?" she asked.

"I'm not really sure how to answer that question actually. I'm not distancing myself from her anymore and she's not dating that guy anymore, but things just seem really off between us."

"How do you mean?"

I didn't really know if I wanted to share all this information with my parents, but I feel like my mom would continue to hound information out of me if I didn't tell her.

"Well, for one, she kissed me," I replied, making sure to leave out all the other unnecessary details. I'd rather not give my mom a stroke anytime soon.

She spat out her water onto the table. Well, at least it wasn't a stroke. Just the good old-fashioned water spit.

"She did *what*?"

"She kissed me. We've been having deeper conversations lately and she had just found out that her boyfriend cheated on her, she had also been drinking, so she was in a vulnerable place. Then, she just kissed me."

"Myles, you stopped it, didn't you?"

"Of course, I stopped it, Mom. She was drunk and upset. I would have been a shit person if I kept kissing her." I didn't tell her that I didn't stop the kissing right away which led to other things, but she doesn't need to know all the details of that night.

"Well, what happened after that?"

"She left and went back to her room. I was honest with her and told her that she needed to figure things out."

"Well, I'm glad that you stood up for yourself, but is she okay now?"

"I think so. We haven't been able to talk about everything since so, hopefully, when I get back from break, we'll try to fix things. Except I don't know if there's going to be a lot of fixing happening. This is kind of something you can't really come back from. Friends don't usually kiss their other friends. I really have no idea what's going to happen."

"And you aren't planning on going to her game?"

"I wasn't planning on it."

"Maybe you should. It's only two hours away, and she'll see how much you support her and are there for her."

"Mom, if she hasn't realized that by now, I don't know what else I can do for her. I've always been there for her. I've gone to every single home game, and she still hasn't realized how much I love her. Maybe it's just not meant to be with her. It's been so hard. Nothing is falling into place and some days I feel like punching a wall. Maybe it's just too stressful."

"Well, that's something that you're going to have to figure out. You're going to have to decide if this relationship is worth it. Do you have any idea of where her head is at in all of this?"

"I don't know all of it but I'm guessing that, because she kissed me, she's at least thinking about it. Why else would she have kissed me? It was just so out of the blue."

"Then you need to figure that all out when you get from break. Just be honest with her. And, if she doesn't feel the same way, it's time to move on. I'm not saying you can't still be friends with her but, if she doesn't have the same feelings back, there's not much else you can do at that point."

"Yeah, I know," I replied.

"Well, we don't have to keep talking about all of this. I shouldn't have brought it up. I just want to make sure you're okay. You haven't been texting or calling as much lately, so I just wanted to check in on you."

"I know. And thank you. I'll be okay. You don't need to worry about me," I replied.

The next morning, my parents and I got up early and went to the mall which was just right down the street from our house. I needed to get both a gift for Christmas, but I also wanted to get something for Prim. No matter what's been happening between us lately, it was tradition to get each other a gift. Usually, the gifts were comical, but I decided to do something a little different this year. I still had some money saved up from lifeguarding during the summers in high school, so my parents went one direction in the mall, and I headed for the jewelry store.

I wasn't looking for anything fancy. Prim doesn't like fancy. She likes simple, at least when it comes to jewelry. The only jewelry that she's ever really worn over the course of the years are necklaces with a simple pendant. So, that's what she's going to get.

As I was looking at the necklaces behind the glass, I noticed the store clerk coming over to me.

"Excuse me, sir. Are you looking for anything specific?" the store clerk asked.

"Uh, not anything in particular. I'm just looking for a simple necklace with a simple pendant," I replied.

"Is this for a family member or a significant other?"

"Neither. It's for my best friend actually."

"Hmm, let me see. These two here are the simpler-looking designs that we have. Would either of those do?"

I looked at the two necklaces that he was pointing at and noticed that each one had a very simple design, but the one on the left was purple, and then one on the right was pink. The pink necklace had a lot more diamonds on it, which is something I know Prim wouldn't enjoy. She doesn't like a lot of flashy diamonds, so I made my decision.

"I'll take this purple one, please," I replied.

"Excellent choice. Give me one minute and I will get this wrapped up for you," he said as he removed the necklace from the glass and went into the back room to get the wrappings.

After I paid for the necklace—*I'm not going to share the price*—I headed back out into the front part of the mall to wait for my parents. I decided to come back sometime else to get their presents because I didn't want them to see what I was getting them.

"You all set?" my mom asked as she and my dad walked up to me.

"All good to go," I replied.

"Is that for Prim?"

"Yeah. I decided to get her a necklace. It's her favorite color and it's simple, so it's right up her alley."

"I'm sure she will love it," my mom replied.

***

We spend the next couple of days catching up on everything that has been happening at school. I tell them about the guitar lessons I have been taking with Casey, and the volleyball team I've been playing for. They seemed genuinely excited for me, so it made me feel really good about my decisions. Since my dad used to play guitar when he was younger, of course, he whipped out his old guitar and asked me to play something for them. I chose to go back to *Wonderwall* by Oasis since it was the very first song I learned how to play with Casey.

They were both very impressed and, honestly, so was I because I didn't think that I would remember how to play that without sheet music. I didn't tell them about the song that I have been writing on my own time. It's not something I want anyone to know about yet, so I'm going to keep that one to myself. For now, that is.

Tuesday afternoon rolled around, and I was helping my mom decide what items we were going to cook for Thanksgiving dinner on Thursday.

"Myles isn't Prim's game tonight?" my mom asked.

"Yeah. The game starts at seven tonight," I replied, guilt forming in my stomach.

"And you're positive that you don't want to go?"

"I'm positive. I just got home a couple of days ago, so I want to spend time with you guys. I've seen her the whole semester. It's fine. I can miss one game."

"Yes, but I just don't want you to regret it if you don't go. It's the championship game, right?"

"Yes," I replied.

"So, that's a big deal, Myles. I'm sure she would love it if you were there to support her."

I sighed. I knew my mom was right. I would regret it. *Fuck.*

An hour later, I was in the car driving two hours back to campus. I figured that I would stay in my dorm room tonight and then come back home tomorrow morning to spend the rest of the break at home. The shit I do for her.

I got to the field ten minutes before the game started, so I made my way to the stands which were already packed. I didn't think all these people would come back for the game, but I guess the soccer teams are more popular than I originally thought. I saw Maverick and Jensen from the basketball team in the stands, so I decided to sit with them for the game. Their season started in early November so I'm sure they may have had to stay on campus during break, at least for a little. The team was taking the field and getting into their starting lines. I looked toward the back of the field and saw Prim, Vesper, and Jax doing their pre-game handshake that they made up. Rem had the ball on the fifty-yard line as the game was about to begin.

During the first half, we scored once, giving us the lead. But, during the start of the second half, Stonybrook got the ball in the box and was able to score. They almost scored again a little later, but Prim was able to take the ball away from their forward just in time. She then passed the ball up the field to Rem. She dribbled, beat the other players, and then scored to give us the lead again. The rest of the second half was a battle back and forth, but we managed to pull out the win. I wasn't surprised. They had only lost one game the entire season. When the referee blew the whistle signaling the end of the game, the entire stadium erupted with cheers and all the fans ran down and stormed the field to see the players. I was not one of them. That's not really my scene.

After the crowd died down, I saw Prim and the other girls walk toward the back of the stadium to the exit that the teams used after the games. I went to the parking lot and drove my car around to the back of the stadium. I was planning to congratulate Prim and trying to relieve some of the awkwardness that has been between us but, when I got to the parking lot out back, Jared was standing in front of Prim. It looked like they were arguing, so I got out of my car and leaned up against my car so I could hear. Not all the lights were on in the parking lot, so they wouldn't be able to see me from where they were standing.

I heard a lot of the conversation. To sum up, Jared was being a dick and trying to ask for forgiveness. I was very glad to hear that Prim wasn't taking his shit and told him to back off. But I could also see that he was getting way too aggressive with her. He got in her face way too many times for my liking. I was trying to be patient with him and let Prim handle herself, which I know she can. But, when I heard him scream and call her a crazy bitch, it took every ounce of resistance I had in me not to run over there and beat the shit out of him. Although, it looked like I didn't need to because Prim wound up and punched him in the face for me. No, not for me. For her. I'm pretty sure that's the second time that she's had to punch him this semester, and the semester isn't even over yet.

That's my girl. Prim has come a long way since the girl she was in high school. She's grown a lot over this semester, but I hate that she's had to do it because of a dickhead like Jared. I'm so proud of her for standing her ground. Honestly, I don't think I gave her enough credit. I thought she would have gotten back together with Jared by now. She's just too nice of a person.

I saw Jared leaving after a while and then, as Prim turned, she looked right at me. Shit. I didn't know what to do because I didn't want her to know that I overheard their argument, so I ignored her calling for me and drove away. A couple of minutes after I got back to my dorm room, Prim texted me and asked me what my problem was for running away like that. Well, she did have a point. I did run away like a coward. But at least she knew that I was there. I told her that I only caught the tail-end of the argument just to make things a little easier. She thinks that I drove away because I saw her and Jared together and thought they were getting back together. That wasn't my intention, but I wanted her to have this night with the girls to celebrate.

Our problems could be solved another day, but tonight was hers.

Chapter 23

Myles

The rest of Thanksgiving break went by way too quickly. Classes started back up again the following Monday, so I drove back to school late Sunday night. We only had a week-and-a-half left of classes before the semester ended and we went into Winter Break, so it was manageable.

The next week was more awkward than I had imagined it would be with Prim. We said that we would talk after break but that still hasn't happened yet. I just don't know how to start our conversation. Should it even be me starting the conversation, or should it be her? I've never felt uncomfortable talking to Prim, but I am now.

I've had two more guitar lessons since we've been back from break and I've almost finished writing the song that I started. The lyrics were all complete; I just needed to finish the last part of the melody. I didn't really think that I would play the song for anyone but I wanted to say that I did it in case anyone ever asked. It was more for me than anyone else. At least, that's what I keep telling myself when I'm playing it on the guitar.

It was the beginning of December, so we were all getting ready to take our finals the next week. All the finals were on Wednesday, Thursday, and Friday of next week. I've heard people saying that there is going to be an end-of-semester party next Friday, so I'm assuming a lot of people are going to stay for that and then drive home the following morning. You would think people would want to go home for break, but nothing stops a college student from going to a party. And I guess that includes me because I also plan on going to the party. I'll probably ask Prim if she wants to ride home with me next Saturday, so she doesn't have to drive. Maybe we can talk in the car. We will have two hours and, if we don't talk, that is going to be excruciating silence the whole way home.

Sabrina, Lawrence, and I spend the entire weekend studying in the library. The only final I wasn't positive about was my Introduction to Statistics class. I'm usually not very good with math, but this was the only math class that I have to take for my psychology degree, so I wanted to get it out of the way during my first year. It's not that the class is hard, but the professor doesn't really do a good job of explaining things. It's like we're teaching ourselves. He puts all kinds of equations and numbers on the board and kind of just makes us figure it out. Not the best. Which is why most of the students in that class have a C or lower. That includes me. I have a seventy-five percent in the class so, if I bomb the final, I will end up having to take the class again another semester. Which brings me here to the library.

Late Sunday night, there was a knock on our room door. Lawrence put his finger on his nose claiming that he wasn't it this time.

"Fucker," I said as I got out of bed and opened the door. It was Remington. She was probably the last person that I expected to be on the other side of our door.

"Hey, Rem. Is everything okay?" I asked.

"Hey, Myles. Everything is fine. Do you have a little bit of time to chat?" Rem replied.

"Uh, yeah, sure," I said as I looked back at Lawrence.

"I'll ask Sabrina if she wants to go grab something to eat at Creek's Corner," Lawrence replied. "I'll let you two have some privacy." Creek's Corner was a small food café that was open a lot later into the night than the school cafeteria, so it was a big hangout spot for the students. He put on a sweatshirt and his shoes and headed to the door.

"Congrats on your win, by the way. I heard your goal was top-notch," Lawrence said as he passed by Rem.

"Thanks, Lawrence," Rem said, smiling back at him. Lawrence nodded and shut the door behind him as he left.

Rem went over to Lawrence's bed and sat down.

"You know, I'm not sure if you want to sit there. I don't know what he and Rebecca do when she comes up," I say, pointing to his sheets.

"Eww, gross. You're right. I didn't even think about that. Why is the male population so disgusting?" she asked as she got up and pulled out my desk chair to sit on instead.

"A question for the generations, I'm sure," I replied. "So, what's up? Are you sure everything is, okay?"

"Everything is fine, don't worry. But I wanted to talk to you about Prim."

"What about Prim?" I asked a little concerned about where this conversation was going.

"First, let me start by saying that I already know about her kissing you the other week," Rem replied.

I started coughing and she came over and patted me on the back. "Easy there, tiger. Everything's all good."

"She told you about that?" I asked after I stopped coughing up air.

"Dude, I'm one of her best friends and we're roommates. Of course, she told me that she kissed you."

"Did she tell you everything that happened?" I asked.

From the smile that formed on Rem's face, I could already predict the answer.

"This is so embarrassing," I said, putting my face in my hands.

"Don't be embarrassed. There's nothing to be embarrassed about. You're both two hot-blooded human beings who got caught up in each other. And, honestly, I'm not surprised. I'm sure all of that tension and emotion has been building for years," she said as she went back to sit down on the chair.

"So, uh, why are you bringing all of this up?"

"Listen, let me also just start by saying that I love you both dearly. You're two of the best people that I know, but you're both also stupid fucking idiots."

"Uh, would you care to elaborate on that, please, before I get offended?"

She laughed. "No offense intended. But, seriously, though, Myles. I know that you're in love with her. You can't fool me."

"I…" I wasn't even able to get the rest of the sentence out before she interrupted me.

"Don't give me any of those bullshit excuses. I know that you're in love with her, but I also know that she's in love with you too, even though she might not realize it yet."

"You think she's in love with me? I don't get that vibe at all with her," I replied.

"Why don't you think she's in love with you?"

"Because she's never shown anything that resembles love in all the years that we've been friends. Of course, she loves me in a way a best friend would, but she hasn't been pining away all of these years like I have."

"Myles, do you know that she sleeps and cuddles with Mr. Tusky every single night?"

"Well, I mean, I know that she has him on her bed."

"And do you know that she's cried over you to me many, many times throughout the semester?"

"She's cried over me. What was she saying?"

"Myles, she loves you. Maybe she hasn't admitted it aloud yet, but she's in love with you."

"I just don't know what to do. That night in my room I wanted to give in to her so badly, but she wasn't in the right state of mind, so I stopped it."

"Yeah, she told me that. I'm glad you did that, though. Jared wouldn't have done that which, I guess, isn't saying very much because he's an asshole, but still."

"I was really worried that she was going to go back to him."

"Honestly, I was worried for a little bit too, but I think she's much stronger than any of us give her credit for."

"She is strong. Stronger than I am."

"She's talked about you every day since everyone got back from Thanksgiving break. It gets quite annoying sometimes actually."

"I wish she would talk to me that much about everything."

"Listen, the reason I came to talk to you is that I wanted to tell you that now is your chance to do something. I have a feeling that, if all the pent-up emotions and feelings come out during a conversation between you two, it would be good for both of you. Honestly, I think it would move your relationship forward. You're both just stuck at a standstill right now. It makes me sad seeing you both being like this because of each other."

"So, what do you suggest that I do about it?"

"I don't know. But you need to talk to her. Don't waste this chance."

"But, Rem, I'm always the one going to her. I've been in this stupid unrequited love thing since high school. If she doesn't have feelings for me, then that's one thing. But, if what you're saying is true, then why shouldn't she be the one to take the lead on this one? It would at least show me how she feels about me and that it's actually real instead of me just guessing."

"And I agree with you. But you're both too stubborn to take the first step. The only reason Prim was able to take the lead the other week and kiss you first is that the alcohol took the edge off."

"She remembered everything that happened, right?" I asked, hoping that the answer was yes.

"Yeah. She didn't have any holes in her memory or anything, so she remembered everything. Even down to the last detail."

"What's that supposed to mean?"

"She said you were a very good kisser, among other things."

"Oh, God. You're doing a shit job of not embarrassing me."

"It's my job as Prim's female best friend."

"I guess you're right."

"I just want you both to be happy and, honestly, I think you would make each other happy. You're a good guy, Myles. I'm rooting for you, I really am. If there is anything that I can do to help, please, let me know. And, in the meantime, I'll try to help Prim figure everything out until you two can talk together."

"Thanks, Rem."

She got up from the chair, patted me on the shoulder, and headed over toward the door.

"You really do love her, don't you?" she asked.

"Ever since freshman year of high school. Hell, even before that. I just didn't know what love was," I replied.

"That's what I thought. Theory proven yet again," she said as she winked and left the room.

Rem didn't have to remind me. That theory was proven to me a long time ago.

Chapter 24

Myles

Tuesday night, I was studying for my first final in the dorm room with Lawrence. I checked one final off the list because our psychology final was our presentation that we had to complete before Thanksgiving. We got the grades back last week. Prim, Sabrina, and I all texted each other in our group chat and congratulated each other on a job well done. That was the most conversation I had had with Prim since classes started again, but at least it was something.

"Wanna take a break and go grab some food at Creek's Corner?" Lawrence asked.

"Yes, please," I replied. I needed a break. We had been studying for four hours straight without even a bathroom break.

When we got there, I ordered a cheese pizza and Lawrence ordered mozzarella sticks. They had been our staple meals ever since we started coming here at the beginning of the semester.

The place was packed so we had to sit in their outdoor seating. Clearly, everyone had the same idea that we did and needed a break from all of the studying.

"So, how are you and Rebecca doing?" I asked Lawrence.

"We're doing really well now," he replied.

"You never did tell me how you two made up after what happened."

"Uh, it was just some personal things that she needed to take care of. They were on her mind a lot, which was another reason she was pushing me away. But we have it all figured out now, so it's all good."

"Good. I'm glad."

We continued eating until I heard a lot of commotion happening around the corner from us. I heard yelling and something that sounded like glass bottles being smashed against the side of the building.

"What the hell is that?" Lawrence asked turning toward the noise.

By this time, everyone who was sitting outside turned their head to see what was happening. A shadow appeared around the corner and when the figure appeared in the light, I realized that it was Jared. Not just Jared. A *drunk* Jared, surrounded by all his soccer buddies. Oh, well, this isn't going to be good.

"Hey, everybody! Where's the party?" Jared yelled as he stumbled over two trashcans outside of the building.

"Listen, man, you need to be quiet. You're causing too much trouble," said one of his friends, holding Jared up by the shoulder.

"I'm just trying to have a good time here. It's almost the end of the semester and I just got dumped. It's such a great time to be alive," Jared replied, pushing his friend off of him.

"Dude, enough," his friend said. "You're trashed."

"Fuck off, Anderson. If you don't like it, then you can go back. I'm just trying to find the party."

Jared made his way to the front of the building and looked right at me. *Oh, shit.* Lawrence looked over at me with wide eyes.

"Dude, we should probably get out of here," he said.

"Agreed," I replied as we both got up and started walking.

"Hey! Myles! You, over there! Where you going so early?" Jared yelled behind me. "The party was just getting started. It's no fun if you leave now."

I turned back to face him. "You're drunk, Jared. Go back to your dorm."

"You know what, Myles. Fuck you too," he said as he made his way over to me and Lawrence.

"How about we take this into the parking lot so we're not around all these people? You're disturbing everyone around you. Why are you so fucking wasted?" I asked.

"Because of you, Myles. Because of a certain girl that you call your fucking best friend, if that's what she really is to you."

I can handle a lot of things in life. But if he was going to stand there in his drunk ass state and insult Prim in front of me, he was dead wrong.

"Lawrence, why don't you go back to the room? I got this handled," I said.

"No, man. I'm staying. I'm not going anywhere," he replied.

"Listen, Myles. We all know the reason that Prim broke up with me is because of you. You've always had feelings for her, haven't you, Myles?" Jared asked.

"Shut your fucking mouth, Jared," I replied, a tone of warning in my voice.

"And do you know what? That's exactly why I did what I did."

"What are you talking about?"

"That's why I cheated on that stupid bitch. I'm sure she's told you all about it by now, right? Of course, she did. You both are always up each other's asses, so why wouldn't she tell you that I cheated on her."

"Jared, I swear to God if you keep talking…" I started.

"The whole situation between you two was really starting to piss me off. You were always around, Myles. I couldn't even get two minutes in peace with Prim before you showed up. You need to work on your personal boundaries, man. No one is going to want to date her with you around."

"I'm glad I was there. At least I knew she was safe with me around."

"She was safe with me too, Myles. But she kept wanting to hang out with you and I just got so damn annoyed, so I found the next best thing. A girl from my study group. Not that there was a whole lot of studying going on, if you know what I mean," Jared said winking back at his buddies.

"You're a piece of shit, Jared. Go to hell. Clearly, you haven't learned your lesson. If Prim knew what you were doing right now, I'm sure she would punch you for the third time now this semester, right?" I said, looking over at his friends. "Oh, did Jared not tell you all that he got punched by Prim? From what I saw, they were killer punches. All that blood? Wasn't very pretty."

Right as I finished my sentence, Jared pushed me up against the wall behind me.

"You need to learn when to stop fucking talking, my man," Jared said.

"Get the fuck off him," Lawrence said as he tried pulling Jared off me.

Jared took Lawrence by the arm and punched him so hard in the face that he flew back and landed on his back.

"You son of a bitch," I said as I also took a swing at Jared and made contact with the right side of his jaw.

By this time, we had gathered a crowd. Everyone that was sitting outside had come around to the back and was watching the scene play out.

Jared got up off the ground and punched me back. There were a couple more punches exchanged between us, and then I pushed Jared back up against the wall so that he was in the same vulnerable position I was in before.

"Don't you dare talk about Prim like that ever again, do you hear me? You're a pathetic piece of shit who got just what you deserved. You don't even deserve the ground she walks on. I'm glad she came to her senses and dumped your pitiful ass."

I could hear the sirens wailing behind me as I let go of Jared's jacket. When I let go of him, he fell to the ground, bent over to his right side, and started vomiting all over the ground. The owner of Creek's Corner came out and ran over to me and Lawrence.

"Are you boys, okay? I saw everything from inside and called the cops. He's been coming here and doing this shit every night and I'm tired of it. I'll go explain everything to the police, so wait here. They're probably going to call you in to make statements."

"Thank you," Lawrence and I said as I massaged the right side of my face. Jared hit me pretty hard, and I could taste copper starting to form inside my mouth.

"Man, you took a nice hit," I said as Lawrence started rubbing his jaw.

"You did too. You should see your face," he replied.

Now, usually, I don't condone violence, but Jared had it coming tonight. It was either going to be from me or Prim. Tonight, it was me. And, I'm not going to lie, it felt good. That was a whole semester's worth of built-up rage toward that guy. I'm just hoping that Prim doesn't find out. At least I didn't start it.

Twenty minutes later and Jared, Lawrence, and I were sitting in the town's police station. This is not how I thought the end of the semester was going to go at all. But here we are.

All of us were holding ice packs up to our faces while the officer was asking us questions about what happened earlier.

"Now, the store owner said that this man started the fight, is that correct?" the officer asked as he pointed over to Jared.

"Yes," Lawrence and I both replied at the same time.

"I didn't…" Jared started but was quickly shut down by death glares from both me and Lawrence. "Fine, I started it."

"Oh, well, look who decided to finally wake up and join us," replied the officer. When Lawrence and I had come into the police station earlier, we saw Jared passed out on the chair that he's sitting on now. "And what made you drink all that alcohol tonight, son?"

"A girl," Jared replied.

"Well, aren't you just the biggest walking cliché out there."

I looked over and saw Lawrence chuckling to himself. I wanted to laugh, but I thought I better not if I wanted to get out of here quickly. So, I held it in.

"Now, Lawrence, Myles, do you wish to press charges against him? It's completely up to you."

I looked over at Lawrence and he just shrugged at me. I didn't really want to get anyone in legal trouble, so decided against it.

"No, sir, not tonight," I replied.

The officer nodded. "Fine. You and Lawrence here are free to leave. We'll let you know if we have any other questions. We'll deal with Jared. Thank you and have a good night."

***

Lawrence's girlfriend Rebecca came to the station to pick us up. She wasn't very happy that Lawrence had gotten into a fight but, as soon as we explained the situation, she was fine.

"Hey, man, Rebecca and I are going to go grab a coffee somewhere. Do you want to come with us?" Lawrence asked as I started to get out of the car.

"No, I'm good. You two go on ahead," I replied.

"Are you going to be, okay?" Rebecca asked.

"Yeah, I'll be fine. Thanks for the ride, Rebecca. I'll see you later, Lawrence."

I waved to them as Rebecca drove away and then pulled out my phone. I had a text message from Prim. It was sent half an hour ago.

Prim–Myles! What the hell happened? I heard you went to the police station. When are you going to be back?

Me–I just got back. I'm going to my room now.

I tucked my phone back in my pocket and walked up to my floor. When I turned onto my hallway, I looked up and saw Prim waiting outside my door.

"Myles, oh, my god, are you okay?" she asked as she ran up to me and put her hand on my jaw. From the pain that I felt when she touched me, I was sure I was going to have a nice-looking bruise on the side of my face tomorrow morning.

"I'm fine, don't worry," I replied, taking out my key and unlocking the door.

"Some girls on my floor were at Creek's Corner and were talking about what happened when they came back. Tell me everything that happened."

"Well, Lawrence and I went there to take a break from studying, but then Jared showed up with his friends and was clearly intoxicated. He kept yelling and getting in people's faces, and then he saw me and Lawrence there, so of course, he stopped to say hello."

"Did he start this?" she asked.

"You think I'm the one who started this?"

"No, that's not what I meant."

"He came over to us and kept talking about you, so I got pissed and said some words back to him. He didn't like that very much, so he pushed me up against the wall and everything just spiraled from there."

"Myles, I'm so sorry. He clearly hasn't learned his lesson from the last two punches I gave him."

"That's exactly what I said to him which set him off, so maybe I shouldn't have brought that up with his fragile ego and all that."

"Where's Lawrence?"

"Rebecca came to pick us up from the police station, so they're going to grab coffee."

"You should have called me. I would have come to pick you up."

"I didn't want you to get involved, and Jared was still at the station when we left, so you didn't need to see that. I'm sure he would have caused another scene if you showed up."

"I'm so sorry he did this."

"Prim, you don't need to apologize. You didn't do anything wrong. This is completely his fault. He should be the one apologizing."

"Did he?"

"What do you think?"

"I'll take that as a no then."

I nodded over at her.

"Here, let me help you. The side of your lip is completely split open. Here, sit still," Prim said as she sat down beside me on the bed. "Do you have a first-aid kit or anything in here?"

"Yeah, over in my closet," I replied.

Prim got the first-aid kit and pulled out some Q-tips and some ointment. I don't know how long any of that stuff has been in there, so I wasn't sure how good it was, but I guess that didn't matter right now. This is the first time that Prim and I have been alone in a while so it felt nice. Even though my heart started to beat out of my chest, at least she was close.

"Hold still, okay?" she said as she put the ointment on one of the Q-tips.

I nodded and looked up at her as she started to put the ointment on the crease of my lip.

"Ouch," I said as I pulled away a little.

"Sorry. Don't be such a baby. I only pressed down a little," she replied.

"Yeah, well, pain shot through my body, so take it easy."

"You're welcome for doing this, by the way."

"You're right. Thank you," I replied.

"That's better."

"You don't have to do this, you know. I can do it by myself if you have more studying that you need to do."

"I don't mind. I want to be here with you. I know things have been weird between us so I, at least, wanted to help you and make sure that you were okay after what happened."

"Thank you. It means a lot. We probably should have talked by now, but I really don't know what more to say to you that I haven't said already."

"I know. Let's not worry about that right now, okay? Let's just get this handsome face back in functional order," she replied.

"Hey, Prim?" I ask.

"Yeah?"

"Thank you."

"For what?"

"For being here."

"Well, you came back for my game, so I figured I owed you one."

"You don't have to owe me anything for coming to your game."

"If you say so," she replied.

She continued to put the ointment on my lip as I stared up at her and thought that there's no way I could fall more in love with her. She continues to prove me wrong every time.

Chapter 25

Prim

I hadn't been expecting to overhear a conversation on my floor about some guys getting into a fight right outside of Creek's Corner. I was in the middle of studying for my English final when I heard girls outside my door talking. I heard the words *fight*, *Jared*, *Myles*, and *Creek's Corner*. That was enough to make me get up out of my chair and go out into the hallway.

"There was a fight?" I asked the girls standing outside their door.

"Uh, yeah. Prim, it was Myles and Jared."

"They fought outside of Creek's Corner? What was the fight about?"

"I'm pretty sure you can guess."

"Where are they now?" I asked.

"I heard that they were all taken to the police station to go over what happened with the officers. The owner of the store called the cops. Apparently, Jared has been getting drunk the last couple of nights and going there and disrupting everyone."

"For fuck's sake. Was anyone hurt?"

"Well, everyone got punched from what we saw, so I'm sure they're going to have some bruises."

"Is Myles, okay? Did you see him?"

"The last we saw, Myles had Jared pinned up against the wall and then the police came and broke everything up."

I texted Myles after that and asked him what happened. I hadn't gotten a response for a little while, so I was starting to get worried. I pulled on my sweatshirt and headed over to his dorm. I knocked on the door, but I didn't hear anyone in the room. Maybe he was still at the police station although, from what I had heard, they had been there for a long time. I decided to wait outside his door hoping that he would come back soon. My phone buzzed.

Myles–I just got back. I'm going to my room now.

He came up to the floor and his face looked terrible. His mouth, lip, and right eye were already starting to swell and bruise. I hated seeing him like that, knowing that they had fought over me. This was so stupid, and when I saw Jared again, I was going to kill him. Okay, maybe not to that extent, but what I said to him after the game hadn't stuck in his dense little brain.

I spent the rest of the night putting ointment on Myles's face. He objected, but I'm stubborn so, of course, I stayed. I wasn't letting him alone like that. He wanted to talk about what had been happening between us, but that wasn't the time for it. I know I keep putting it off, but I don't think attending to someone's wounds was a great time to hash out feelings and emotions.

The night felt strangely intimate though. We were so close in proximity, and the way he kept looking up at me made me melt a little inside. I know I have thought about this before and I know that I've talked to Rem about this, but I knew that I was in trouble. I've known it for a while, but I've never wanted to admit it loud so maybe this was the time. *I like Myles.* And who knows? Maybe it was a little more than that at this point.

***

This is what I need to do. I need to go out tonight, get drunk, and blow off some steam. I haven't talked to Jared since the championship game when he came up to me afterward. That definitely put a dampener on the rest of that night, and I was still pissed off that he would confront me about everything literally minutes after we won the championship. I can't believe he started that fight with Myles. I'm glad I haven't seen or spoken to him because I'm sure we would all end up in the police station again. What a fucking idiot.

I mean, we had only been dating for two months, but it was my first relationship since high school, so I thought that it meant something to me. I should have known better. Who would be lucky enough to meet their soulmate during the first month of college? Well, let me tell you. It's not me. Even if he is on the boys' soccer team and I'll have to continue to see him both outside and during soccer seasons.

And do you know what? It's time to celebrate. The girls and I won the title championship this season so it's time that I forget about all the negative stuff and focus on tonight and my girls. Since everyone else at school was home for break the night of the game, we weren't able to have a proper celebration until now. We thought that tonight was the perfect night for it since it was the night before everyone went home for Winter Break. I'm going to lose myself in the music, probably too much alcohol, and, of course, all of the beautiful soccer ladies. I can't believe my freshman season is officially over, but I am looking forward to being able to devote more time to making money tutoring. I couldn't tutor a lot this semester because of the season and my bank account has slowly dried out.

The only other thing I'm worried about is Myles. Well, not so much worried but, ever since I admitted to myself that I have feelings for him, my heart races anytime I see him. I haven't been able to figure out how to handle that, so, again, I've been avoiding. I think I knew that I had feelings for him even before I showed up at his dorm the night, I found out Jared cheated on me, but I didn't plan on feeling all of this so quickly and strongly. He was just the first person I thought of. But, of course, I would go to Myles. He's my best friend. Right. But he's the best friend that I kissed. I actually *kissed* him and, well, a little more than that. Was I drunk? Yes. Did I ever intend to kiss Myles? Nope. Jesus. And now? Well, now I was starting to think about what it would be like if we were more than friends. As I said before, I think I'm in trouble. Big trouble.

I'm sure Myles and I will talk soon. We're going to have to. We can both feel the tension especially after the other night when he was hurt. We've seen each other in class over the last couple of days since we've had to take our finals, but I think we're both too embarrassed to talk. I don't think either of us knows how we would even start that conversation. But I've certainly been replaying over and over in my head what he had said to me in his room the night I kissed him. *"No, not like this."* His thoughts were clear. He wanted to kiss me, and I wanted to kiss him. I'm sure that if he hadn't stopped us, one thing would have led to another and, well, you know.

But I can't think about that right now. Tonight, I'm going to try and forget about all of my troubles. The senior girls have a house that they use for parties and, tonight, it's going to be used for that very purpose. They invited pretty much every single student on campus, and almost everyone agreed. The women's soccer team was beginning to get more popular, especially now that we had won the championship title. The title hadn't been won by the women's team in over ten years, so this was a big accomplishment. Not to toot our own horn or anything. Okay, well, maybe a little.

I walked in the front door, put my jacket on the hooks, and saw Remington over by the stairs. She scored our game-winning goal to give us the title, so she deserves a little extra love tonight.

"Hey, Rem! I thought I was supposed to meet you outside?" I asked.

"Sorry! I got caught up helping make drinks and forgot to text you," she replied.

"How many more people do you think are going to show up? There's barely enough room in here as it is, and the place is already packed. I hope the captains are all right with this."

"Of course, they are! We fucking won, dude. They are all stoked to party. And it's the end of the season, so the coaches aren't as keen on catching us drinking as they were during the season. Drink up!"

"Here, here!" yelled Jax and Vesper as they approached us. They were carrying two extra drinks, so they handed them over to me and Rem.

"Thanks, ya'll," I said, taking the cup and downing the first drink of the night.

"Sheesh, Prim, take it easy. We have the whole night," laughed Vesper.

"I'm just trying to enjoy my drink since we can finally drink again. It's been a while and I need it."

"How are you holding up with everything?" asked Jax.

"So far so good. Haven't seen Jared since he came up to me at the stadium but then, after what he did to Myles, I hope I never see him again," I replied. "But Myles is more the problem now."

"Myles?" asked Vesper and Jax in unison looking at each other and then back at me.

I froze. *Oh shit.* I never told Ves and Jax about what happened with Myles, only Remington. Great going, Prim. Now they're staring at you. You're going to have to tell them now. Heat flushed up the back of my neck.

"I, umm, I may have kissed Myles when I was drunk the other week," I replied.

"Myles? Like your best friend since elementary school Myles? That one? The one that goes to this school with you and is always with you?" asked Vesper.

"Rub it in a bit more, Ves," I replied.

"Damn. Uh, how did that happen?" asked Jax.

"Well, it was the night that we saw the picture of Jared and that girl Shelby in the parking garage. After I left you guys in the room, I just roamed around campus for a little because I didn't know what else to do at that point. I know I should have stayed in the room and talked to you, but I just needed space and I felt like I couldn't breathe. I chugged the alcohol and then ended up in front of Myles's room."

"Prim, that was straight vodka," replied Vesper.

"That would explain how I got so drunk," I replied, looking around the group nervously. "Although, by the end of the night, I definitely sobered up."

"Okay, so you ended up in Myles's room. What led to you kissing him? Wait, the more important question is, did he kiss you back?" asked Vesper.

"Can I finish telling the story?" I asked.

"Sorry, sorry. You can't just spring something like this on us and not expect us to ask questions! This is, like, umm, pretty big news," replied Vesper.

"No, it's not big news. It's not a big deal, so, please, keep your voice down," I replied.

"So, what all happened?" asked Jax.

"Please don't be mad at me for not telling you, okay? The only reason Rem knows is that she was there in the room when I got back, and I didn't want everyone knowing because I was embarrassed."

"It's okay, Prim. You've been going through a lot lately. You can tell us now," replied Jax.

"Well, we did kiss, but we also did a little bit more…" I trailed off.

"Oh, my fucking god, did you have sex with him?" Vesper asked, a little louder than I would have liked.

"Jesus, Ves, shut the hell up. I think my mom didn't quite hear you back at our house," I replied. "No, we didn't have sex. But I did get on top of him, and I may or may not have felt his erection underneath me."

Before any response could be made by the group, Vesper spilled her drunk all over the front of her shirt.

"What the hell?" yelled Vesper, looking behind her.

I looked up to see Theo had just knocked into the back of Vesper. Theo. Vesper's least favorite person in the world. Those two had this weird tension thing ever since they first met, and it always seemed like they were both out to get each other for some odd reason. I couldn't quite understand the relationship that they had with each other but, the last time I asked Vesper, she said that she hated him. I have yet to ask her any more questions about that. I think it's best if we tread lightly with that one.

"Theo, what the hell? You did that on purpose, you asshole!" yelled Ves.

"Sorry, Miss Valedictorian. Didn't mean to tarnish your royal clothes," replied Theo.

"Shut up. How were you even invited to this party?"

"Uhh, because I'm incredibly attractive and your teammates love me."

"Shouldn't you be getting a head start on studying for next semester or something?"

"I should ask you the same thing. Or have you given up your academic supremacy?" asked Theo.

"Never," replied Vesper with a death glare.

Theo winked and then walked away. I looked over and saw Ves roll her eyes. Although, I could have sworn that I saw a faint smile start at the corner of her lips. Maybe not.

"*Anyway*," I chimed in, "where's Cade tonight, Jax?"

"Oh, he's probably in his room playing games or something. I asked him to come but I don't think he will show," replied Jax.

"Well, at least you tried. You both have classes together, right?" I asked.

"Yeah, we have a graphic design class together. Our majors are similar, so we'll have classes together over the next three years."

I glanced over at Remington, and we shared a smirk.

"What's that look for?" asked Jax.

"Come on. Don't play dumb. You both love games and you basically have the same major. You both spend a lot of time with each other. You don't see what we're getting at here?" asked Vesper.

"Come on. We're just friends. I swear. No romantic feelings at all. Like, at all," replied Jax.

Remington laughed, "If you say so."

"All right, enough dumb talk. Let's go dance," I said, trying to ease the awkward tension. And because it looked like Jax really could use saving. Her face was bright red.

"Thanks for saving me," Jax said as she took my arm and dragged me to the dance floor. "But you know that we aren't letting you get away from us without telling us the rest of your story with Myles, right?"

"I wouldn't have expected anything less," I replied.

Chapter 26

Prim

The room was dark except for neon lights that were hanging at the top of each of the walls. There were so many people packed into this room that I was having a hard time trying to tell who was who. As we were all dancing, I looked over at the wall beside the stairs and thought that I caught a glimpse of Myles. Remington kept giving me drinks and I happily accepted, so my focus returned to the group in front of me. We kept dancing and enjoyed the company of whatever guy came up behind us to get our attention. I kept dancing, but I couldn't help but continue to glance up and look over to where I saw Myles leaning against the wall. So, it was Myles. Heat started to spread through my chest and neck. But what I was seeing looked like a creepier version of Myles which I wasn't used to. What was he doing? It looked like he was just staring at me. Why does he look upset?

"Hey, guys, I'll be right back," I said, leaning over toward Remington so that she could hear me. She nodded and went back to dancing with the guy behind her.

I pushed my way through the crowd on the dance floor over to where Myles was leaning against the wall.

"Myles! Come dance with us," I said. I don't know what was giving me such confidence tonight, but I'm assuming it had something to do with the alcohol. But I also felt weirdly comfortable going up to Myles, even after everything that has gone on between us the last couple of weeks.

"Uh, no, I don't think so. You seem like you're having a good enough time without me," replied Myles, motioning behind me to the floor.

"Now, why would you say that?" I asked.

"The other guys seemed to be enjoying it."

A weird thought came to me then. Is that why he looked upset?

"Are you jealous?" I asked Myles.

Myles cleared his throat. "No, I'm not jealous. Why would I be?"

Before I could answer, one of the guys that I was dancing with earlier came up to me and tapped me on the shoulder.

"Wanna head back out to the floor? I thought we were having a good time out there," said the frat boy as he stared down Myles.

"No, she doesn't," interrupted Myles. "She's going with me."

"But I thought you said…" was all I could say before Myles was pulling me into the middle of all the people dancing.

He spun me around so that my back was to him and then pressed his body into mine. The song playing over the speakers was now *Losing Myself by* Stephen Cornish, so it was definitely one of those songs where everyone gets hyped up and starts dancing all up on each other. And that is exactly what happened. No surprise there. We started to move to the music, but I kept wondering to myself whether or not Myles was drunk. He never acted like this, and I have never seen him angry at someone like the way he was with the frat guy. Although I have to say, Myles is a pretty good dancer. I don't think we've ever danced like this. At least, not this close. He pressed more of himself into me, and I could smell the strawberries. You know, I think that was becoming one of my favorite scents.

I continued to move my hips on Myles, not even realizing that I didn't know where the other girls were. They must have gone to get some more to drink. But, honestly, at this moment, I didn't really care where everyone else is. For whatever reason, this felt really good, so I was going to chase this feeling.

I decided to lean my head back on Myles's chest and continue to move against him. I could feel his hands start to rub along my hips and then to my waist. Was it getting hotter in here or was it just me? I don't think the heat is only related to the amount of alcohol that I've consumed tonight. Am I fucking horny? I felt this way when we were kissing in his room. God, I wanted him to touch me. He just felt so good. This felt right. And is that what I think it is? Myles was getting hard behind me. *Oh, fuck.* This is turning me on even more. I felt Myles leaning down and pressing his lips to my ear.

"Prim, I…" whispered Myles.

"Shh, no talking. Just dance," I replied, continuing to grind on him. He continued to rub me with his hands as they made their way up my stomach and to my...

"I think we should stop," said Myles, starting to back away, apparently taking notice of the fact of where his hands almost explored.

"No, don't stop. Please," I said, pulling Myles back into me.

"Are you sure? I don't want to do anything you're uncomfortable with."

I didn't answer. I couldn't answer. No words were coming to me. I was just feeling the moment, feeling the music, and feeling Myles as he continued to press his erection on me. The friction between us was unmistakable, and I could hear his breaths becoming more labored behind me.

"Oh, God, Prim. This feels good, but I don't think we should be doing this here," said Myles, evidently feeling the same thing I was.

I ignored him and started to dig my hips harder into him. I was into this just as much as he was now. What was happening? I know we had done some things in his room, but this felt different. This was on a different level. I keep telling myself that it is just the party, it's just that we are both drunk, and it's the music's fault. Yes. Absolutely, the music's fault. No, it wasn't the music's fault. I liked this. And I liked that it was Myles behind me. I kept picturing me grabbing his hand and putting it in between my legs in his room. God, I was so wet. I couldn't take this anymore.

"Let's get out of here," I leaned up to say to Myles.

"Wait. What?" Myles asked with a look of shock on his face.

"You heard me."

Myles still looked like he didn't know what to do, so I grabbed him by the arm and led him through the crowd of people to the front door. I grabbed my jacket and then kept holding onto Myles's arm as I dragged him through the front door and to the other side of the street, to my dorm.

"Prim, are you sure? What are you doing? Where are we going?"

"Myles, yes, I'm sure. Please. I just don't want to think tonight, okay? I want you. I've wanted you for a long time, especially after what we did in your room. I can't get it out of my head," I replied, surprised that I put that out there in the open. Well, I guess I figured out how to start the conversation that we needed so desperately. It wasn't, "Hey, Myles, let's talk about what we are to each other." Nope, it wasn't that. I decided to start the conversation out with a bang. I guess quite literally, if what's about to happen is what I'm thinking is going to happen.

Myles stopped dead in the middle of the hall as we got to my room door.

"You what?" asked Myles.

"Don't make me say it again, please," I replied.

"Umm. But since when? How long have you been feeling this?"

"I don't know. It's not important. Look, do you want to fuck me or not?" I asked, more sternly than I intended to.

Myles didn't say a word. He stayed silent and followed me into the room while I locked the door behind us.

"Rem won't be back for a while. I saw her making out with some guy before we left," I said. "I'm sure she will be preoccupied for the rest of the night."

I walked over to turn on the lamp beside my bed. It was the only light on in the room, so it seemed very fitting for a situation like this. Jesus. I was about to have sex with Myles. And the weird thing is that I want to have sex with him. I've never once felt this way during our friendship. What's changing? For a minute, neither of us said anything. Honestly, I think we both didn't really know what to say in a situation like this. Were we actually going to go ahead with this? Was Myles going to be okay with this? I know a lot of people joked about us liking each other as we were growing up, but Myles had always ignored it and denied it. Myles cut the silence.

"Prim, what are we doing? Don't you think we should talk first, at least? This isn't the only thing that I want. I hope you know that."

"I don't know. I'm, uh, I'm really confused about everything. I mean, you're my best friend, but lately…" I trailed off.

"Lately, what?" asked Myles.

"Lately, I've been feeling differently. I want to be around you. I want to kiss you. I want to touch you. I just…" I broke off. "Never mind, forget it. I don't want it to ruin the night."

I decided that the best option in this situation would be to take off my shirt. So, that's exactly what I did. I took off my shirt, got on my bed, and then laid back on the pillow, looking at Myles watching me the whole time.

"Are you sure about this? We don't have to if you're feeling drunk or whatever," said Myles.

"Yes, I'm positive. Please just come here," I replied.

Myles took off his shirt, got onto the bed, and then slowly raised himself over me as I pulled him closer to me. Well, this was a new angle of him. He was staring down at me like he wasn't sure about anything. It was new territory for both of us, but he looked incredibly nervous. I was also nervous, but I think I would need to lead this one.

"Prim, I..." started Myles.

"Shh, just kiss me, Myles," I replied.

Myles took one last look into my eyes before he leaned down and kissed me on my forehead. Then he moved and kissed the corner of my mouth.

"Myles, please..." I started.

"I also just wanted to clarify something for you. I don't want to fuck you," said Myles.

I didn't really know how to take that statement. I started getting up and leaned up onto my elbows.

"You should have just said something if you didn't want to," I said continuing to try to move off the bed.

"No, no! That's not what I meant," replied Myles.

I lay back down on the pillow, unsure of what he was going to continue saying. Was he saying that he didn't want to have sex with me?

"Then what did you mean?" I asked.

"I mean, I don't want to *fuck* you. I want to make love to you. I know that sounds fucking corny as hell, but I mean it. Prim, this is what I've wanted, and it's been so hard trying to find the words to tell you. I just didn't expect me to say them during something like this."

My heart is fluttering in my chest at this point. Umm, where is he going with this conversation? Why am I feeling shy right now?

"Then do it," I said with all the confidence I could muster in this scenario. I could see the heat flare in Myles's eyes at that statement. The atmosphere changed and I could see the veins in his arms and neck flexing.

"What do you want me to do to you?" asked Myles, breathing heavily in and out.

Wow. This was a side of Myles that I have never seen before. Was he like this with the girls he dated in high school? My cheeks are absolutely getting red right now, I just know it. Heat is flaring throughout my whole body, and I could feel myself getting wet just by him asking me that question.

"I want to feel you in me," I replied, looking Myles right in the eyes.

"Yeah?" asked Myles.

I nodded and then Myles started to slowly unbutton my jeans.

"Is this, okay?" asked Myles.

"Yes, keep going," I replied.

Myles pulled the zipper down and took off my pants.

"Panties too?"

"Yes, take them off," I replied, fully appreciating this conversation. Why was he being so gentle? I was going back and forth between wanting him to continue to be like this or if I wanted him to ravage me.

As Myles was taking off my panties, he started to softly kiss my navel and then down to my thighs.

"Oh," I said without realizing that I was moaning as he caressed my thighs. "Please keep going." Goosebumps formed all over my arms and down my legs.

I couldn't quite explain the look that Myles had on his face after I moaned. It looked almost animalistic.

"Now, what do you want?" asked Myles, licking his lower lip.

"I want you to feel me."

"How? Like this?" asked Myles, slowly inserting two fingers into me as I arched my back at his touch.

"Oh, Myles, more," I squealed.

"More?"

He then inserted a third finger and continued pumping his fingers as I continued to writhe underneath him. This felt so fucking good. I hope this sensation never stops. I was leaking all around his fingers, and I felt like I was so close to coming already. I looked down and realized that Myles's erection was bursting through his jeans, and it looked uncomfortable.

"Why don't you take your pants off? That seems painful," I told Myles.

Myles took his fingers out of me and put them in my mouth so that I could taste myself.

"Mmm, you taste so good, don't you?" he asked, a low growl forming deep in his throat.

I was so aroused right now. He removed his fingers and took off his jeans and boxers.

"Better?" I asked, barely able to get out the word.

"Much better. Open your legs more for me, Prim baby. I want you ready for me."

Wait. Did he just call me baby? And why was that such a turn-on? His words were melting me all the way through. He was so dirty, and I was enjoying every single minute of it. I did what he asked and opened my legs and as soon as I did, I felt Myles's mouth on my center. I had no time to prepare.

"Oh, Myles, God. Yes," I moaned.

I could feel all the sensations throughout my whole body. I had never experienced all these sensations and emotions at one time before. What was happening between the two of us? Myles kept licking, sucking, and kissing my center. He pulled at my clit with his teeth and that about did me in. I realized that I was almost at the edge of release.

"Yes, yes. Don't stop. I'm almost there." As soon as I said that Myles lifted his hand and slowly started circling my clit while his tongue was still inside me. This was the best feeling ever.

"Fuck, Myles! Oh god," I yelled as I orgasmed around his mouth.

Myles waited until I was done with my release and then he kissed the top of my opening. It sent a shiver through me. I started to pull at his arms.

"Oh, no. Not yet. I'm not done with you," he said.

Holy fuck.

He wiped his mouth the back of his hand, and then leaned back down and softly took my clit between his teeth again. I moaned and dug my fingers into his shoulder blades. As he was sucking on my clit, he pushed three fingers into me and continued to fuck me.

"Come for me, baby," he said. I exploded and squeezed around his fingers. He didn't stop fucking me with his fingers until I was completely done and out of breath.

"Get up here. It's your turn," I said as I pulled Myles up to me and kissed him. I could taste myself on his lips which was actually hot as fuck. I sucked on his tongue as he wrapped his lips around mine. "I have condoms in my stand if you want to grab one."

Myles opened the drawer and took out a condom from the box.

"Do you want to put it on, or do you want me to do it?" asked Myles, looking as if he was smirking.

"You do it," I replied.

"I can't promise I'm going to last very long because that was the sexiest thing I've ever seen," said Myles as he ripped open the condom and put it on himself.

"What?" I asked.

"You. Watching you being pleasured. It was really hot," replied Myles.

"Just come here and fuck... oh, sorry, *make love* to me," I said as I smiled up at Myles.

"Yes, ma'am," said Myles, and then lowered himself and entered me slowly.

I moaned and arched my back as he filled me completely.

"Are you okay? Tell me if I'm hurting you."

"Yes. I promise. You don't have to be gentle with me," I assured him.

As if on cue, Myles started to speed up his thrusts as he kissed my neck and lips. I was totally into this. This. This is what I've been missing in my life.

"Fuck, Myles. Yes!"

"Oh, Prim. God, you're so beautiful," grunted Myles as he continued thrusting in and out of me.

"Harder, Myles, harder. I need more," I begged.

Myles continued to pound into me until it seemed as though he was close to climax. I felt my third release slowly coming as heat prickled at the base of my spine.

"Myles, I'm about to come. Are you close?"

"Almost there," replied Myles, almost out of breath.

My body tensed and I could feel myself tightening around Myles inside me. That, apparently, was all that Myles needed to spur his own climax.

"Prim, I'm coming. I, I'm coming," Myles blurted out as he released inside of me. He collapsed on top of me. "Holy shit, that was amazing."

At that moment, I didn't realize what was happening or why, but I started crying. So many emotions overtook me, and I was just starting to put two and two together. I just had sex with my best friend. I've known this guy since third grade. What was going to happen after this? Would he still look at me the same way? Panic creeped up every inch of me. Myles saw my breakdown and turned to me, looking panicked.

"Prim, oh, my god! What's wrong? Did I hurt you?!" asked Myles.

"No, you didn't hurt me. But Myles. What did we just do? Oh, my god, this is going to ruin everything, isn't it?" I asked.

"What do you mean, ruin everything?"

"Our friendship. Friends don't do what we just did," I said, the panic evident in my voice. "I know we've kissed already, but this is so much different. This is… this is, well, I don't know what this is."

"It's not going to ruin anything. We will just have to talk about it and move forward with whatever decision we make. What would you like to do? Do you want to talk about whatever is going through your mind right now?" asked Myles.

"Not right now, no. I think I would like to be alone. Rem is going to be back soon anyway. You should probably leave before she gets back. I'm sorry. I shouldn't have brought you back here. It was a mistake." Did I think it was actually a mistake? No, it wasn't a mistake. But I wasn't ready to admit to him that this was everything in my life that I didn't know that I needed. This was terrifying.

I could see all the color draining from his face. "You think this was a mistake?" asked Myles with a hurt tone in his voice.

"I'm sorry, Myles."

I don't think Myles knew what to say after that. He looked so hurt that I almost wanted to take back what I said. But I didn't know what to say either. I just needed space and time to think about what we just did. My body was shaking, I was so panicked. I needed him out of here so that I could cry without anyone seeing me. I looked over and saw that Myles had gotten off the bed and was throwing away the condom in the trash can. He started to get dressed and then walked toward the door. After opening the door, he turned to face me.

"I don't think this was a mistake. Nothing like this with you could ever be anywhere close to a mistake," Myles said.

I looked up at his eyes and noticed that some tears were filling his eyes. "Are you going to be okay tonight?" he asked.

"I'll be fine," I replied. I didn't intend to sound so short with him, but I don't think I could have continued the conversation without crying and I didn't want to keep doing that in front of him. This was already embarrassing enough.

"Okay. I'll talk to you later then. Goodnight, Prim."

"Goodnight. I'm sorry," I said, but it was no use. Myles had already closed the door.

What am I supposed to do? Why do I keep pulling myself away from the one person I know won't ever hurt me? I'm making this so difficult for both of us. I know how he feels. I know how I feel. But, still, something keeps stopping me. I know I'm being a coward. He deserves someone who isn't as fucked up as me. I turned over and grabbed my elephant stuffed animal and pulled him close to my chest.

"What do I do now, Mr. Tusky? I think I'm in love with him."

***

The next morning, I rolled over on the bed and picked up my phone off the bedside table. I kind of was expecting this. I had a text from Myles. All the events from last night kept coming back to me. The orgasms. Myles kissing me. Me pushing him away, again. Him leaving my room with tears in his eyes.

Myles–I know that I shouldn't be texting you right now, but do you want to ride home with me for break or are you going to take your car?

Well, I *was* planning to ask Myles to get a ride from him so I didn't have to pay for gas but, after what happened last night, I can't do that.

Me–No, I'm going to drive my car back. Thanks.

Myles–Okay. I know we might not be in the best place right now, but am I going to get to see you over break?

Me–Umm, I think I'm going to need some time to think about things. I'm sorry. It's not you. I promise.

Myles–We're going to need to talk at some point. We can't keep putting off these conversations, Prim. This keeps happening, and I don't know how much more of this I can take, especially after what happened last night. That meant something to me, and you pushed me away like I was nothing to you.

Me–I know, and we will talk. I didn't mean to push you away like that, but I just need some time. Have a good break, and I'll see you when we get back.

There weren't any more responses from Myles. Crying into my pillow, all I could think of was that I was losing my best friend.

Chapter 27

Prim

I had only been back home for less than twenty-four hours before my phone started buzzing. I looked at my messages and realized that it was from the group chat that I have with Rem, Vesper, and Jax. We all had plans to meet up at some point over Winter Break. We had over a month off, so we wanted to make sure we saw each other at least once during the break. We also had plans of exchanging Christmas gifts, so I reminded myself to go shopping later.

Rem–Prim, did you hear the news?

Me–What news?

Ves–Oh, my god, Prim. You're going to freak out.

Me–What the hell are you talking about?

Jax–Rem, would you just tell her?

Rem–Jared dropped out of school.

Me–Oh, my god. Are you serious? Why?

Rem–I overheard it at the grocery store yesterday afternoon when I got home. Some of my friends from high school were talking about it in the aisle next to me, so I listened in.

Me–How do they know?

Rem–Well, I told you he went to my rival high school, and was very popular, so word travels fast since our schools are only fifteen minutes away from each other.

Jax–I knew he was a piece of shit.

Ves–Wait, wait. You must explain why.

Rem–His parents were pissed that he caused all that shit at school, so they made him drop out. I didn't hear much else of what they were saying, but I'm pretty sure he's going to transfer. Either that or take a year off and then go back to school after that.

Me–His parents made him drop out just because of him being drunk and getting into a fight?

Ves–Damn, Prim. How haven't you heard all of this yet? That's not all he did!

Rem–He had a meeting with the Dean on Friday before he left and, apparently, he got in her face about everything and was claiming bullshit on the fight, even though everyone knew the police were involved. He was trying to say that it wasn't him. School security had to escort him off campus, but not before he threw in a couple of punches. His parents found out about everything when the Dean called them so, when he got home yesterday, they told him that he was dropping out.

Me–What the actual fuck.

Jax–Well, bright side. At least you won't have to see him at school anymore!

Me–This is crazy.

Ves–I wonder if Myles has heard about it. Have you talked to him at all since the party?

I hadn't told the girls what happened between me and Myles the night of the party. I saw them before we left for break and they asked me where I had gone after the party, but I just said that I came back a little early because I wasn't feeling very well and had too much to drink. They didn't question me after that because they had all had too much to drink too. Rem hadn't come back that night, so she didn't have to see Myles doing the walk of shame out of our room. It was a walk of shame that I had forced on him, so I did feel a pang of guilt about that.

Me–No, I'm sure he left the party with Sabrina and Lawrence. He did text me the morning after to ask me if I wanted a ride home, but I decided to drive my car home instead.

Jax–You still owe us the full story of what happened between you two… you're gonna spill everything when we get together.

Me–And here I was hoping that you all had forgotten

Jax–Not when that's the most exciting news we've heard all semester. Sorry, love. Not going to happen.

Two minutes after we stopped texting, Rem called me.

"So, first, I wanted to check-in and ask if you are, okay?" Rem asked. "About everything with both Jared and Myles. How are you holding up?"

"Well, with Jared, I really don't care. Any feelings that I had for him have gone out the window at this point. Rem, I honestly can't believe that I dated him. What was I thinking?"

"Prim, you must stop blaming yourself. You did nothing wrong. Now, you get to move on and onto something better. Speaking of…" she trailed off.

"Yes?" I asked.

"I know about you and Myles."

"What do you mean? Of course, you know about Myles. I told you that we kissed."

"No, that's not what I mean. I know you two slept together."

"What? How?" I asked, panic rising in my throat.

"Well, thanks for confirming that for me," Rem replied as I could hear her laughing on the other end of the phone.

"Shit. How did you find out?"

"I saw you two leave the party together. I wasn't quite sure, but I felt like something else would happen between you two. I just didn't know when. I came back to our room a little later, and I, uh…"

"You what?"

"I may have heard you two having sex."

"Oh, my god. You did not," I replied, thankful that she couldn't see my face. This was so embarrassing.

"I mean, I just kind of put two and two together. You both left the party and then I heard you in the room, so I figured it was Myles. From what I could hear, he seems to be excellent in bed."

I could almost see her mischievous grin as she said those words.

"Please, never mention this ever again. Can you die from embarrassment?" I asked.

"I'm so sorry. I had to tease you," Rem said as she started laughing aloud. "But, seriously though, what are you two right now?"

"I don't know. I may have kicked him out afterwards."

"What? Why?"

"Because I panicked and freaked out that I had just had sex with my best friend. I know it's stupid, but I was fine in the moment and then, when we were done, I just freaked and started crying."

"Oh, Prim, I'm so sorry."

"That's not the worst of it, though. I told him that it was a mistake."

"Yikes. How did he take it?"

"I'm not sure. He left soon after that."

"Well, what are you going to do now?"

"Try to figure out what we are, I guess, and what I want us to be."

"Prim, babe, I think you already know the answer to that. I think at this point, you need to move past the fact that he's your best friend. The friendship boundary has already been long since crossed with you two. You're getting too caught up in that aspect, so it's clouding your judgment as to what you two could be."

"I know, you're right. It's just hard to move past having a friendship with him for over ten years and then, now, suddenly, being intimate with him.

"I understand that. But you must admit. You have been going back and forth with him lately. I'm sure that's hard on him so as much as it's hard on you."

"I know I haven't made this very easy for him. Honestly, I'm surprised he still wants to talk to me."

"I'm not surprised at all. That kid is head over heels in love with you. He worships the ground you walk on, and you know he would do anything for you."

Everything that Rem was saying was true. I have been too hard on Myles, and he just keeps coming back no matter how many times I keep trying to push him away. It was time to decide.

***

A week-and-a-half later and I found myself three days before Christmas. I probably shouldn't have waited until the last minute to go shopping, but better late than never. I know I needed to get something for my mom and dad, and I should probably get something for Myles. We always do, and I've never missed a year. I can't start now. Before I head to the mall, I decide to stop at the local bookstore down the street from my house. I haven't been able to read a lot that wasn't academic related during the semester so, now that it's break, I'm going to try and get back to my roots. I've been coming to *Used and Loved* bookstore since I was younger, so this has always felt like a safe space for me.

I walk into the store and greet the owner. She recognizes me, of course, from all of my visits growing up, so we catch up a little and then I start browsing the shelves. As I walk into the fiction aisle, I notice that there's a guy holding two books in his hand and staring between them. I also notice that I recognize this guy. *Chad*. My ex-boyfriend from high school. The one who broke up with me after graduation. Well, this was going to be awkward. Chad looked up with a look of recognition on his face.

"Prim, hey!" he said as he walked closer to me. "It's been a while. How have you been?"

"Hey, Chad. I've been doing well. Just enjoying break as much as I can. How about you?"

"I'm doing great, thanks. Although, I could use your help with something. I told my mom I would get her a book for Christmas, but I can't decide which one of these books I should go for. Any advice?"

I look at the two books; one is a romance and the other is a thriller.

"I think your best bet would be the romance book. I think I remember your mom's tastes, and romance is definitely up her alley."

"Good idea. Thanks," Chad replied as he put the thriller back on the shelf. "So, I know we haven't seen each other in a while, but would you want to grab a coffee or something and catch up?"

"Uh, sure, yeah. That sounds good. Now?" I asked.

"Yeah, unless you're busy."

"No, now is fine."

"Great. My treat."

Luckily, there was a coffee shop right across the street. That was the nice thing about living in a small town. All the shops were local and very close to each other. We went up to the counter and ordered two lattes and two scones. There were a lot of people in here, so the only empty seat left was right in front of the window. I normally didn't like sitting in front of the window in places because I always felt like someone was watching me and it didn't feel as private.

"So, seriously, how have you been Prim? We haven't talked at all since the beginning of the summer," said Chad.

"And whose fault is that?" I asked, my tone more serious than I had intended it to be.

"Touché," he replied. "Okay, I deserved that one."

"Sorry. I shouldn't have said that. Anyway, I can't say that I've been doing great, but I can't say that I've been doing awful, so somewhere in the middle of those," I said with a little laugh.

"What's going on?"

"Well, I was seeing someone at school, but we broke up a couple of weeks back."

"I'm sorry to hear that."

"It's okay. I'm over it now. He wasn't the greatest."

"Well, then he doesn't deserve you. Speaking of someone who didn't deserve you, I'm sorry about everything that happened over the summer."

"I've already forgiven you and, honestly, I think it was for the best. We wouldn't have been able to work throughout college, so it was the right decision."

He nodded in agreement. "So, do you still keep in touch with Myles or get to see him at all?"

"Well, of course, we do. It would be kind of hard not to see each other at the same school, don't you think?"

"Wait, I thought you went to Silver Creek. Didn't Myles go to Lakewood University?" he asked.

"No. We both go to Silver Creek. What are you talking about?"

"Oh, I overheard Myles talking to his counselor in high school about going to Lakewood. It was his dream school. He had the acceptance letter and everything. He must have changed his mind, I guess."

I really didn't know what to think. Why didn't Myles tell me?

"He told me he only wanted to go to Silver Creek. Why would he do that?" I asked.

"I'm going to hazard a guess and say that it was to follow you. But, hey, what do I know."

"What do you mean?"

"Come on, Prim. Everyone knows that Myles was in love with you in high school. Since he followed you to school, I'm going to say that he's still in love with you."

"How was I the only one who didn't realize this until now?" I asked.

"Honestly, I have no idea. It was obvious," Chad replied. "Why do you think he hated me so much?"

I feel so stupid. Of course, he loved me. No wonder he didn't get along with any of my boyfriends in high school. I just thought it was a best friend thing and he was trying to protect me. I am the dumbest person on the planet. It was also pretty obvious why he never told me about getting into Lakewood. I would have made him go there, especially if I knew that it was his dream school. *Shit.*

"Chad, I'm sorry, but I have to go. Thanks for the coffee. It was nice catching up with you," I said as I grabbed my jacket off the back of the chair, threw the cup in the trash, and walked across the street to my car.

I didn't know what I needed to do, but I just knew that I needed to do something. I was feeling a mix between heartbreak and anger. Heartbreak for not realizing how Myles felt about me sooner or how I felt about him. Anger for Myles lying to me about Lakewood and following me to school. Damnit, Myles, what were you thinking? I didn't know which emotion to act on first, so I just drove home.

When I got home, my parents were both sitting in the living room watching TV. I slowly walked up to them, looked at them, and then burst into tears.

"Prim, what's wrong?" asked my mom.

"I'm so stupid. This is all my fault. If only I had realized sooner, none of this would have happened."

"Slow down, honey. What are you talking about? What's your fault?"

"Did you know?" I asked.

"Did we know what?" asked my dad.

"Did you know that Myles was supposed to go to Lakewood and not Silver Creek?"

They both looked at each other and nodded.

"We knew. I found out from your advisor, and then he confirmed it before he came to campus the first day."

"Why didn't you tell me?"

"Because we didn't think it was our place to tell you, and he asked us not to say anything. We couldn't break that promise."

"You should have told me. No, better yet, he should have told me. I'm so mad at him right now."

"Honey don't be mad at him. He has his reasons for keeping it from you."

Tears stream down my face and my mom reaches up and brushes them away.

"You know why he kept it from you, don't you?" asked my mom.

I nodded, not able to form any words because of all the sobs.

"Mom, I've been so selfish. All of these years, and it's taken me this long to realize how I feel about him. It was right in front of me."

"And how do you feel about him, Prim?"

I look up into her eyes and admit the one thing I haven't been able to say aloud to anyone else.

"I love him, Mom."

She nodded. "We were hoping you were going to figure it out sooner rather than later. That boy is madly in love with you."

"You knew that too? Was no one going to clue me in as to what was going on?"

"We talked to Myles about this before, but you needed to figure that out for yourself. You had to make your own decisions and figure out how you felt on your own. We couldn't do that for you, and we didn't want to force you into anything if you really didn't feel the same way back."

"So, he told everyone else how he felt except for me?" I asked.

"Prim, he might not have said the words out loud to you, but just think back over the years. Think about everything that you've been through and everything that he's done. They say that actions speak louder than words."

"I just wish I would have known sooner. I never would have… I could have…" I shook my head, not being able to finish my sentence.

"How do you feel about him? Is this something that you would want to pursue with him?"

"I hate what we're going through right now. Everything has been so awkward between us ever since we got to school. I guess I now know why. Mom, I love him. I love him so much, and I'm so mad at myself for not realizing it until now."

"Then, sweety, I think you need to tell him."

I nodded. Like I said before, it was time to decide. Well, I just made the decision. I stood up from the couch.

"Uh, I need to go. I, uh, I'll be back later," I said as I grabbed my car keys from the table and rushed out the door.

Chapter 28

Myles

Prim thought it was a mistake. She actually thought that it was a mistake. Does she not feel anything for me? I'm lying in my bed at home playing that night over and over in my head. I got home from school about a week-and-a-half ago, and my parents definitely realized that something is wrong with me. I haven't really wanted to do much since I've been home. I'm afraid that if I go outside or around town, I'll see Prim. I even texted her and offered to take her home since we only live ten minutes from one another, but she turned it down. I guess I understand that. She's embarrassed. But I want her to realize that I'm embarrassed too. But it's also something that we need to talk about, which I told her before we left for break.

I just can't believe that she kicked me out of her room. She started crying that night and I freaked out because I thought that I hurt her or something. But she panicked. I was freaking out a bit too, but I wish we could have done it together. We keep getting ourselves caught in this endless cycle or pushing each other away. Then, we avoid each other for weeks on end.

Prim and I had sex. That hadn't really sunken in fully until a couple of days after I got home. She initiated everything and I went along with her. Of course, I wanted to have sex with her. But it wasn't just about that for me. I wanted the emotional connection too. I know that our friendship is officially ruined. If it was ruined after the night of the kiss, it was certainly ruined now. No coming back from this one. This was make or break. I keep replaying that night over and over in my head and I'm trying to figure out where it went wrong. When Prim first suggested that we go back to her room, I was too surprised to say anything. But everything just felt so natural. Maybe I fucked it up by talking too much. Maybe I came on too strong. I don't know. It just felt so good. She felt so good. And not just having sex with her. Just being that close to her. This is going to be the longest break ever.

It was three days before Christmas, and my parents were starting to wrap presents. My grandparents, aunts and uncles are all coming over Christmas day, so we've been getting the house cleaned and ready for the visitors. I was getting a little hungry, so I decided I would go pick up some lunch and coffees for us. It's the least I could do as I haven't been very good company since I got home.

"Hey, I'm going to head to the coffee shop in town. Do you want me to pick up some sandwiches and coffee for you two while you're wrapping?" I asked.

"Sure, honey, that would be great. Thanks," my mom replied.

"What coffee do you both want?"

"How about two peppermint mochas?" asked my dad.

"I didn't know you liked those holiday drinks?"

"Of course, I do," my dad replied.

"Sounds good. Turkey sandwiches, okay?"

"And some of that banana bread if they still have any."

I pick up my car keys and wallet and head out the front door. I could use the time outside. I haven't really left the house for anything since I've been home. My parents are going out shopping again later because they still need to buy a couple more gifts for the family, but I also turned them down for that. So, really, this was the least that I could do for them. I really need to snap out of whatever this mood is. I don't want it to spoil the holidays. But I'm just not sure when I'm going to get to see Prim again. She said she needed space, which I completely understand, but this is just a really shitty time to ask for space.

I turn onto Ridge Lane and park my car across the street from the coffee shop. *Coffee and Things* was the name of the place. The "things" part really did mean what they are advertising. The shop had so much more than just coffee so, if you wanted to, you could get a three-course meal here. It was basically half-coffee shop, half-deli. Prim and I would always come here during high school on the weekends and then we would go to the bookstore across the street. I think seeing her browsing through the shelves was one of the first things that made me realize that I was in love with her. She was so happy. She would spend days on end in a bookstore if you let her.

I get out of my car and I'm about to cross the street when I notice two people that I recognize sitting at a table by the window. One of them was Prim. The other one was Chad. *Chad?* What the fuck was Prim doing with Chad? Chad, aka Prim's ex-boyfriend who dumped her two weeks after graduation because he wanted to "spread his wings" and be free during college. That was obviously code for 'I'm going to hook up with as many people as possible and don't want to be tied down to anyone while I'm doing it.' I lean against my car and watch them for a couple of minutes. From the outside, if anyone were watching me, it would look like I was some kind of a creep. I guess I wouldn't blame them if they saw me like this. I start to wonder how long she has been talking to Chad or if she just casually saw him. I was also wondering whose idea it was to hang out in the first place. I hoped it wasn't hers. I'm so fucking tired of seeing them together. I'm so fucking tired of seeing her with any guy, let alone one of her ex-boyfriends. That should be me with her, not them.

Fuck this. I got back in my car and headed down the street further into town. No way was I going in there. I did not want or need that kind of confrontation. Plus, I don't know how I would be able to handle myself around Chad, so I better not risk it. They're probably talking about when they were dating in and catching up on all of that. How sweet. First Jared and now Chad. Their names even scream "asshole." I give up. No matter how hard I try, these things never work out in my favor and I'm so sick of it.

I get home after picking up coffee and turkey sandwiches that were *not* from *Coffee and Things*. My parents were still in the middle of wrapping gifts.

"Mom, Dad. I need to talk to you about something that I've been thinking about for a while," I said as I sat down on the chair next to both.

"Okay. Is everything all right?" my dad asked.

"Not really, no. I'm sorry I've been in a shit mood ever since I got home, but things with Prim aren't going well and I don't have many options left."

"What brought all of this up?"

"I saw Prim with her ex-boyfriend at the coffee shop."

"Oh. I'm sorry, Myles," replied my mom.

"I started thinking about this back at school a month or so ago, but I think that the best decision for me would be to transfer schools."

"You want to transfer?"

"Yes. I've already been in contact with Lakewood, and they said all of my credits would transfer, so I wouldn't be behind in anything."

"Wow. So, you have been thinking about this for a while."

"I have, yeah. I made a mistake going to Silver Creek. I never should have accepted. I should have just told Prim about Lakewood and none of this would have happened. I can't keep seeing her with other people. I'm in too much pain and I can't do it anymore. I thought I could handle it when we first went, but I also didn't expect her to start dating someone so soon into the semester. I got up to school and then, there he was. Literally, in her dorm room. It was a great first impression," I said sarcastically.

My mom and dad both looked at each other and then back at me.

"Myles, this is your decision to make, so we're not going to get in your way. We just want to make sure you're thinking about this thoroughly before you make any decisions," my dad replied.

"I have thought it through. We've only been in school for one semester and it's already unbearable. I literally didn't hang out with her because I couldn't stand seeing her with Jared. I can't keep doing that. I would never be able to see her if that was the case. I can't do it anymore. It hurts too much."

"I'm so sorry this is happening, honey. I didn't realize you were in so much pain," my mom said.

"I guess I didn't realize how much pain I was in until recently either. I just kept avoiding the issue. What should I do?"

"Again, this is completely your decision but, if you feel that this is something that you need to do, you have our full support. We just want you to be happy, son," my dad replied.

***

Thirty minutes later, I get a text message from Prim.

Prim–Are you at home? I need to talk to you.

I'm sure she was going to tell me all about her little date with Chad, so I decided to ignore her message. I threw my phone down on my desk and fell into my bed. Another buzz from my phone.

<u>Prim</u>–Myles Aratis. You better fucking answer me right now.

Another ignore. I don't care if she used my last name. Although, I was a little curious to find out why she was so adamant on contacting me. Another buzz. This time it was a phone call. I clicked the button on the side of my phone and let it go to voicemail. I wasn't in the mood.

Five minutes later, I heard the doorbell ring. My parents were both getting ready to go out shopping, so I ran downstairs and opened the door.

Prim.

Chapter 29

Prim

If Myles doesn't answer me one more time, I'm going to lose my shit. I've texted him twice and tried calling him, and he still isn't answering me. I know he ignored my call because it went straight to voicemail. I'm five minutes away from his house. This is going to be really awkward if I just storm up to his house and he isn't home. Then, I'll be stuck trying and failing to explain the situation and why I seem so upset. Because I am upset. He lied to me, and I have some words to say.

I pull up in front of his house, park my car on the side of the street, and walk up to his front door. Both his car and his parent's car are in the driveway, so I know at least someone is home.

I ring the doorbell and wait until someone answers. I hear someone running down the stairs, so I'm going to assume it was Myles. I don't really think either of his parents would willingly run down the stairs to get the front door. The door opened and Myles came into view. He stared at me for a couple of seconds before he said anything.

"Prim, what are you doing here?" he asked.

"There are many reasons why I'm here, Myles. One of them being, why the hell are you ignoring my messages? We'll get to the more important stuff later," I replied.

Before I could say anything else, I saw Mr. and Mrs. Aratis come into view behind Myles.

"Oh, Prim, honey, it's so nice to see you. How are you?" asked Mrs. Aratis.

"I've been pretty good, Mrs. Aratis. How about you?" I replied.

"We've been good but busy. The family is coming over for Christmas, so we're trying to get everything ready. We're actually about to head out to the mall to do some more shopping."

"Is Myles going with you?"

"No, he said he didn't want to go this time. Did you need him for something?"

"Yeah, if you don't mind," I replied as I glared over at Myles who had started to move behind his parents for, what I could only assume was, protection from me.

"He's all yours. We should be gone for a couple of hours, so feel free to order something for dinner, if you want," said Mrs. Aratis. She patted me on the shoulder as she walked out the front door followed by Mr. Aratis.

"Hi, Prim. Nice to see you," said Mr. Aratis.

"You too. Have a nice shopping trip," I said as they got in their car and drove off down the street.

I turned back toward Myles as soon as they drove away, and he started backing away from me.

"I'm going to go make some coffee. You want some?" he asked without waiting to hear my answer. He walked toward the kitchen.

"Myles, we need to talk. You would have known that if you read my messages or picked up my phone call."

"I saw your messages."

"Then why didn't you respond to any of them?"

"Because I didn't want to, okay?"

"And why didn't you want to?"

"A lot of shit has been happening lately. You kick me out of your room after we had sex and you're just still expecting me to always be here whenever you need me. I'm tired of doing that, Prim. You said I was a mistake. And then you freaked out and acted like that night didn't mean anything to you. I know you felt something. You initiated it, remember?"

"Yes, I did initiate it. But that's not why I came over here. I mean, it's part of why I came over here, but there's something else."

"Oh, you mean like how you were hanging out with Chad earlier?"

"How did you know that I was with Chad?"

"That's not the point. But, if you must know, I saw you two sitting in the coffee shop. I went to go pick up coffees and sandwiches, but I happened to see you two instead, so I didn't go in. I didn't want to cause any confrontations."

"And when you saw us, you thought that it was because we were getting back together? Is that why you're so upset right now?"

"Maybe."

"Myles, that's ridiculous. Why would I want to get back together with him?"

"I don't know, you tell me."

"I saw him at the bookstore across the street and he asked me if I wanted to grab a coffee and catch up. It was all innocent. I helped him pick out a book for his mom for Christmas and then we walked across the street."

He nodded and looked down at the ground. I don't blame him for misunderstanding the situation though. If the roles were reversed, I would think the same thing.

"Speaking of Chad, he told me something very interesting while we were having coffee."

"And what was that?"

"Myles, when were you going to tell me about Lakewood?"

I could see his entire body tense after I finished the question. His face flushed and he was looking anywhere in the room except at me.

"What do you mean Lakewood?" he asked.

"Don't play dumb. Chad told me that you were accepted to Lakewood and that it was your dream school."

"I see he's still being an asshole," he replied.

"Don't change the subject."

"Listen. I never wanted you to find out about this. It wasn't a big deal. Yes, I wanted to go to Lakewood and, yes, it was my dream school because of their psychology program. You were just so happy when you thought that we were going to Silver Creek together, that I couldn't risk not seeing you anymore. I was planning to tell you when I got to your house the day we accepted for Silver Creek, but then I saw your face and I knew I couldn't go to Lakewood."

"Why didn't you tell me that you wanted to go there instead of Silver Creek?"

"Do you still really not know why? After everything that we have been through lately, and you still don't know why I chose Silver Creek over Lakewood? Goddammit, Prim. I would have followed you anywhere. Why the fuck do you think I've kept this from you the whole time?"

My breath got caught in my throat.

"Because you have feelings for me," I stated. It wasn't a question. I already knew the answer.

"Do you want to know something? Do you know how I wanted space and distance from you?"

I nodded.

"Do you know how hard that was for me? We have never had to do anything like that before. Ever. Prim, I've even looked into transferring schools next semester because I can't bear to see you with someone else again. I can't keep doing this. I'm so tired of seeing you be happy with other people who aren't me."

"You're transferring?" I asked, the taste of bile rising in my throat at the thought of being away from Myles.

"I haven't made my final decision yet, but Lakewood said it would be an easy transfer if I wanted it."

"You're going to leave me?"

"You think I want to leave you, Prim? The whole fucking reason I chose to go to Silver Creek was so that I could be with you. The thought of not being near you every day makes me nauseous. But I hate seeing you with other people. They aren't good enough for you. None of them are. I'm surprised I only punched Jared, let alone kill him."

"Jared dropped out of school," I replied, knowing that this wasn't the best time for me to say this, but I wanted to make sure that Myles had all the facts straight before he made his decision.

"He dropped out. Why?"

"His parents made him because of everything that he did at campus. Apparently, he caused some more trouble with campus security and the Dean when he got back to school, so his parents pulled him out. I just wanted you to know."

"Prim, what else do you want me to do? Do you want me to get on my hands and knees in front of you and tell you how much I'm in love with you? How much I think about you every fucking day. How I can't get you out of my head no matter how hard I try. How I wanted to murder Jared the entire time you two were dating. How every time you come close to me my heart races and I start to sweat all over my body. How ever since we first kissed, I can't stop replaying it in my head. How I will literally bend over backwards to do anything and everything for you to be happy. How your smile lights up the entire room whenever you look at me."

At this point, there were tears streaming down my face and I couldn't help the sobs that were coming out of me. I must tell him.

"You have no idea how much you mean to me, Prim. If you can't see that you are my entire world, I don't know what else to tell you. Of course, I wasn't going to go to Lakewood. How could I go there if the one person I loved the most in the world was somewhere else? I didn't know what to expect and I didn't think that we would ever be together, but I still wanted to be near you. I needed to be near you, even if that meant watching you with someone else. But it's gotten too hard to do that. I was in so much pain when you were with Jared because I knew how much of a dick he was."

"Myles, I…"

"Please, let me get this out, Prim. I've been holding it in for so long and you need to hear it."

I nodded.

"You mean everything to me. I am deeply and excruciatingly in love with you. Sometimes it hurts me just how much I love you. What else do you want me to do or say? Tell me, please, and I'll do it. I'll do anything."

"You don't need to say or do anything else. You've already shown me over the years just how much you love me, and I was too stupid to see it. It's my turn now."

"Your turn for what?"

"My turn to tell you how much I love you," I replied.

"What?" he said as he looked me in the eyes.

"I love you, Myles. I'm *in* love with you. I'm so sorry I didn't realize it until now, but I'm so in love with you. You're everything I never knew that I needed. You've always been right here with me and, I guess, I chose to ignore it because I didn't know anything else. I've spent most of this semester hating the fact that you and Sabrina were together all the time. I was jealous and, at first, I couldn't understand why, but now I know. I love you. I think I've always loved you. It just took everyone else around me to find out before I could accept it. I was so afraid that this was going to ruin our friendship, that I couldn't see past it and into the future. I couldn't see how great you are, and I couldn't see how amazing you would be with me."

A tear fell out of each of his eyes, and I moved closer to him, lifted my finger to his cheek and wiped them away. He leaned his cheek into the palm of my hand.

"Myles, I'm so sorry for everything. I'm so sorry that I kept pushing you away because I thought it would be easier than facing how I felt about you. I'm sorry that we've wasted so much time when we could have been together because I didn't see what was right in front of me. You mean so much to me, Myles. I fucked this whole thing up. It's my fault. I've hurt you so much over the years and I can't say I'm sorry enough."

"It's not your fault, baby," he replied. I closed my eyes as he gently put his hand on my cheek and traced a path down my neck.

"Call me that again," I said as I ran my hand up the length of his arm.

He bent down until his mouth was right at my ear.

"Baby," he whispered. My knees may have almost given out.

I think he could feel my body trembling, so he picked me up and sat me on top of the counter.

"Well, this feels just like the Halloween Party. Someone thought I wouldn't recognize him. Except I would much rather prefer this counter than that tiny bathroom sink. My ass was sore after that."

"I just needed to kiss you that night. And I need to kiss you now."

"I love you," he said as he kissed my forehead.

"I love you," he said as he kissed my cheek.

"I love you," he said as he kissed the corner of my mouth.

"I would say you have no idea how much I love you back, but I don't think that would be true. I think you do know," I replied.

"So, where do we go from here?" he asked.

"I think we should go upstairs," I replied.

He put his head down on my shoulder and laughed.

"What? You asked me where we should go and I told you," I said.

"I meant, where do you and I go from here. Like where does this leave us?"

"Oh," I replied, my cheeks heated from embarrassment. "Well, what would you like us to be?"

"Well, we can't necessarily go back to being just best friends now, can we?"

"I think we've completely smashed that boundary line between us, so I'm going to agree with you."

"So, Prim, would you..." I cut him off.

"Nope. I told you it was my turn to show you, remember? Myles, will you be my boyfriend?"

Another tear slid down his cheek. I wiped it away and then kissed the spot where it had just been.

"I'll be your boyfriend, Prim. You have no idea how long I've been wanting this to happen," he replied as another tear slid down his cheek.

"Baby, don't cry," I replied as I felt tears swelling behind my own eyes.

"I love you, Prim."

"I love you too, Myles. You make me so happy. I hope you know you're stuck with me from now on."

"I've never wanted anything else," he replied as he leaned in and kissed me.

"It's you baby. You're the one," I said.

"You've always been the one."

He kissed my neck and then made his way up to my earlobe. Heat started to rise throughout my body and up my neck. My nipples were poking through my shirt, and I felt myself already getting wet as he made his way down to my shoulders and chest.

"Myles, please. Take me upstairs," I said, out of breath already.

"I'm going to take my time with you tonight. No need to rush, love."

He slid my pants and underwear off, and then slowly started to pull my shirt above my head. I lifted my arms to give him easier access. He leaned me back on the counter and then put one of my legs over his shoulder. I didn't even have time to think about what we were doing before his mouth was on me. He licked the length of my folds, and I squirmed underneath him.

"Oh, Myles," I moaned.

He stopped licking and started kissing up my stomach until he reached my nipple and started sucking. He put my nipple between his teeth and tugged, and I arched my back as I felt a mixture of pleasure and pain roll through me.

"Myles, I want you in me. Please fuck me."

He put two fingers and then a third into me and pumped slowly at first but then sped up until I was on the edge of orgasm already.

"Fuck, Myles," I cried as tears formed behind my eyes. "Almost there."

He leaned his face down and sucked on my clit while he was continuing to palm my breast and pump into me with his fingers.

"God, Myles, yes!" I cried as I clenched around his fingers.

Myles removed his fingers from me and kissed my throbbing clit, sparks shaking through my body at the touch.

"God, you are so sexy. How have we not been doing this for years?" he asked as he got a paper towel to clean me up.

"Well, we have all the time in the world. Take me to your room," I replied as I wrapped my legs around him. I grabbed my clothes just in case his parents came home a little earlier than expected, and he carried me upstairs. "It's your turn now."

Chapter 30

Myles

We barely made it into my room before Prim had already pulled off my shirt and was kissing my neck as I slowly lay her down on my bed. I had just started working my way up her stomach when my phone buzzed in my pocket.

"Fuck. It might be my parents." Prim nodded. "Hello?" I said as I answered the phone and tried to slow down my breathing. I was right. It was my mom.

"Hey, honey. We just wanted to let you know that we're going out to dinner in about an hour after we finish up here at the mall. Will you and Prim be okay there at the house?" my mom asked.

I looked down at Prim while she covered up her laugh. This girl was going to be the end of me, but in all the best ways.

"Yeah, I think we'll be fine. I'll order us something in a little bit after we're done." Prim's eyes widened in horror. *Fuck.* "We're playing video games right now," I continued, trying to cover up what I had said before and hoping my mom didn't catch on.

"Okay, well, have a good time. You both should do something tonight," my mom replied. Oh, we'll be doing something all right.

"We will, mom. We'll see you later," I replied as we ended the phone call. "Now, where were we?" I leaned down and parted Prim's lips with my tongue so she could take me in. She wrapped her legs around my waist and pulled me down closer to her.

"You have too many clothes on," she replied.

My erection was straining so tight behind my zipper that it hurt trying to take off my pants. As soon as we were both naked, she grabbed me and threw me down on the bed and got on top of me.

"Now, let's try this again," Prim said. "And this time, hopefully, you won't stop us halfway through."

"That was completely different, and you know why I stopped it," I replied.

"Yes, and I love you even more for it." She leaned down and ran her fingers through my hair as she kissed me. "Do you have any condoms?"

"Yeah, they're in my bag. It's on the floor beside my bed."

"Why do you have condoms in your bag?" she asked as she raised an eyebrow at me.

"Students were going around on campus and stuffing condoms in everyone's bags, and I never took them out. It's a good thing I didn't," I replied noticing the tension leave her face. "Don't worry, I didn't sleep with anyone else. Who would I have slept with, hmm?"

"You could have you know. I mean, you had every right to."

"I know, but I didn't want to. I was too busy pining after you."

She leaned down and kissed me deep and slow. I was already dripping pre-cum, and Prim must have noticed because she leaned over and grabbed a condom out of the bag. She put the condom on me and then slowly lowered herself on top of me until I completely filled her.

"Oh, god," I moaned as I squeezed my eyes shut and enjoyed the sensation as I felt her around me.

I grabbed her ass as I slowly picked her up and down as she continued to whimper and moan as I pumped into her. Her tits were bouncing in front of me as she rode my cock, so I figured I would start sucking on her nipples for some added stimulation. I tugged on her right nipple, and she threw her head back in pleasure.

"Myles, yes," she moaned. "I'm almost there."

I quickly flipped us over so that she was underneath me and continued thrusting in and out of her as I circled her clit with my thumb. She started picking up her breaths, so I knew that she was about to come. She squeezed around my cock, and I knew that I was almost gone. I was right. Four more hard pumps into her and I came with a force so strong that it shot chills down my entire spine.

"Fuck, that was good," Prim said as I fell down on the bed beside her. "I think you're going to have to change your sheets."

"I think you're right. But not yet. Round two is coming up soon," I said as I turned over and winked at her.

"I like the way you think, Aratis," she replied. "Let's go get in the shower."

Five minutes later and I was already hard again as Prim was on her knees in front of me sucking my cock. She was so beautiful as she looked up at me. I had to hold onto the side of the shower I came so hard. She took it all in and swallowed. Goddamn, that was sexy.

"You could have spit it out in the shower if you wanted to," I said she stood back up.

"I usually do, but it's you, so I'll make an exception."

I leaned in and kissed her, tasting the saltiness of my release on her lips. She deepened the kiss and put her arms around my neck as we got lost in each other.

After we were done in the shower, we got dressed and then lay on my bed, her head laying on my chest and her leg intertwined with mine.

"Are you happy?" she asked, looking up at me.

"Baby, there are no words to describe how happy I am right now," I replied. "Are you happy?"

"I'm very happy. You know, I didn't even tell Rem all of this, but there were times during the semester where I fantasized about being with you. Not just the sexual stuff, although those were nice thoughts too, but things like this. Lying on your chest, cuddling with you, just being with you."

"Oh, yeah?"

"Yeah. It was weird to think about at first because I had never thought of you in that way before, you know? But the more I thought about it, the more it just felt right. Rem knows about us, by the way."

"How does she know we're together? We just got together. Unless you texted her after we got out of the shower."

"No, uh, she heard us the night of the party before we went on break. I guess she did end up coming back to the room, but she heard us having sex, so she left."

"Are you serious?" I ask, starting to laugh. Prim started to laugh too, so I figured they had already talked about everything. "Rem came to me after Thanksgiving break and told me that I should keep going after you. She told me not to waste this chance."

"She's been playing matchmaker the entire semester, hasn't she?"

"I mean, I don't really mind now that it got me to you."

"I'm glad she did too."

We both nodded and smiled at each other.

"Did you always think that this was going to happen?" she asked.

"No, but I hoped, every day," I replied as I leaned down and kissed her forehead.

"Theory proved," we both said at the same time.

***

Two weeks later and we had rung in the new year. It was January 6th and Prim's parents were holding New Year's dinner today, since they were both working at the hospital on the actual holiday. This happened most years, so I wasn't very surprised. The only difference this year was that Prim and I were officially a couple. It had been eleven years in the making but we were finally here. Ever since Prim and I got together, I keep waiting for the other shoe to fall and for her to tell me, "Hey, just kidding!" but that doesn't happen. I'm never letting her go.

I got to Prim's house and was welcomed in with her running up to me, jumping on me, and wrapping her legs around my waist. She leaned down and kissed me.

"I'm glad you came, boyfriend."

"I'm glad I'm here, girlfriend." I put her down and noticed both of Prim's parents smiling in the background. My cheeks flushed red, and I rubbed the back of my neck and cleared my throat.

"Nice to see you, Margaret. Sam," I said as I walked into the kitchen holding Prim's hands. Her parents weren't traditional by any sense of the word, but it still felt a little awkward kissing Prim in front of them. My parents were the same way, so we did feel a little freer in that regard.

"It's nice seeing you like this," Margaret replied.

"Like what?" I asked.

"Happy," Margaret and Sam said in unison.

I leaned over and kissed Prim on the cheek and started helping in the kitchen to get all the food ready. Prim's grandparents had come for dinner as well, so we sat down and devoured the ham dinner that was prepared.

"So, Myles, are you still thinking of transferring for the upcoming semester?" Margaret asked. Well, I'm glad I told Prim about this or that would have been a really awkward conversation.

"Uh, no, I don't think so. Not anymore," I replied as I looked over at Prim and squeezed her hand under the table.

"I didn't think so."

"So, Prim finally came to her senses, huh?" asked Sam, nudging Prim in the side of the arm.

"Dad, it wasn't my fault," Prim replied.

"No, I know. I'm just teasing you."

"We're together now and that's all that matters."

"It's about damn time. That boy's been in love with you for years," Prim's grandma said.

"Grandma!" Prim said as her cheeks flushed red. She was so cute when she got embarrassed.

I have gotten to know Prim's grandparents a lot over the years, and I saw them a lot during the holidays, so I'm sure it wasn't very hard to see how I felt about Prim. I'm sure my eyes lingering in her general direction all the time probably gave it away to them. I was like a little puppy following its owner around, but I didn't care at all. I would be her puppy if she wanted me to. I was already drooling over her all the time anyway, so I might as well tack the label onto it too. She was finally mine. No one else's. Mine. I didn't have to see her with another man ever again. I was going to make sure it stayed that way.

Later that night, I took Prim out for coffee and a date at the bookstore. I sat on one of the benches in the store as I watched her go through each of the aisles. If browsing through the shelves was her heaven, watching her get excited over the books was mine. The way her smile spread all the way across her face and up to her eyes. She made my heart melt.

"I have a surprise for you," I said as we walked hand-in-hand back toward our houses. It had started snowing, so being on this date with her felt even more romantic.

"You do? What is it?" she asked.

"You know how my aunt and uncle have that cabin?"

"Yeah, we used to go there all the time in high school."

"Well, I asked them if we could use it next week."

"Seriously? Just you and me?" she asked, her eyes shimmering with excitement. I loved seeing her like this.

"Just you and me. For a whole week," I replied. "How does that sound?"

"Yes! Oh, my god, Myles. Yes! Can we go tubing too?" she asked as she jumped up and down.

"That's what I was planning on," I said as I leaned over and kissed her on the cheek.

There was a ski resort about ten minutes from the cabin and Prim and I used to go there all the time when we were younger. I had one of my birthday parties there in middle school, so the place holds a lot of sentimental value. And I wanted to have this with her. We didn't have a lot of money since we were still in school so this was the best, I could give her. At least for now. I would give her the world if I could. It was worth it just to see the look on her face.

I love this woman with my entire soul.

Chapter 31

Myles

The day before we left for the cabin, Prim and I decided to go shopping for new snow boots. Most of mine had worn out and hers started to tear on the bottom, so we figured it was a good idea if we didn't want to get frostbite. We turned into the shoe aisle and, as we did, I heard a familiar voice coming up from behind us. I turned and looked at the guy behind us and had to do a double take.

"Mr. Keller. Is that you?" I asked walking up to him and the woman who was standing beside him.

He gave me a curious look and then I could see the realization that dawned on his face. "Myles Aratis. Wow. Look at you all grown up," he replied. Prim and I haven't seen Mr. Keller since eighth grade. After he taught us in third grade, he took a teaching position at our middle school. So, when Prim and I got to eighth grade, we had him as a teacher for the second time. We didn't mind. He was one of our favorite teachers.

"How have you been?" I asked, with Prim coming up beside me.

"I've been great. How about you? Oh, my gosh, is that Prim O'Brien?"

"Hi, Mr. Keller. It's nice to see you," Prim replied. "I'm surprised you recognize us after all these years."

"Of course, I do. I remember all my students. Especially those who I've taught twice," he said looking over at the woman beside him. "Myles, Prim, this is my wife, Shannon. I don't think you've ever met her before."

"Nice to meet you both," Shannon replied as she held out her hand to shake both of ours.

"These two have been best friends ever since they were in my third-grade class. It was a little bit of a rocky start, but they seemed to figure things out," Mr. Keller said. "What are you two doing here?"

"Oh, we're looking for snow boots. We're going up to my family's cabin tomorrow," I replied as I saw him look down at where Prim had her hand on my back.

"Wait. Are you two?" he started, motioning his finger between me and Prim.

"Are we dating? Yes," I replied.

"Well, look at that. You finally figured it out. I better be invited to the wedding." Now, most people who are only in their freshman year of college would probably choke on their water if something like that was ever said to them but, as I looked over at Prim smiling up at me, I felt comfort in knowing that both of us just knew somehow.

"You'll be the first one invited," I replied taking Prim's hand in mine.

We said our goodbyes to Mr. Keller, found the snow boots we were looking for, and then headed out to the car.

"Did you mean what you said back there?" Prim asked as she turned on the heat.

"What do you mean?"

"Back there, when you were talking to Mr. Keller about a wedding," she replied.

"Of course, I did. Prim, you're it for me. I hope you know that. There's no one else in this world that I would want to be with. I would be living half of a life with anyone else. You're it, baby."

She smiled, leaned over, and whispered into my ear, "You're it for me too."

***

We were finally at the cabin. It took us an extra half-an-hour or so because it had started snowing on our way here, so we got delayed a bit behind all the snowplows. My aunt and uncle had taken really good care of it over the years, so it looked exactly like it had when we came here the last time. We hadn't been able to get up here in the last couple of years, so the last time we had been here was our sophomore year in high school.

"I am so excited! Oh my gosh, look at this place! I'm so glad we came back," Prim said as she ran through the cabin and looked into every room.

The last room she came across was the guest bedroom. She looked in the door and stopped.

"Myles, what's this?"

"What do you mean?"

"What is all of this?" she asked as surprise lit up her face.

I walked up to her, wrapped my arms around her waist, and kissed her cheek. Before we left to come up here, I called my aunt and uncle for a favor. I wanted to make this week special for Prim and me, so I had them put rose petals all over the room and light some candles so that Prim would see them when we got here. They only live ten minutes away, so I tried to time it so that the candles wouldn't be burning for very long without us here. I told them our estimated time of arrival and then sent off a quick text message telling them about our delay when we stopped for gas.

"I wanted to make this week special. It's our first outing as a couple so I wanted to do this for you. I had my aunt and uncle come to do this while we were on our way here," I replied.

She turned and faced me. "I love you. So much it hurts."

"I know the feeling," I said as I nuzzled my face into her neck and sank my teeth in.

"Myles, we just got here," she said, even though I could feel the goosebumps forming on her skin as I kissed the spot where I had just bitten her.

"Let me show you just how much I love you. We must make up for all those years of lost time, don't we?"

"Yes," she replied, but it came out more of a quiet gasp.

I started sucking on her neck. "Take your clothes off, baby," I said.

She stepped back and took her clothes off so slowly that I thought I was going to come undone right then and there. God, she was so beautiful. When she had taken off all her clothes, she lay back on the bed on top of all the rose petals.

"Come watch me, Myles," she said as she put her hand in between her thighs and slowly put one and then two fingers into herself.

"Prim, oh, my god," I said as I heard a low growl form in the bottom of my throat. She was already so wet. "You're so fucking sexy."

I stood in front of the bed and watched her pleasuring herself as I took my pants off and started fisting my cock. I wanted this to last a while, so I did long, slow strokes so that I wouldn't come too soon.

"Oh," Prim moaned as she started circling her clit with her other hand. I could tell that she was close.

"Let me see you come all over those fingers," I replied, picking up the pace of my hand on my cock.

She let out a loud cry and I could see her body shake as her orgasm ran through her body. I got on the bed, spread her legs apart again, and placed a small kiss at her opening. She shuddered underneath me, so I took her clit between my teeth and gently tugged.

"Myles, I need you in me," she cried.

"Not yet, baby. One more orgasm for you and then I'm all yours. You just look too sexy right now."

I started pumping two fingers into her and then picked up the pace when I saw that her breaths were getting shallower. In went a third finger. She moved her hand to her chest and started making circles around her nipples.

"Fuck, Myles, I need to come," she moaned.

I curled my fingers inside her as I massaged her clit and, five seconds later, I felt her squeeze against me.

"Yes! Myles!" she screamed as she climaxed, her juices running down my fingers.

If I didn't get inside some part of her soon, I would explode without any other friction. She was *gorgeous*.

"Myles, fuck me," Prim said with rose-colored cheeks.

I pulled out a condom from my bag, put it on, and then bent down and teased at her entrance.

"Myles, please," she begged.

"Patience, baby," I replied. She glared up at me, so I decided to stop teasing her and give her what she wants.

I pushed into her slowly and watched as she arched her back and whimpered below me.

"You feel so good, Prim."

"Fuck me, Myles."

"Yes, ma'am," I replied as I sped up my thrusts into her. In and out. In and out. She came again right before I did, and then I crashed down onto the bed beside her. We were silent for a couple of minutes after that, trying to catch our breaths.

I leaned over to Prim and pulled her closer to me so that she was resting on my shoulder. I kissed the top of her head, and she smiled up at me.

"Did you think that we would ever be this comfortable with each other?" Prim asked.

"What do you mean?" I replied.

"I mean, we went from being friends to being in a relationship with each other. Now we're having sex. I never would have imagined us doing this a couple of years ago. But do you know what? It's not weird at all. I would have thought that it would be weird, but it feels so natural."

"It does feel natural. I also didn't know you were so dirty in bed," I said as she nudged me in the arm.

"I could say the same thing about you. You're incredibly sexy when you talk like this," she replied.

"I guess you just bring it out in me. You're right, though. This doesn't feel weird. It feels right. You feel right," I said as I pulled her closer to me.

"So, what do you want to do for the rest of the day? It's probably almost time to eat dinner, and I'm starving."

"How about steaks?" I replied.

"From Samson's?" she asked.

"That's what I was thinking." Samson's Steaks had been a restaurant that we had gone to whenever we came up here to the cabin. They were right down the street, and they had dinner rolls that were to die for. "How about delivery this time around?"

"Deal. I'm too tired to go anywhere anyway," she said as she lay her head down on my chest while I ordered on my phone.

***

It was three days into our trip and the snow had built up enough on the ground that it was the perfect weather for tubing. Prim and I both got dressed and then drove down to the ski resort. We liked going tubing at night, so we waited until it got dark outside. When we reached the resort, I went up to the window and paid for two hours. We got two tubes, but we spent the majority of the time going down the hill in one tube together. This was the most fun that I had had in a really long time, and I was so happy that I was sharing this moment with Prim. At one point, I just sat at the bottom of the hill and watched as Prim ran all the way up and then tubed down.

Watching someone do something that they love to do is one of the best things to experience in life. It was even better that the person I was watching was Prim. I know we both said that we love each other but I don't think she will ever understand the depth of my love for her. My heart aches when I'm with her, and my heart aches when I'm not with her. I just have so much love for her. I was taken out of my thoughts when I looked up and saw Prim speeding down the hill right toward me. Luckily, the snow wasn't as icy on the bottom of the hill, so the tube at least slowed down a little before she plowed into me. Okay, maybe I'm being a little dramatic. She didn't plow into me. I moved just in time, but the closeness of her tube knocked me off my feet and I landed right on top of her as she fell out of the tube.

"Hi, there," I said as I looked down at her. Her cheeks and nose were red from the cold, but I couldn't remember a time when she looked more beautiful.

"I have something for you."

"You do? Right now?" she asked.

"Here," I replied as I took the necklace out of my pocket. It was the necklace that I had bought her over Thanksgiving break. We couldn't spend Christmas day together because we were with our respective families, and I hadn't found the perfect time to give it to her yet. I took the necklace and put it around her neck and clasped the chain together in the back.

"You got me a necklace? Myles, this is too expensive," she said, picking up the pendant and looking at it. Purple with diamonds. Her favorite color. "It's beautiful. Thank you."

"Merry Christmas, baby," I replied.

"I love you."

"I love you more," I said as she pulled me in for a long, slow kiss.

Chapter 32

Myles

Prim and I spent the rest of the week at the cabin tubing, eating, talking, and loving each other. It was the best week, and I plan to have many, many more like that. We have about a week-and-a-half before we have to go back to school to start the second semester, so Prim and I are about to head to Vesper's house to catch up on what's been happening and to exchange gifts. Vesper's house was right in the middle of everyone, so we figured that was the best place to meet. Rem is the only one who knows about me and Prim so far, so this should be a fun surprise for everyone. Not that we're hiding our relationship or anything, but she wanted to wait until we saw them in person to tell them.

When we got to the house, Rem and Jax were already there so we pulled into the driveway behind them. I followed Prim up to the front door and she rang the doorbell. We heard laughter getting closer to the door, and then Vesper opened up the door to greet us.

"Hey, Pr... " Vesper started before she looked over at me with a confused look on her face. "Myles, hey. What are you doing here?"

Oh, yeah. That's another part of this surprise. Prim didn't tell them that I was coming along with her.

"Hey, Vesper. Nice to see you," I replied.

"Uh, let's all go inside first," Prim said as she led us all inside.

Jax and Rem saw us coming in the door, so they got up from the couch and came over to greet us.

"Myles, hey! We didn't know you were coming," Jax said waving at me as they walked over.

"Well, I didn't tell you guys on purpose. We have something to tell you," Prim said as she leaned over and took my hand. "Myles and I are dating."

I started to look around at all of them to gauge their reactions, but they weren't reacting like I thought they would.

Vesper started laughing. "Was that your big surprise that you were telling us about, Prim?"

"It was," Prim replied.

"This isn't a surprise. This is just common sense," said Vesper.

"What do you mean?"

"My gosh, woman, we've all been rooting for you two to get together the entire semester."

"It's about time, really," Jax replied.

I looked over at Rem and she was smiling at both of us. "Rem, do you have anything to add?"

"Well, I don't have anything sarcastic to add to the conversation, if that's what you mean by your question. Promise. I'm just happy for you too. Except I did not like hearing your sex noises," she replied.

"Wait. What? You heard them having sex? When? Didn't they like just to get together?" Vesper asked.

"Uh, Myles, Prim, I think you two better take this one. If not, she might poke someone's eyes out," Rem replied.

"We hooked up the night before we left to go back home for Winter Break," I said.

"Oh, my god. You've already had sex and you didn't tell us?" Vesper asked, looking over at Prim.

"Geeze, Ves, don't have a coronary or anything," Rem said.

"But this is like big news," Vesper replied.

"I knew you weren't sick at that party," Jax said, pointing a finger at Prim. "No wonder you left so early. Must have been pretty good dick."

I cleared my throat. "Okay. How about we all go sit down and exchange gifts and then we can tell you all about it," I said, looking up at all of them.

"Good idea," Rem said, grabbing the food off the counter and taking it back into the living room.

I spent the rest of the night watching the girls exchange gifts and fielding questions about Prim and my relationship. Honestly, I didn't really mind that much. I could talk about Prim forever. All the gifts that they exchanged were books. *Shocker*, I know. The books that Prim got at the bookstore on one of our dates must have been the ones she gave the girls now. I've never seen people freak out about books more than the people in this room.

"You'll just have to get used to it if you want to keep dating me," Prim said after I commented on how many books she has in her bedroom at home.

"I'm already used to it," I replied as I leaned down from the couch in front of me and kissed her. The girls decided to sit on the floor. I felt like I was intruding in their girl time, so I stayed on the couch. The only reason I came today was because Prim was so excited to tell them about us.

"Wow. You two are disgustingly adorable," Jax said.

"I'm jealous," Rem replied.

"Speak for yourself," Ves said. "Relationships aren't my thing." Everyone looked over at her. "But, of course, your relationship is just beautiful and I'm so happy for you," she said as she looked between the two of us.

"Thanks, Ves," I replied. "I'm glad we have your stamp of approval."

"You better not hurt her."

"I would do no such thing."

"I'll hurt you if you do."

"I would let you hurt me, don't worry."

"Good. Just so you know."

A little later, the girls were all talking about what they had been doing during break, so I decided to go out front on the porch to give them some privacy. I was in mid-thought when Rem came out onto the porch with me.

"Hey, there," she said as she handed me one of the peanut butter cookies she had made for tonight.

"Thanks," I replied.

"I see you've had a pretty good break so far."

I smiled. "Yeah, I would say that I have."

"I'm happy for you, Myles. I know how hard this past semester was for you, so it's nice seeing you smile."

"It's nice being able to smile for a change. It's been rough, but we finally got here."

"I'm surprised you didn't give up over the years."

"Never. I'm no quitter," I replied.

"I really admire you, Myles. I know love is real and, I've been in love before, but I never knew it was able to withstand all of this. My relationship didn't work out, but I'm so happy that yours is. I hope you both are really happy together."

"We are. Thanks, Rem. I appreciate you being here for us. And thank you for looking out for Prim during the semester. She's really lucky to have you as a friend."

"You're damn right she is. Oh, and I also just wanted to say. If you break her heart, I'll break something of yours that you hold very near and dear. Got it?" she asked.

I gulped. "Understood."

She started laughing and then nudged me in the arm. "I'm just teasing you. I thought it was my right as the other best friend."

"You don't have to worry. I promise. I won't hurt her. Now that I have her, I'm never letting her go. And I'm going to do whatever it takes to keep her," I replied.

"I know you will."

Chapter 33

Prim

"Are you happy to be back?" I asked, as I played with Myles's hair as he lay on my lap.

"I'm not happy that classes started again, but I'm happy to be here with you," Myles replied, pulling me in closer to him.

Classes started a little over a week ago for the second semester. I don't have any classes with Myles this time around, but we've been able to see each other every day, mostly, in part, to me not having soccer practice. And we live right beside each other, so that helps too. I was sad to be back after the amazing break that we had together, but it's nice to get settled into a routine with him.

The afternoon we got back to campus, we went to drop Myles's stuff in his room. One thing led to another, and we started making out on his bed. He had just taken off my shirt when Lawrence walked into the room. Talk about a surprise entrance. He stared at us for a minute and then grabbed his phone out of his pocket to make a phone call.

"Sabrina, uh, I think you need to come see this. We're in our room. Oh, yeah, everyone is all right. Come quick," Lawrence said as he hung up the phone.

Not even one minute later, we heard Sabrina running down the hallway and then saw her appear in the doorway.

"What the hell?" she asked.

Myles and I looked at each other and then back at Sabrina.

"Surprise!" we said together.

"Wait, you two are together now?" Lawrence asked.

"Yes," I replied.

"When did this happen, and why didn't anyone tell us?" asked Sabrina. "I'm gonna kick your ass, Aratis."

"It was about a week-and-a-half after we went home. Things just happened and then we got together," Myles replied.

"But like what brought this on. How did you end up getting together?" Lawrence asked.

"We, uh, kinda hooked up the night before break," I replied.

"Hooked up as in you had sex?" asked Sabrina.

Myles's grin was all that Sabrina needed to confirm.

"Holy shit, look at you guys. It took you fucking long enough. Christ. But the question still stands. Why didn't anyone tell us?"

"Well, I was going to text you guys, but we were kinda busy during break," Myles said as he smirked over at me.

"Oh, my god, eww. Gross. I didn't need that image in my head," replied Sabrina.

"Nice," Lawrence replied nodding his head up and down and giving Myles a thumbs up. Sabrina leaned over and slapped him on his arm.

"Guys are so weird," I replied.

"Agreed," said Sabrina.

"I take offense to that," Myles added.

"Of course, I wasn't talking about you, baby," I said turning to Myles and kissing him.

"Damn. Look at you two," Lawrence replied. "You're so disgustingly in love I feel like I might vomit but, still, I'm happy for you guys. Prim, thank you so much for getting together with him. Maybe now I won't have to hear him whine all the time about you."

Myles chucked a pillow at his head. "I'm going to kill you, Lawrence."

Ever since then, we've all been hanging out together as one big friend group. Sabrina and Lawrence have joined our group. They even brought their significant others to introduce to us. Sabrina asked Myles and I if we wanted to go on a double date with her and Bethany, so Myles and I have been lying in bed until we needed to meet them at the restaurant.

At six-thirty p.m., we pulled up to a local restaurant and walked in to find Sabrina and Bethany who were sitting at a table in the far-right-hand corner. They saw us come in the door and waved us over.

"Apparently, corner tables are our thing this year," I said as Myles and I took the two empty seats across from them.

"I thought that it was only fitting," Sabrina smiled.

We talked to them for a couple of minutes until our server came up to the table and took our orders. We decided to order cheese fries to split between all of us as an appetizer, and then each of us ordered burgers as our main dish.

"So, what all did you two do over break?" Bethany asked, taking a sip of her beer.

"Well, we spent a lot of time together, had New Year's dinner at my house with my family, and then Myles took me to his family's cabin. We spent a week tubing and trying not to freeze to death," I replied as laughter went around the table.

"That sounds romantic. Nicely done, Myles," Sabrina said.

"I can be romantic from time to time," Myles replied.

"More like all the time. I knew you were in love with her from the moment I sat down beside you two in class last semester."

"Honestly, I really thought I kept it hidden pretty well. She didn't even realize it until recently," Myles replied, pointing over at me.

"And that's why you two are perfect for each other," Sabrina said.

Myles and I smiled at each other. "So, were you two able to do anything fun over break?" I asked.

"Actually, we spent the two weeks before the end of break in South Carolina at Bethany's beach house. I've never been to the beach outside of the summer season, so it was nice to walk on the beach and not have a crowd there," Sabrina replied.

"Oh, that sounds really nice," I replied. "It's so nice to do this with you two."

And I meant it. It was nice to do this. Be out in public on a double date with my friends. Looking back over the course of last semester, I never realized how much I needed something like this. How much I needed interaction. How much I needed Myles. How much I needed stability in my life.

As we were driving back to campus, Myles started to stroke my leg and then ran his fingers up under my dress. He started massaging over the top of my opening, and heat started to run up my back and neck. I bit the bottom of my lip and arched my back against the seat as he hit the sensitive spot. He got one finger inside me before I told him to pull over. We had to search for a minute or two before we found an alley that seemed promising.

Three orgasms later—two for me and one for him—we were driving back to campus again basking in the glow of each other.

***

A month later and I had just finished tutoring for the afternoon. I decided to tutor for both English and Education, so it was taking up a lot of my afternoons after classes. I was making pretty decent money from it, so I thought it was worth it. I had just gotten to the cafeteria for dinner and sat down beside Myles, Rem, Vesper, and Jax. We made it a goal this semester to have dinner together in the cafeteria every night, if we could. Since there was no added stress of going to soccer practices and games, it was nice to just relax and hang out with the group.

Myles pulls me in closer to his side, leans over and kisses my neck as I continue to eat my sandwich.

"I thought you didn't like PDA. You always gave me shit for it before," I said looking over at him.

"I didn't like PDA when you were doing it with other guys. I like it now," he replied, rubbing my back.

"I love you," I said.

"I love you too," he replied, nuzzling his nose into the side of my neck.

"Uh, hello. Earth to the lovers over there. You know we can see you, right?" Ves asked.

She snapped her fingers, and it brought me back to realize where we were.

"Shit, sorry," I replied, as my cheeks started to burn.

"Oh, leave them alone, Ves. They're still in their honeymoon phase. I'm sure all the lovey-dovey stuff will wear off at some point," Jax replied.

"Not if I can help it," Myles said.

"Why are we talking about lovey-dovey stuff at the dinner table?" Cade said as he came up to the table with his tray and sat down next to Jax.

"Hey, Cade. Ves is just jealous over here because Myles and I are showing affection to one another," I replied.

"Well, as long as I don't have to spit out any of my food while it's happening, we're all good," he said.

I liked Cade. Jax and him had become fast friends during last semester but he didn't come out of his room a lot. This was one of the rare times that he made an appearance, but we all seemed to get along well so we accepted him in as one of our own. He and Jax both liked playing video games so most of her nights this semester so far had been with Cade playing online with other players.

"Uh, oh, here comes trouble," I said as I looked up and saw Theo coming up to our table.

Vesper looked behind us, saw who it was and rolled her eyes.

"Hey, all. Did you have a nice break?" Theo asked as he approached us.

"Are you asking us seriously or is there some kind of a sarcastic joke behind your question?" Ves replied.

"The only person at this table that I'm ever remotely sarcastic to, is you, Ves. But, no, I was being serious," Theo replied. "Ves, do anything fun over the break?"

"No, not really. My dad had a bad cold over the break, so we just stayed in," she replied.

"Ves, you didn't tell us your dad was sick while we were at your house. I hope we weren't too loud," I said.

"No, it's okay. He had taken some sleeping pills, so he was knocked out the entire time."

I nodded, unable to miss Ves's smile disappear almost as soon as it had appeared.

"We aren't holding you up, are we?" Ves asked looking back up at Theo. "I'm sure you have better things to do with your time than stand here and talk to us. We see each other in class every day. Don't you think that's enough?"

"Not near enough. I like getting under your skin, Ves. It's fun seeing you get all worked up," Theo replied.

"I'll show you worked up," she replied as she got up and chased him out of the cafeteria.

"Someone should write a book about those two. People would eat that shit up," I said as we all laughed watching Ves and Theo running all the way back to the dorm.

CHAPTER 34

Prim

It was the middle of April, and I was wrapping up my last tutoring session of the year. We only had a month left until summer break and I needed to focus all of my free time on finishing up my internship at the elementary school. The student I had been working with all semesters was able to bring his English grade up from a D to a B in the end, so I will call that mission accomplished. At least, now, he would be able to stay on the football team. We weren't able to get to a lot of the football games last semester because of interfering sport schedules, but his face lit up whenever he talked about football, so I wanted to make sure that he passed. Also, Myles and I were planning on splitting a beach trip this summer, so a lot of the money that I had made this semester was going toward that.

I grabbed my bag and headed out the door, only to find Myles waiting outside for me.

"Hey, what are you doing here?" I said as I leaned up and kissed him.

"I missed you and wanted to see you," he replied as he took my arm and pulled me down the hallway.

"Wait, what are we doing? Where are you taking me?" I asked as we stopped in front of one of the building's supply closets. "Uh, Myles, what are we doing in front of the supply closet? Do you need another notebook or something?"

"Nope. I need you," he replied as he opened the door and pulled us both in, locking the door behind us.

He didn't even turn the lights on. The only light that I could see was the light shining in from underneath the door. He pinned me against the wall and started kissing me.

"Myles, what if someone walks in?" I asked.

"It's a supply closet. I don't think as many people come in here as you might think," he replied. "And it's the end of the day. Just relax and let me take care of everything."

He bent down and unbuttoned my jeans and pulled them down. He took one leg out of my jeans and put it over his shoulder.

"Myles, I..." I tried to finish my sentence, but he moved my panties aside and stuck his tongue in me. I let out a whimper and had to cover my mouth so no one would hear if they walked by the closet.

"Oh, Myles, that feels so good," I said as I started grinding my hips against his mouth. I needed more friction.

He replaced his mouth with two fingers as he pumped in and out of me. I felt my legs start to shake so I knew that I was close to coming. Myles must have sensed it too because he started circling my clit with his thumb as he continued to pump his fingers.

"I'm coming. I, I..." I quickly put the back of my hand over my mouth to cover up my moans as I clenched tight around Myles's fingers inside of me. He had to hold me up as the last of my release shook the lower half of my body.

"Nothing like an orgasm to take the edge off after your last day of tutoring," Myles said as he stood up and kissed me. There was something oddly satisfying about tasting my own release on my lips as he parted them and stuck his tongue in my mouth.

"Taste good?" Myles asked as he pulled up my pants and buttoned them.

"I don't mind it as much as I thought I would," I replied. "What about you? I can't be the only one who gets an orgasm."

"Lawrence went to visit Rebecca, so my room is free. You in, O'Brien?"

"Totally in," I replied.

***

It was one week before the end of the semester and, today, I had to say goodbye to all the kids I have been working with at Pheasant Hill Elementary School. I got a lot of little hugs from all the kids, and a glowing recommendation letter from Mr. Simmons. Throughout the semester, he gave me a lot of teaching advice, and I had scribbled through almost two notebooks with the information. I was able to lead a lot of the classes, and, by the end of the internship, I had decided that maybe elementary education wasn't the best way for me to go. Don't get me wrong, I loved talking with the kids and doing all of the activities, but I started to realize that I wanted to teach books, novels. While I loved reading the children's books to the second-graders, it wasn't making me as happy as I thought it would. I decided that next year I would declare Secondary Education as my major with an English minor. I guess this is what interning and experience was all about. Figuring out what works for you and what doesn't.

The end of the day bell rang, and Mr. Simmons dismissed the class as all of the students headed out to their busses. The class had a going-away party for me earlier this week, so the students hugged me again before running out the door. I shook Mr. Simmons's hand, thanked him for everything, and he wished me the best of luck with my future.

I stepped outside into the sunshine and saw Myles walking toward me. He was taking me out for a late lunch today, so I wore a nice sun dress. It was getting warmer outside, but I still had to throw a jean jacket over top.

"Hey, baby," Myles said as he came up to me and kissed my cheek. "Was it a good last day?"

"It was. A little emotional, but it was good. I'm gonna miss these kids. They were so great," I replied.

"And I'm sure they're going to miss you too. But you'll have another internship, don't worry. And then, someday, you'll have your own classroom, and you won't have to leave."

"You're right. Okay, are you ready to go?"

Myles nodded and took my hand as we walked over to his car.

"Miss O'Brien! Miss O'Brien! Don't leave yet!" I heard as I turned around to see Madelyn running toward us.

Madelyn had been the first student I talked to when I first came to this school, so I guess it was only fitting for her to be the last. We had bonded a lot over this semester, and she always helped me in the classroom. She was my little helper. I had even met her parents during one of the school plays. They thanked me for taking her under my wing. She had been struggling to make friends since this year was her first year at this school. We had always walked out to recess together and, throughout the semester, I was able to see her branch out with the other students. Just last week, I heard that she went to a sleepover with a couple of the girls from class.

"Hi, Madelyn. Aren't you going to be late catching your bus?" I asked as she slowed down in front of us.

"I wanted to give you this before you left and I forgot that it was in my backpack," she replied as she handed me something she had just taken out of her bag. It was a purple and green bracelet. My favorite colors.

"Madelyn, this is beautiful. Did you make this yourself?"

"I made it with my mom last night. I wanted to make you something to match the purple necklace you always wear," Madelyn said pointing to my neck.

"Thank you. I love it," I replied. "Actually, this guy right here got me this necklace."

"Oo, is this your boyfriend, Miss O'Brien?"

"It is," I said bending down to meet her level. "Do you remember before Thanksgiving when I came here, and we were talking about my best friend?"

"I do remember. Is this Myles?"

"It sure is," I replied.

"And he's your boyfriend now?"

"I am her boyfriend now," Myles replied waving at Madelyn. "I see you two have already talked about me."

"She said you were her best friend," Madelyn said. "And then I told her that you were going to be her boyfriend one day. I think I should get a prize."

Myles put up one finger as he reached around to his back pocket and pulled out some candy. "Here you go."

Myles always carries around candy with him. I never know if I'm going to taste Jolly Ranchers or Starbursts whenever he kisses me. Today, it was a blue Jolly Rancher. That's going to taste good later.

"I like this prize," Madelyn replied. "Okay, I gotta go catch my bus, but I just wanted to say goodbye again and tell you that I loved having you in class. I'm going to miss you," she said as she wrapped her arms around me to give me a hug.

I am not going to cry. I am *not* going to cry. *Shit*. I'm crying. I bent down so that I could properly hug her back.

"Thank you, Madelyn. I'm going to miss you too," trying to hold back the tears as I felt one fall down my cheek. We released from the hug, and I stood back up.

Madelyn turned toward Myles. "Be good to Miss O'Brien, okay? She really loves you."

"Well, that's good, because I love her right back," Myles replied.

"It was nice meeting you, Myles. 'Bye, Miss O'Brien!" she said as she turned and ran back toward her bus.

"You, okay?" Myles said as we turned back toward the car.

"I'm more than okay. This is what I'm meant to do," I replied.

Myles leaned down and pulled me into a soft kiss. "And you're going to be great at it."

***

It took us about an hour to load up all our belongings into our cars, but we were finally done. Rem, Ves, Jax, Myles, and I were some of the few students still left on campus, so we had just gotten back from our last lunch together as a group before summer break.

"Can you believe freshman year is already over?" I asked.

"I can. Too much shit happened this year. I'm ready for a fresh start," Ves replied.

"I'm going to miss you guys," Rem said as she pulled all of us girls into a hug. "Be sure to text over the summer, okay? You too Myles."

"Have fun training for next season," Jax said.

"Shit. I forgot about that," I replied. "Maybe we can all go running at the same time so we can help motivate each other."

"Deal," all three of them said in unison.

"Myles, take care of our girl, okay?" Rem asked.

"Always," he replied as he kissed the top of my head.

"You guys and your kissing," Ves said. "Makes me sick. I'm just kidding. Have a great summer, you, guys."

We all waved at each other as Rem, Ves, and Jax walked to the other side of the parking lot where their cars were parked.

"Well, are you ready to go?" Myles asked.

I looked back at the two dorm buildings that had been our whole lives over the course of this year. So many nights laughing. So many nights crying. So many nights wondering what would happen in the future. And it all came down to this. Myles here next to me, just like it's always been. Except now, when I looked at him, I didn't see a best friend. I saw much more than that. I saw my soulmate. The person I've been searching for my whole life only to realize that he was standing right beside me this whole time. I know our relationship is just starting out and things are fresh and new, but I have a feeling that this one is going to last a long, long time.

"Ready," I replied as I wrapped my hands around his neck and pulled him down for a kiss. It was soft and tender, just like him. "I love you, Myles."

"I love you too, Prim."

We both got into our cars but, before I drove off, I took Mr. Tusky off the seat next to me and pulled him into my chest.

"See, I told you I was in love with him," I whispered. "Theory proven."

Epilogue

Myles
Four Years Later

"See you later, Brendan," I said as the school bell rang.

"'Bye, Mr. A. See you tomorrow," Brendan replied as he ran out of my office and down the hallway.

I've been working as a therapeutic staff support, better known as a TSS, ever since we graduated from Silver Creek. I help students who have behavioral and emotional needs in a school setting. I'm actually working at Stanson Elementary School, which just so happens to be the elementary school that Prim and I went to. So, it has some sentimental value for me. The classrooms haven't changed one bit since we were here. Once I decided during senior year that I wanted to be a school psychologist, I interviewed with this school during our spring break. I figured I would get my foot in the door and make some money while I was taking classes to get my master's degree. I have six months left of my program and then the principal at Stanson said that I would be able to stay on the staff as one of their School Psychologists.

After graduation a year ago, Prim and I both moved back to our hometown. Prim then accepted a position teaching freshman English at our high school. We spent the next ten months working and saving our money and, then two months ago, we were able to afford a place together. It was a three-bedroom apartment, so it wasn't anything fancy, but we didn't care. It was good enough for us. We would be renters for life but, honestly, with this economy, who could blame us? Plus, I've been saving up for something else.

I got home a little after four o'clock and I already knew that Prim would be home. The high school let out at three o'clock, so she was home by three-fifteen every day. I opened the front door to find three pieces of chocolate sitting in the bowl on the cabinet. Every day, since we moved in together, I've found some kind of candy inside the front door when I come home from work. I do have a big, sweet tooth but I have an even bigger one for her. Speaking of which. I heard music playing from Prim's office, so I walked down the hall and saw her sitting at her desk with her glasses on the bridge of her nose.

"Hey, gorgeous," I said as I leaned over her desk to kiss her. "What are you working on?"

"Oh, I'm just grading some essays that were due today. But I can always take a break. I think I might need a de-stressor after today," she replied looking up at me with that face that I can never resist. *Fuck, this girl.*

I bit my bottom lip and moved my eyes over her whole body as she stood up. As she moved from behind her desk, I noticed that the only thing she was wearing was a black silk robe. *Holy fuck.* How did I not notice that when I came into the room?

I cleared my throat as my cock hardened against my zipper. "Did you, uh, have a bad day?" I could literally feel the brain rushing from my head.

"Oh, it's not that. I've just been a very naughty girl today," she replied as she started walking slowly over to me. Each step accentuating all her curves. I was in trouble.

"You... you've been n... naughty?" I asked, barely able to get the words out.

"Very naughty. We had a staff meeting today and I didn't listen to one single word that the principal said. Do you want to know why?" Her voice was so calm and steady. This was so fucking sexy.

"W-Why?"

"Because the entire time all I could think about was your cock pounding into me. I didn't listen at all. I think I deserve to be punished, Mr. Aratis," she said as she came so close to me that I was pinned against the wall. I didn't even realize I had been backing up the whole time. She grabbed my cock over my pants, and I let out a low growl. "How about we do something about that?"

She licked her lips and looked up at me with those soul-crushing eyes, and I couldn't resist. Not that I was going to resist anyway. I picked her up, threw her legs around my waist, and then turned us so that I was pinning her up against the wall in midair.

"Does someone need to be punished hard?" I said, lowering my hands to lower my pants.

"Fuck me, Myles," she replied. "I'm dying over here."

"Mhmm," I moaned as I slowly pushed her panties aside. I pushed one finger into her and watched her squirm up against the wall. "Like that?"

"Myles, more!" she screamed.

"Someone does deserve to be punished. So, demanding," I replied as I hovered my cock right at her entrance and thrust upward into her.

We fucked so hard against the wall that two of her pictures fell down and broke all over the floor.

Forty-five minutes later and we were lying on top of our bed after round two.

"That was some good discipline," Prim said as she curled up next to me, laying her head on my shoulder.

"Glad to be of service," I replied as I wrapped my arm around her. "I love you."

"I love you too."

"Oh, don't forget, I have that conference tomorrow, so I probably won't be home until around five o'clock."

"Sounds good," she replied.

"Do you want to go out to dinner when I get back tomorrow?" I asked.

"Yeah, sure. Do you want me to call and make a reservation somewhere while you're gone? It's going to be busy since it's Friday."

"I'll take care of it, baby. Thank you, though," I replied as she slowly drifted off to sleep in my arms.

***

Okay, I may have lied to Prim. I don't have a conference today. I'm planning on meeting with Rem, Ves, and Jax instead. We're meeting for lunch. I have something to tell them. I told Prim that I didn't have to leave until eight o'clock this morning, so she already left a little while ago for school. I grabbed my work bag, took the little black velvet box out of the small pocket, and headed out the door.

"Oh, my fucking god, are you serious?" Vesper asked.

"That is absolutely beautiful," said Rem.

"She's going to freak out," Jax said.

I put the box back into my jacket pocket and waited until all the squealing and clapping ended. Yep. I'm going to propose to Prim tonight. This has been a long time coming. I've wanted to propose to her ever since we got together during freshman year, but I thought that would have been a little too eager. I wanted her to have time to fall in love with me just as much as I had fallen in love with her all those years ago.

"So, you think she'll say yes?" I asked, looking up at the three of them with a playful look.

"Considering you both live together and are completely in love with each other, I'm going to say, hell, yes," Rem replied. "You two are soulmates. We've all known it for a long time."

"Yeah, well, I've felt it for a long time," I replied, taking a sip of my water. I was not going to get choked up here. I'm sure that would come later. "Obviously, Prim would let you know but I guess this is your unofficial invite to the wedding. Oh, and, by the way, good luck fighting over the maid of honor position. 'Bye," I said as I got up and walked out of the door before, they could say anything else.

But I wasn't that much of an asshole. I peeked my head back in the door. "Thank you. Seriously though. It means a lot to me that you met me here. I just wanted to make sure you all knew what was happening before I did it."

"Good luck, Myles. We're rooting for you, buddy," Ves replied.

I shook my head and walked out of the restaurant. I had one more stop to make before I went home to pick up Prim.

I pulled into Margaret and Sam's driveway a little past four o'clock. Now, I know that Prim and I aren't traditional, and neither are her parents. I'm not here to ask for permission to marry her because no one does that anymore. I just figured that, after everything that we have been through and everything that they helped me get through, they, at least, deserved to know my plans ahead of time.

They both greeted me as I came into the house, and we went to sit on the couch. I had texted them beforehand that I was coming over and had something to tell them, so they were already expecting me.

"So, Myles, what did you have to tell us?" Sam asked.

"I think it may be better if I just showed you," I replied, removing the box from my jacket and handing it over to him.

"Wow, Myles. This is a beautiful ring," said Sam as he handed it over to Margaret.

"I'm sure you both know how much I love Prim. I'm not asking for permission because we all know how patriarchal that is, but I just wanted to tell you as a courtesy. You've seen Prim and I grow together over the years, and I wanted to let you know that I am the luckiest man to have her in my life. I'm planning to propose tonight after dinner. So, hopefully, if she says yes, you can expect a phone call."

"I'm so happy for you, Myles," Margaret said, tears starting to form in the corners of her eyes. "We're really excited for you both."

I spent the next thirty minutes describing how I was going to propose and trying not to cry after they kept telling me how much I meant to both of them. I looked at the clock and realized that I told Prim I would be home in fifteen minutes. Well, here goes everything.

***

I went home, picked up Prim, and then headed to the restaurant. I had put a change of clothes in my car earlier this morning, so I changed at Prim's parents' house. There weren't any hiccups during dinner, so the night was going very smoothly. Although, the nerves were starting to set in. I didn't think she was going to say no, but there's always a slight chance with these things. With what I had planned for tonight, I hoped it would be a night to remember.

"Where are we going?" Prim asked as she noticed me driving past our apartment.

"I have a surprise for you," I replied smiling over at her.

"Wow, dinner, and another surprise all in one night? I'm a lucky girl."

A couple of minutes later, I pulled into the parking lot next to the playground at the elementary school.

"Why are we at the elementary school?" Prim asked.

"Come on, I want to show you something," I replied as we got out of the car, and I took out my guitar from the back seat.

"You brought your guitar?"

"It's all part of the surprise, gorgeous."

As we walked over to the picnic tables, I patted my jacket when she wasn't looking to make sure that the ring was still there.

"Okay, so, for the surprise, I need you to sit right here," I said as I pointed to the table on the right. "So, do you remember in college when I started to take guitar lessons?" She nodded.

"Well, I never told you this, but I wrote a song of my own after I had been practicing for a while. And the reason that this is a surprise is that the song I wrote is for you."

"You wrote me a song?"

I nodded. "Do you want to hear it?"

"Of course, I do!" she replied. "Let's hear it."

I took my guitar out of the case and sat down on the table across from her. I had been practicing this song on my lunch break at work for the last month so, hopefully, I didn't butcher it at the last minute. "Okay, here it goes." I started playing the melody and the first couple of lines.

From that day when we were kids until now, it's always been you.

I played the entire song and then looked up to find tears streaming down Prim's face. I went over to her and kissed her.

"How was that?" I asked.

"Myles, that was beautiful," she replied.

"I'll let you in another surprise. That's not the only reason I brought you here tonight."

"It's not? What's the other surprise?"

"What do you remember about this playground?" I asked.

"It's our elementary school playground," she replied.

"Yes, but more specifically, what happened here?" Realization showed on her face.

"When I told you on you to Mr. Keller and got you in trouble?" she said as she laughed.

"Yes. And I'm so glad that you did," I replied, pulling out the box from my pocket and getting down on one knee in front of her.

"Myles, what are...?" she started as her hand went up to cover her mouth.

"Prim, if you never would have paid attention to me in third grade and told Mr. Keller on me, we might not be here right now. I wanted to do this here because it's the place where it all started for us. This is all I've ever wanted out of life. I think I've loved you ever since that day on the playground," I started, and she started giggling at that.

"Okay, maybe not exactly when you told on me, but after you apologized. I've spent all these years falling more and more in love with you every day. I wake up each day next to you wondering how on earth I could possibly fall more in love with you than the day before. But every day I do. If you couldn't already tell, I'm so completely and hopelessly in love with you. You are the best thing that has ever happened to me, and I have loved every minute of this journey we've been on together. Your smile, your laugh, your big brain, your kindness. I knew from freshman year of high school that you were the one for me, probably even before. I just hadn't realized I was already in love with you. You take my breath away every time I look at you. You're my soulmate, Prim. So, at this point, there's only one thing left to say. Prim, will you marry me so that I can spend forever showing you just how in love with you I am?"

Prim got up from the table and knelt with me. She took her hand, pushed the strand of hair out of my eyes, and brought her lips to mine. She moved her head until her mouth was right beside my ear. "Yes," she whispered.

"But you haven't seen the ring yet," I replied, mostly teasing her.

"I don't care. I would marry you even if there wasn't a ring. You're my home, Myles. My safe place, my soulmate, my best friend. And I would choose you every single time."

I started to breathe again. All the emotions building up throughout the day came to a head as a tear ran down my cheek. I opened the box and put the ring on her finger.

"It's beautiful, Myles," she replied.

"We made it, baby," I said as I put my forehead to hers.

"I love you, Myles."

"I love you more."

We went home and made slow and tender love to each other. When Prim fell asleep, I lay there and looked at her and asked myself how a stupid little third grader was able to grow up to have someone this amazing beside him.

She's the best part of me and always will be.

Prim
One Year Later

Everyone was here. All our friends, all our family, in one place. Since our engagement, Myles was able to graduate with his master's degree and get promoted at the elementary school. We didn't want to have a big wedding, so we only invited around fifty people. The majority of those were family and close friends. We chose to have the wedding at a winery about an hour away from our apartment. We originally were going to have the wedding at Silver Creek University on the quad, but we figured that our engagement was sentimental enough to last a lifetime. It was enough to just have all of our close friends and family here. Myles and I decided that we were going to walk down the aisle together instead of doing it traditionally, so we did the first look before the ceremony. We had our backs to each other and, when we turned around, we both started crying. I even had to redo my makeup.

"You're so beautiful," Myles said as he cupped my face and kissed me.

"You're not so bad yourself, baby," I replied. "Well, are you ready to do this, Aratis?"

"I've been ready for a long time, O'Brien."

I'm glad that Myles and I decided to walk down the aisle together because that's how we had always gone through life. Walking side-by-side through hell or high water. It took us a while to get here but we finally did it. We turned the corner and looked out into the crowd who had come to celebrate us. They were celebrating our love. I had known Myles for almost fifteen years now so, when I looked over at the person that was standing beside me, it was the most comfortable feeling in the world. I was always meant to be his and he was always meant to be mine. I just arrived a little late to the party, that's all.

I looked out in front of us and saw Rem, Ves, and Jax all standing up front in their lavender-colored dresses. I couldn't pick just one maid of honor, so I chose to have them all be my maids of honor. They were my girls and always would be. Sabrina was also standing up there beside them. I had gotten really close to her after freshman year of college, so I thought it only fitting that she was with me today. Plus, she and Myles were still really good friends, so it was a win-win situation. I looked at the very end of the aisle to see Mr. Keller standing and waiting for us. Yes, we decided to have him officiate our wedding. Of course, we did. We're sentimental people and having him be able to do this for us meant so much. If he never would have made that phone call to Myles's mom...

We walked up to where Mr. Keller was and then turned to face each other in front of everyone. Mr. Keller started the ceremony and then it was time to say our vows. Myles and I decided to write our own wedding vows because, why not? Traditional weddings, be damned. I took out the piece of paper from the pocket of my dress and unfolded it. Yes, my wedding dress has pockets.

"Myles, for as long as I can remember, you've always been my very best friend. You've been with me through highs and lows, successes and failures, and everything in between. Who knew that one day on the playground in third grade, I would have met my soulmate? Here we are all these years later getting married. And guess what? You're still my best friend. But that has taken on a new meaning now. You're not just my best friend. You're my safe place. My confidant. My support system. The one who makes everything better on a bad day. The love of my life. Growing up, I never thought of you as anything other than a friend. Or so I thought. It was just always so comfortable falling into that friend role, that I never dug deeper into what I was feeling for you. But now, looking back at everything that we have been through together, I know that you were always the person that I was meant to spend my life with. We care for each other so deeply. You're the person that I always want beside me, and I'm so glad that you learned to curse all those years ago or else I never would have had to tell Mr. Keller on you."

I paused for a minute so that everyone could laugh. I looked back over at Myles, and he was giggling to himself too. I am literally the luckiest woman in the entire world. God, this man.

"Thank you for never giving up on me. Thank you for being so patient with me while I caught up to everything. I can't imagine the emotional struggle you went through for all of those years, but I'm here now, baby, and I'm not going anywhere. You're stuck with me. I can't wait to continue to do life with you by my side. I love you, Myles."

I folded my paper back up and put it back in my pocket. I looked up at Myles to see a tear falling down his right cheek. I lifted my hand to his face and wiped the tear away. He leaned into my palm and kissed my hand.

"Prim, for the longest time, I never thought that this day would ever come. I thought that I was going to have an unrequited love forever. Just having you as a friend was enough for me for a while. But then, it became harder to just be your friend because there was no way I could just be your friend while feeling everything that I was feeling inside. I was just so scared of messing everything up and losing you for good, so I never said anything to you. I don't regret going to Silver Creek to be with you. I'm glad you found your way to me. I know it took a while, but here we are. I wouldn't trade any of it for the entire world because it led us to today. You are the best person that I know and I can't believe how lucky I am to spend the rest of my life with you. I can't wait to continue showing you just how much I'm completely head-over-heels in love with you. You are everything I could have ever dreamed of and more. You're so beautiful and you're just the greatest person ever. You have no idea how happy you make me every day. I love you, baby."

I don't think that there was a dry eye in the entire place. Including me, of course. Myles and I smiled at each other as Mr. Keller pronounced us husband and wife and instructed us to kiss. Well, he doesn't have to tell me twice. Myles leaned over, took my face in his hands, and gave me the softest and most tender kiss that shot shivers down my spine. As we pulled away from the kiss, there were tears in both of our eyes as everyone started to clap for us.

"You really do love me, don't you?" I asked.

"Always, from then until now… and forever."